THE GUARDING STATE

Ron Vergona

This is a work of fiction. Names, characters, places, and incidents either are the product of the author's imagination or are used fictitiously, and any resemblance to actual persons, living or dead, events, or locales is entirely coincidental.

Published by:

Shepherd Hall

Coeur d'Alene, Idaho

To my wife Addie, and children Jessica and Michael, for their love and support.

CHAPTER 1

A BRINY SEA BREEZE CLASHED with the lingering aroma steeping in the brackish waters of the estuary. No match for the stale tobacco traces shrouding both figures. At this time of night, the Lakewood complex was deserted. Security guards, pockets heavy with cash, were taking an unscheduled break.

To the west, the light traffic on the Garden State Parkway added to the familiar low-level drone. The sporadic wailing of a distant tugboat herding a loaded barge to port echoed in the alleyways surrounding the buildings. The actions of the two men crouching in the shadows were about to transform the darkness.

"What're we waiting for?" the heavier man said. "Come on."

His partner raised a hand to silence him. A flickering reddish glow reflected from their eyes.

The heavier man shrugged and retraced his steps toward the window. An extended arm grabbed his shoulder, wrenching him to the ground. A jarring force shattered glass in every window of the building as the erupting flames triggered a deafening flashover, engulfing the entire structure. Raining shards of sparkling glass filled the air.

Containers of flammable liquids added to the dissonance, succumbing to the intense heat. Like a den of angry serpents, the twisted copper tubing of the failed sprinkler system ripped open. Scaled fluids turned to steam, spewing the impotent mixture onto the raging inferno.

A big improvement over the Cedar Knolls job.

The heavier man sputtered for words while pulling himself back to his feet. His gestures were overridden by the pumped voice of his partner.

"Much better. This proves the damn thing's reliable. Just gotta remember the details. You find the papers?"

The heavier man nodded with an instinctive shudder, glancing up at the ominous clatter of the crumpling roof. Dense clouds of ash and embers spit out from the burning structure, choking off more of the air supply.

Both men picked up their pace, distancing themselves from the fireborn climate of destruction that crushed the former calm of the night. Their eyes stung from the churning particulates, and their lungs strained for lost oxygen in the unfurling waves of smoke.

"Okay. Let's get out of here. Once we're clear, I'll get word to the marshal. He'll handle the rest." He grabbed the heavier man's arm. "Did you give him the envelope this morning?"

The heavier man found his voice as he climbed into the driver's seat of the Lexus. Turning the key, he punched the pedal to the floor almost before his partner's door slammed shut. They heard the sounds of approaching emergency vehicles getting louder, then fading into the night as the Lexus sped away.

"Yeah, Marty. His sticky fingers had no problem grabbing hold of it. Can we get something to eat now?"

"Not yet, Tony. We got one more job to do. Remember? It's garbage night. Besides, you don't need to worry about missing a meal."

Tony Funetti and Marty Calebrese distanced themselves from the millworks at the Lakewood complex and headed north on the Garden State Parkway to their next destination in Morris County. Things were heating up and the boss demanded results.

* * * * * *

Absently checking the tension on his seat belt, Steve Casella gazed out the jetliner's window and pondered his good fortune. It doesn't get any better than this.

Spend the next day or two sifting through the remnants of a few suspicious fires. Tell the man what he's already concluded. And then the rest of the time— relaxing, taking in the touristy sites Edie talked about. It might even be fun seeing her family again. After all, it would soon be his family too. The only family he had left. Right now, he couldn't think of any better place to be.

Steve nodded to himself and leaned back, allowing a contented smile to spread across his face. This wasn't the first time he'd gotten it all wrong. If he were lucky, he'd live long enough to figure that out for himself.

The non-stop United Airlines flight from San Francisco to Newark completed a sweeping turn over the Golden Gate Bridge and climbed toward its cruising altitude. Edie Pauling tapped Steve on the shoulder. He twisted his body away from the receding landmarks of his home in the Bay Area and looked at his fiancée.

"I've been wondering, Steve. We've been together for for about two years now, I guess. How come you've never made fun of the way I talk?"

The grin lingering on his face neutralized when he turned his head. No longer surprised by whatever Edie blurted out, Steve ran a hand over his scattered dark brown hair and carefully phrased his response.

"I was trying to avoid being racially insensitive?"

"I'm tawkin' about my Jerzy accent. You saying I've got a black dialect?" Edie whispered loudly; traces of a smile emerging. She pushed herself higher in the comfy first-class seat and leveled her amber eyes straight into Steve's riveting gaze.

"Huh. There's a difference? I've always tried to catch about every third word out of your mouth. And then remove those beginning with the letter 'd'. Like *dem* and *dat*. And then break up anything with three or more syllables. It'd help if you'd talk a little slower." Steve shrugged. "I'm going to check out this New Jersey guidebook you gave me."

He paused and held up the book, thumbing through the pages. "Wasn't there a part describing the finer points regarding the indigenous language of the local population?"

"See if you can understand—what—I'm about—to say—now."

As Edie's smile grew, she gave a not-so-gentle tug on Steve's seat belt. "I've got a captive audience for the next several hours. Guess it's time to take advantage of the situation and educate your California-schooled Sicilian brain. Especially since you don't have your little white girl around to run interference."

Edie was referring to Steve's pure white German Shepherd Dog, now unhappily tucked away below in the luggage compartment. Steve figured they'd be paying for that little indiscretion when they got Amber out of her crate after landing in Newark.

"Yeah?" Steve said. "Now that you mention it, how is it we're sitting in this comfortable first-class cabin, and she's stuck down there with the ninety-nine percenters?"

"You mean the ninety-eight percenters. But anyway, Mr. Casella," Edie said and poked an extended thumb over her shoulder. "Those poor folks you're referring to are sitting right behind the blue curtain. And I'm guessing Amber has better accommodations in the baggage compartment."

Edie had once spent an overwhelmingly claustrophobic flight in the economy seats behind a similar curtain on her first trip to the San Francisco Bay Area. Steve recalled that most of her apprehension had more to do with what would happen after she reached her destination than any physical inconveniences of squeezing her trim frame into one of those ever-shrinking airline seats. Both their lives dramatically changed after that first shaky confrontation in Steve's front yard.

"Speaking of that, Ms. Pauling, I'm surprised you couldn't get Amber up here with us." He nudged Edie's arm. "Are your ratings slipping? Or have you squandered all your political capital?"

"In case you haven't noticed, there're only two seats on this side of the aisle. If Amber were here, you'd have to choose which girl you wanted to sit next to."

Steve imagined he'd be on the floor looking up at his two favorite females, but he let that one go as a foregone conclusion.

Edie brushed a few errant strands of straight black hair away from her face. "Besides, this is your show. I'm just along for the ride and to make sure the story gets properly told, like any good journalist."

She paused and patted Steve's arm. "By the way, you never finished describing how Capt. Jordan reacted when the vice president called him."

CHAPTER 2

AFTER A QUICK DEPARTURE FROM the fiery scene at the Lakewood complex, the two men in the Lexus made good time to their next destination. As Tony Funetti and Marty Calebrese exited the car, overcast skies hid any intrusive glow from the moon. There were no streetlights until one reached the intersection of the county road a half-mile west of their present location. Shrouded in black clothing, Tony lifted the lid on the gray trash bin at the end of a long driveway in the quiet, rural neighborhood in Morris County.

"For chrissakes, Marty. Why the hell we gotta put this stinking garbage in my trunk?"

"Keep your voice down. We may be in the boondocks, but there're still houses around. Let's take this stuff someplace where we can look through it without getting caught by any of the nosy neighbors."

In a final gesture of protest, Anthony Funetti, who some called Tony Two-Step, slammed down the trunk lid of his metallic silver Lexus and climbed back in behind the wheel. Deciding not to draw any undue attention from the quiet neighborhood, Marty The Mouth Calebrese chose not to shoot his partner and slid into the front passenger seat.

Marty signaled for Tony to move out. "Let's get over to the landfill and see what we got."

"Crap. All the way over there? I can smell the shit already. And Paulie only detailed this ride last week."

"Just open the damn window and drive." Marty's fingers flirted with the fabric on the jacket covering his pistol.

Tony Funetti was twenty-four and putting on the pounds. If his current diet and drinking habits remained constant, his first heart attack would strike before he reached the age of forty. On the other hand, with his present career choice, which began when he dropped out of the eighth grade, he could easily preempt that prediction.

Fit and trim at twenty-six, Marty Calebrese had fought his way through Army Ranger school. A high school guidance counselor had persuaded Marty to channel his energies into a military career, hoping the training and discipline could corral the darker side of the young man's temperament.

Marty had the intellect to tackle almost anything; that was never his problem. His scholastic aptitude, especially in science and computer classes, only suffered when his mind wandered due to boredom. He considered himself smarter than everyone else, including his teachers. In the mind of the guidance counselor, Marty might be a productive adult if he learned to curb his socially deficient attitude.

At first, he excelled in the Ranger program and completed the grueling training course. There came a point when he couldn't keep his underlying conflicts to himself. It began with a simple disagreement with his commanding officer. This escalated into an emerging disregard for all military authority and gained him an inevitable dishonorable discharge.

Ejected from the army, Marty packed his duffle and hopped on a bus back to New Jersey, leaving Fort Benning, the First Battalion, and the Rangers behind. Before heading home, his foremost skill had earned him a designated marksman status during his abbreviated stint with the Seventy-Fifth Ranger Regiment sniper team.

* * * * * *

Marty Calebrese and Tony Funetti entered the landfill via their usual private entrance and sifted through the three large black plastic trash bags pulled from the oversized gray container in the rural Morris County neighborhood. After a frustrating thirty-minute effort inspecting the contents, the only thing accomplished was the rare squelching of Tony's voracious appetite.

"What the hell are we looking for, Marty? I hope you don't want me to count the number of fuckin' condoms." He kicked one of the empty trash bags over the strewn garbage pile at his feet. "Jesus. Why the hell doesn't the guy flush 'em down the toilet like any normal American would?"

"Doesn't anything I teach you ever stick? You gotta be more vigilant. Maybe for once you'd even learn a thing or two." Marty shook his head and pointed a finger at Tony. "Remember the big tanker truck we saw pull up his driveway last week? The one with the funny saying on the side? They were getting their septic tank pumped out."

"Chrissakes," Tony said, crinkling his face. "How the hell could I forget that? It stunk up my car more than this here garbage. But so what. Who cares about this guy's septic tank?"

"That's what I'm trying to tell you. This is why he doesn't flush the condoms down the toilet. He doesn't want to clog up his septic and have the crap back up into the house."

"Is that so? Here I figured everything flushed in New Jersey got dumped in the ocean—where it belongs,"

Tony said, shaking his head. "Besides. You've lived in Newark your whole life. You're a city boy. What the hell do you know about septic systems?"

Marty tossed a crumpled milk carton at him.

"Ah fuck," Tony said, checking for any rancid drips clinging to his shirt. He then arched his brows and looked at Marty. "How does any of this help us stick something to these people? Didn't you say Big Al's getting pissed off at us for spending all this time and coming up with nada?"

Marty had no good answer and shrugged. "I'm trying to tag as much detail as we can. And possibly educate you in the process."

"Fuck you, Marty."

After three weeks of surveilling the house, following the two occupants to work, and at one point snooping around inside the place, Tony Funetti and Marty Calebrese had accumulated a lot of useless information. They had even planted several listening devices in the house. Other than learning more than they wanted to know about their quarry's personal relationship, which appeared energetic and healthy, Tony and Marty didn't come up with a single damn thing to use against her. They did, however, have a good picture of the couple's daily routines and work schedules, as well as upcoming travel plans.

Nonetheless, Marty Calebrese's brain worked overtime as he tied together the details of what they'd picked up. Not at the house, but at the high school where the husband worked. Surveillance at the school may have been more dangerous in terms of exposing themselves, but there was a good chance it could pay off. The wife,

CEO of the company targeted by Marty's boss, had not given them a great deal to work with, but taking down the husband might be the best place to start.

The first modicum of a potential plan took root. But so far Marty kept this to himself, not even filling in Tony on what he had in mind. He didn't need any of Tony's editorial comments. With everything else coming up empty, it was time to call the boss. He imagined the smile on Big Al's pasty white face when he ran this idea by him. The heat was about to be turned up even more than the firestorm they'd created earlier this evening at the Lakewood complex.

CHAPTER 3

STEVE REMEMBERED TELLING THIS STORY to Edie but smiled as he turned away from the jetliner's window and the rugged peaks of the Rockies far below their flight path. He cleared his throat and replayed the recent conversation between Capt. Jordan of the San Francisco Fire Department and Tyler Griffin, the vice president of the United States.

* * * * * *

"Yeah? And I'm the fucking Pope," Capt. Jordan barked into the phone.

The C shift squad working at the Dogpatch fire station in the Potrero Hill section of San Francisco was sitting down for their evening meal. Steve Casella was the hazmat response team coordinator for the station, and it had been his turn to cook dinner for the squad.

The call came in on Capt. Jordan's personal cell phone as he placed a fork of Steve's prized veal parmesan into his mouth. The squad always ribbed Steve about his Sicilian heritage and pretended to be wary of his supposed mafia connections, but the truth of the matter was that as far as Steve knew he was the sole surviving member of the Casella clan. The previous summer, his last known living relative, Uncle Bob, had been killed when he got caught up in a vicious terrorist plot in the Idaho panhandle. Both Steve's mother and father were also deceased.

After several choice words and gestures, Capt. Jordan scrawled something down on his napkin and pressed the end button on his phone.

"You guys are going to be paying for this childish stunt. Washington, D.C.—my ass. Wait till I find out who the hell's responsible for this prank."

He looked straight at Steve when he said this, but instead of waiting for a response, he punched in the number off the napkin and gave his name to the person answering the call. Thirty seconds later Jordan rose from his chair so forcefully it flipped backwards and crashed onto the glossy black and white tiled floor. Clanging echoes filled the quiet room. All eyes stayed on the captain.

"Ah. No, sir. It was nothing...," Jordan mumbled, minus the earlier venomous tone.

Jordan stood at attention, looking ready to salute the phone. After several minutes of additional muted and submissive responses from the overactive, alpha leader of C shift, he shoved the phone back into his pocket, yanked up his chair, sat down, and resumed tasting Steve's creation. After taking his first bite, Jordan smacked his lips and leaned forward, inhaling the savory aroma of Steve's secret sauce. The rest of the squad stared at the captain while Steve kept his eyes down, toying with the food on his plate.

Without another word, Capt. Jordan finished his veal parmesan and brought his empty plate over to the sink. After rinsing it off, Jordan casually called out over his shoulder.

"Hey, Casella. Let me get the dishes for you tonight. Seems you need to get ready to go on a little trip. Investigating suspicious fires? Sounds like another vacation with Edie's political pals—if you ask me."

Amber sat straight up at Steve's side and barked twice at the captain. Steve never changed his deadpan expression.

* * * * * *

Still gazing at Edie, Steve finished up his story by saying, "As I understand it, the vice president told the captain that this investigation was a personal matter, and he was simply asking him for a favor. I finally convinced Jordan I'd be using my own leave time for this trip and swapping shifts with the rest of the squad when I got back. But to tell the truth, he might still be standing at attention."

He hiked his eyebrows. "By the way. Are the taxpayers picking up the tab for all this luxury; not to mention the other expenses we're sure to run up?"

"No way," Edie replied. "Tyler Griffin doesn't even want these expenses on his family's company books. This is all personal for the vice president."

Steve nodded and a slight smirk transformed his face. "So, I'm looking forward to seeing what you did with the condo."

Edie traveled extensively between coasts for her work and had purchased the condo unit she had been renting before meeting Steve. It was the lower left-side apartment of a four unit restored Victorian building near the southeast section of the Morristown Historical District.

"Right. If I didn't tell you all about my redecorating adventures, you wouldn't have appreciated the difference," Edie teased. "Speaking of which, there are a few manly chores I need help with."

Steve gave Edie's hand a gentle squeeze, reached into the seatback pocket, and opened up his New Jersey guidebook, again thumbing through the pages. Edie sat back and closed her eyes. She smiled inwardly as her mind grew hypnotized by the droning sounds of the jumbo jet's engines mixing with the subsonic rushing air being thrust aside.

Their wedding plans needed finalizing. Little details like when and where still had to be discussed. Steve insisted they get married in New Jersey so her family wouldn't be inconvenienced by any long trip to San Francisco or Idaho.

Edie still remembered the surprise of seeing her family, when unbeknownst to her, Steve flew them out for a surprise engagement party late last summer in Coeur d'Alene, Idaho. As the result of Amber's indiscretions, Edie suspected Steve would be proposing. After Steve had stashed away the ring, Amber had sniffed it out and brought it to Edie. Edie figured out the script but kept her silence. Steve never noticed the tooth marks on the box. Edie had almost failed to recognize her family lined up under the pavilion when Steve pulled into the outdoor event area called Alder Creek Grove.

One thing remained a constant trouble for Edie. It saddened her that Steve had no family to invite to the wedding and share in their happiness. On this subject, something had been germinating and, now and then popped to the surface. Before Edie slid into a restful sleep, she convinced herself to follow up on those thoughts.

CHAPTER 4

EDIE AWOKE TO THE SUBTLE change in cabin pressure as the jumbo jet began its initial descent into Newark Liberty Airport. Her head remained nestled against Steve's shoulder until the captain's voice crackled over the cabin's speaker system announcing their final approach. Edie glanced out the window at the familiar sight of the Statue of Liberty and waved, lipping a silent hello.

She hadn't visited the Statue of Liberty since grade school, but perhaps she and Steve could find the time for a quick tour before returning to the West Coast. Although Steve downplayed his impending investigative tasks, she had a gnawing sensation he'd be in for some intense undertakings over the next couple of days. A tour of the Statue of Liberty might be a great way to unwind. Too bad the inside of the statue had been closed to the public again for needed repair work. It would've been fun to climb up the spiral staircase and get a birds-eye view of the entire metropolitan area.

Edie remembered once peering out of Miss Liberty's crown at the thrilling harbor views; the crisp winds billowing the long strands of hair about her face. She and several other adventurous kids in her sixth-grade class had tried sneaking up the arm to get into the off-limits upper torch area, but two stern looking security guards had put a quick stop to their quest. She wondered when the last time anyone else conspired to do that. Given all the enhanced security measures now in place, she doubted they'd be successful.

* * * * * *

After walking down the extended jetway into Terminal C, Steve and Edie headed to the baggage claim area to pick up their luggage and rescue Amber from her travel crate. They had opted for the direct concierge transfer service rather than subjecting Amber to any prolonged waiting in the cargo area of the airport.

As they exited the security zone, Steve and Edie were confronted with a surprising picture of two familiar figures: A large black man with a completely shaved head kneeling in the corner holding a leash, tussling the fur on an animated white German Shepherd. In addition, two serious looking airport security guards stood about fifteen feet to the left. Steve and Edie's luggage lay scattered in a heap directly in front of the guards.

Steve turned to Edie and whispered, "If we head straight for the side door... it's possible they won't see us."

Before the last word had left his lips, Amber jumped from Sampson Pauling's side and headed straight for them. Sampson didn't release the white German Shepherd's leash fast enough. With a resounding thud, the large man wound up stretched across the floor. The harsh terminal lights reflecting off his glossy head. His uttered expletives echoed throughout the area.

After an enthusiastic greeting, Amber relaxed at Steve's side, and the three headed over to Sampson Pauling. He sat on the floor gingerly rubbing his left elbow and right knee.

Edie shrugged and said to her older brother, Sampson, being sure to include the two security guards in her remarks, "Ah, thanks for getting our luggage?"

Looking satisfied that the crazy white dog was now under control, the two security guards walked closer. The one holding a clipboard coughed and then addressed Steve while the other guard's hand rested on his holstered service revolver.

"Sir. Please show me your identification."

Steve pulled out his driver's license and dropped it onto the offered clipboard held by the outstretched arm. The man scribbled on the form and checked the appropriate boxes. He then extended the clipboard and license back to Steve.

"Sir. Please sign at the bottom by the X. The damn dog and the yellow copy are all yours."

Steve did as instructed and handed the clipboard back. He folded the yellow paper and stuffed it into his pocket along with his driver's license. Looking as if the weight of the world had been lifted from their shoulders, the two guards scurried off with repeated nervous glances at the dog.

With Amber padding by his side, Steve walked over and reached out to help the two-hundred-seventy-pound Sampson Pauling back on his feet. Both Steve and Edie stood staring, waiting for her brother to explain.

Sampson pointed to one of the security cameras.

He rubbed his hands together and said, "I'll bet if you find a copy of the airport's security disc, you'd have a damn good chance of getting it shown on *Red Eye*. That is if the show's still running."

He was referring to the late-night cable show that often featured amusing animal videos to preface a news story.

Steve and Edie never budged, so Sampson kept talking.

"I didn't see how it happened, but I believe the genius who wheeled the crate from the conveyor system thought it would be a good idea to... well. Somehow the door on the crate opened and Amber... well. You can see for yourself. Anyway, doesn't appear she's suffered any ill effects from the long flight."

Edie nodded and looked over at the crowd still gathered around the luggage carousel; the one with their flight number flashing on the digitized sign. The passengers milled about waiting for the carousel to turn. Everyone kept a wide berth from where Amber sat.

"How'd you get our bags out here, Sampson? Nobody else has gotten their luggage," Edie said.

Sampson's hawk-like eyes grew large, and a smile spread across the smooth chocolate skin of his squarish, round face. "It was really something. When I came through the terminal door, everybody was yelling and running all over the place."

He glanced down at Amber. "I guess Amber didn't recognize me, or maybe she was too busy to pay me any attention. Here she was scurrying about, nose in the air and then—bang!" Sampson clapped his hands once. "She scooted herself onto this carousel here and scrambled to the top. Then she disappeared into that opening in the center." He clapped his hands again. This time Amber added a few barks. "I heard a lot of commotion from somewhere inside, and a little while later—out she comes with one of those bags. Then back in she goes again. After a few trips, it became routine. I even got used to the irritating screeches of her nails slip-sliding on the shiny metal surface. Unfortunately, the guards didn't appear amused."

Sampson paused and pointed to his left. "I trust she didn't miss any. Did she?"

Steve and Edie looked over at the pile of bags and then back at Sampson, simultaneously shaking their heads.

Sampson strode over to their luggage and said, "I'll give you a hand with these. My car's right outside in the waiting area."

Edie grabbed Sampson's arm and gave him a quick hug. "It's great to see you, bro. Thanks for meeting us."

Edie took a step back and stared up at her brother. "Now. What in the hell are you doing here? I don't recall giving you our flight information."

She glanced over at Steve, who shook his head but remained silent. Edie continued, "We have a rental car waiting, and then we're headed over to my condo in Morristown."

"Well, that's not gonna happen." Sampson hiked his shoulders. "Besides, I canceled your Avis reservation. There's been a slight change in plans."

With most of the luggage in tow, Sampson looked over his shoulder as he approached the revolving doors. "I'll be your limo driver for this evening. Sorry, but I forgot my cap."

CHAPTER 5

THE VICTORIAN CLOCK ABOVE THE revolving door ticked past two o'clock. The lunch crowd had thinned as the maître d' escorted the two men to a booth in the back corner of the Old Ebbitt Grill. Philip Lucchesi and Albert Rozano slipped across from each other onto the wine-colored velvet seats. The historic Washington, D.C., restaurant was conveniently located, not only near the White House, but was also close to the headquarters of many high-profile lobbyist groups, including the national union headquarters of the Consolidated Brotherhood of Tradesmen, or CBT.

Over the long years of the restaurant's existence, countless brokered deals occurred in this very dining room: many with long-lasting consequences for the nation. Not all those deals had turned out as expected for the participants.

Both men wore similar charcoal gray pinstriped business suits, but even a casual observer could never mistake one for the other. Philip Lucchesi, the national president of the CBT, stood over six-foot-two, and though in his early sixties, he projected a fit and trim two-hundred-pound image.

Across the mahogany table sat the pasty, white figure of Albert Rozano, the head of the New Jersey chapter of the same union. The fact that people referred to him as Big Al spoke volumes for what lurked behind the wire-rimmed glasses highlighting his roundish face and slicked-back, thinning brown hair. While not technically fat, his short stature helped present him as an inconsequential looking bureaucrat. Those who knew him personally or were familiar with his reputation were aware of how dangerous a conclusion that would be.

After the server returned with cocktails and took their lunch orders, Lucchesi placed his manicured fingers on the edge of the table and leaned his formidable frame closer to Big Al. To someone passing by he portrayed the image of a cobra poised to strike at a chubby little mole.

"Sounds good, Al. It's a masterful scheme. I'm pleased by your initiative."

With Philip Lucchesi's Botox-induced eyes and freeze-framed smile over the backdrop of a leatherized tan, Big Al Rozano had trouble differentiating any pleasurable expression on the face of the union president. Rozano nodded his head, lifting the martini glass to his lips. He had no problem accepting credit for Marty Calebrese's idea.

Although impossible to say, Lucchesi may have intended to keep the smile as he continued, "Like I always say, if you can't find the dirt, you gotta haul it in."

A hint of a chuckle emphasized his words. "And the underage part is good too. The press will tear the guy a new asshole. This is going to bring his pretty little white wife down with him. Kristie Pauling. Or is it Kristie Griffin-Pauling? She still hyphenating her last name? I hope so. Makes our job much easier. There goes the wholesome image of the vice president's family business. She'll wish she never married that black high school teacher in the first place. Not only will her political career be stopped in its tracks, but can you see the headlines when the husband of the company's CEO gets his ass hauled off to jail?"

He paused. Big Al Rozano waited for Lucchesi's expression to change. It didn't, but his voice lowered as he leaned forward. "And you're sure this kid you're playing will grab the bait?"

"Oh yeah," Rozano replied, smiling. "We got a few details to work out, but one way or the other this is gonna happen."

Big Al Rozano remained confident about that part. Tony Funetti and Marty Calebrese had guaranteed it with their lives. At least Rozano looked at it that way. Didn't matter if Tony didn't understand what the hell was going on.

"And we're making headway with the workers in Griffin's company," Rozano added. "I'm talking about not only the mills, but the entire retail operations too. The boys have turned up the heat and are making their typical convincing arguments. Won't be long till the employees vote us in. Marty Calebrese can be very charming. He has a way of convincing people to do what he wants. We're still working on Tony Funetti's people skills. His parole officer has had several helpful suggestions."

With the same expression fixed on his face, Philip Lucchesi nodded and said, "Got big news today. Comes from our guy in the White House."

Lucchesi's voice lowered even more while Rozano instinctively glanced around the room. "I can't confirm when they plan to make this public, but the word is that President Andersen will not be running for reelection. She's been diagnosed with a chronic disease. So far the president's office has kept a lid on it. Well, except for this little leak."

Big Al Rozano tried to process how this impacted his immediate plans.

Before the news had a chance to sink in, Lucchesi said, "And there's a twist that complicates this whole thing. The word we're getting is the president plans on endorsing Tyler Griffin. This would normally make sense, him being the vice president. But due to the circumstances of how they both got into office last year—especially with them being in opposing parties—when this gets out, there will be one hell of a feeding frenzy."

After a pause and a prolonged glare at Rozano, Lucchesi said, "Our job is to determine how we can work this to our advantage. I'll tell you one thing. As you can guess, Vice President Tyler Griffin is no friend to big labor. If he gets elected, our progress could be set back indefinitely. But he may have more to contend with than just us. The mainstream republicans can't figure out what to make of Tyler Griffin either; him being the so-called leader of the Restraint in Government Alliance. If they even have such a position. And after Griffin accepted the vice-presidential role in a democrat administration, who the hell can figure out what the RGA faction is even thinking? So we may be in a position to hammer the hell out of the republicans and make sure we tear them apart once and for all."

Similar words to that effect had been echoing around this room for years, as each party tried to spin every new crisis to their own advantage.

Big Al Rozano said, "When those scandals ripped apart the White House and they indicted President Connor, I assumed we'd be screwed for a good long time. But those republican jerkoffs can't seem to do anything right. When they strut around threatening to investigate a scandal, we all feel a lot safer. Those morons can't find their assholes with a wad of toilet paper. What a fucking shame."

Philip Lucchesi picked up his martini. Finding it empty, he cleared his throat. "Too bad about the president, but she wasn't on our side anyway. What the hell was she thinking, trying to do the right thing for the country? Hard to believe her career got started in your home state. I thought you Jersey guys all lock-stepped to the same tune. Do-gooders like Alice Andersen will spoil a good thing. Not to mention the other guy from your state. Tyler Griffin. Soon people are going to think the whole damn state is conservative. Time to put a rest to all this nonsense."

Lucchesi slowly nodded before adding, "I can appreciate your current plan. Once Kristie Pauling's name gets smeared over the news because of her husband, the vice president is going to wish he never had a sister. Nothing like family problems to put the screws to Tyler Griffin's goals."

Both men clicked their empty glasses and leaned back as the server arrived with their food. Before leaving, he had taken orders for two more martinis.

CHAPTER 6

STEVE SAT UP FRONT NEXT to Sampson Pauling while Edie climbed in the back seat with Amber. Sampson fired up the engine and pulled away from the curb, heading for the airport exit lane.

Edie leaned forward and addressed her brother. "Nana's house? We planned on seeing her in a day or two. After Steve had time to settle into the investigation. She knew that. I talked to her yesterday morning."

Sampson glanced in the rearview mirror and caught Edie's eye. "Right. But believe it or not, this request didn't come from Nana."

"Request? Who's doing this requesting?"

* * * * * *

As Sampson drove through the tree-lined residential neighborhood of Newton and turned onto Nana's street, Steve remembered the first time he had visited her house. He looked over at Sampson's profile, and the vision of his imposing figure opening Nana's front door popped into his head.

As if reading his mind, Sampson, still looking straight ahead said, "Did I really scare the hell out of you that day?"

Sampson turned his head to Steve. "I can still see that honky look fixed on your face."

"No, you're a pussycat, Sampson. Your sister—now that's a different story." Steve felt a sharp pinch on one earlobe, followed by a wet tongue lashing on the opposite side.

After glancing again in the rearview mirror, Sampson whispered, "You care which one did what?"

"No, I can live with either one."

Edie changed the subject and asked Sampson, "Is Thomas going to be at Nana's house?"

"No, sis. You're stuck with me. The good-looking big brother. Thomas is out of town. He's at a science teacher's convention in Philadelphia. Kristie's with him too. You turned out to be quite the matchmaker. Those two are inseparable. Now the Paulings are tied to the vice president's family."

Edie raised her eyebrows. "Are you considering asking Kristie for a job in the mills?"

"No, I could never stand all those splinters. But there're lots of opportunities in Washington for someone with my abilities."

Sampson pulled to the curb in front of Nana's Craftsman-styled bungalow. Steve noticed the weathered shaker siding had been power-washed and resealed. But what pleased him most was that the old and dry cedar split-shake shingle roof, a potential fire hazard, had been replaced with a dark brown metal shake replica design. Before he had the chance to make any comments, Edie opened the door. She and Amber scooted out.

Edie leaned back in and said, "I'll go get Nana. You two juveniles can wait here and continue your previous discussion. Steve? Decide if you want to remain sitting up front and having me, Nana, and Amber lined up behind you. Nana might be old, but she's still quick."

Amber was sitting at the front door by the time Edie sprinted up the steps.

A short time later, Edie reappeared at the front door. "Change of plans. Nana's fixed us lunch. Come on inside."

Steve turned to Sampson. "What the hell gives? Didn't you say we had to pick up Nana and head directly over to meet with Tyler Griffin?"

Sampson shrugged. "Hey, he might be the vice president. But who you gonna listen to? Him or Nana? Besides, Edie did say we're having lunch. I'm sure I could eat a bite or two of Nana's home cooking. Wouldn't want to hurt her feelings now, would we?"

Without waiting for an answer, Sampson bounced out the door. Steve, three steps behind him, closed the gap.

After a hasty greeting Steve regarded as oddly out of character for Nana, they seated themselves around the mahogany dining room table. Amber settled onto an oversized dog bed. One Steve had never seen before; stuffed in the corner of the dining room next to the stone fireplace. Steve also took note that although Amber rested on her new bed, her ears stood erect, swiveled forward; focused on Nana.

Every time Steve observed Nana's image, his heart skipped a few beats. His mind contemplated the future. He pictured himself, a half century from now, sitting in a cozy rocking chair similar to the one parked on the other side of Nana's fireplace. The one with the plump, hand-embroidered pillow on the seat. He'd be looking up at Edie, who was bringing him a tray filled with chips, salsa, and an icy cold bottle of beer. And he'd be staring back at the identical face he was seeing now on Nana. Edie would pour his beer into a chilled glass mug and hand it to him. Well… the face resemblance was at least possible.

Nana interrupted his daydreaming. "Now, you children stop fretting and enjoy the food I've prepared. I'm sorry to make you late for your meeting with Vice President Griffin. When we're done here, you kids can go on by yourselves. I don't need to be involved in whatever you'll be discussing. The only reason he invited me in the first place was because of Alice." Nana was referring to Alice Andersen, the president of the United States and her dear friend.

"There was something Alice wanted you to hear. And she asked that I be the one to tell you. She didn't want you hearing it on one of those senseless news programs that run twenty-four hours a day." Nana stopped and smiled. "No offense to you, Edie. I always enjoy listening to your stories. And at least you haven't lightened your beautiful black hair. Lord knows, there are enough blond reporters around."

That last sentence put an unbidden image into Steve's head. He avoided looking at Edie, afraid she might read the lurid expression on his face. He almost jumped when he felt the ever-so-light touch of Edie's fingertips on his knee.

"Now where was I?" Nana said in a clear voice, sharp eyes fixed on her guests.

Steve's face burned from Nana's penetrating stare. An exceedingly rare response. Edie pulled her hand away.

"Anyway," Nana continued, lowering her voice. "I can just as well tell it to you here, so I'll get right to it. I'll do all the talking. So please keep eating."

No one made a move to touch their food, so Nana shook her head and said, "What I have to say is in complete confidence. You understand? I'm not sure when

Alice wants to make all this public. The vice president can fill you in on that. Last night, Alice decided not to seek her party's nomination for president. She'll carry out her term but will not run for reelection. Alice has just undergone a number of tests, and the findings from the movement disorder specialist sealed the deal. She's been diagnosed with Parkinson's disease, so—"

"Oh, Nana. I'm so sorry. How… is she—"

"Edie, just listen, dear. It's in the early stages and the doctors anticipate her living a normal life for many years. So once the new president is sworn in, Alice will be heading to her farm in Virginia. I hear it's a lovely place. So far, I haven't gotten the chance to visit it. Alice keeps saying she must come up with a good excuse for me to make the trip. She tells me it's the perfect place for her to write her memoirs. And as we all can appreciate; she's got plenty of colorful stories to tell."

Nana picked up her napkin and smoothed it out on her lap. "She's being philosophical about this whole thing. Did you realize Parkinson's occurs twice as much in males? And it is fifty percent greater in whites compared to blacks? Also, at her age the numbers are usually much lower. But I'll tell you what Alice said. The odds of her becoming the first African American female president because her running mate was impeached, removed from office, and later thrown in jail were much greater." She paused and coaxed out a small smile. "So, Alice figures she can live with whatever gets thrown at her from here on in. She just doesn't think it's fair to the American people to have a leader who can't give one hundred percent all the time—"

This time Steve interrupted. "I'd take fifty percent of her anytime, but for her sake, she deserves the chance to have a more peaceful existence. Dealing with all the D.C. stupidity she's been trying to fix would only exacerbate her condition. She's earned the right to sit back and let somebody else try and steer the nation back on track."

Nana wiped away a tear with the corner of her napkin and looked around the table. "I told Alice... now I'll be fully committed to looking for that man I've always promised I'd find for her. So, let's eat. I'm sure the vice president has other important things to tell you too. I'm hearing his family business is experiencing labor relations problems—New Jersey style. But you kids are probably aware of all that. I'm supposing it's why you're here. The vice president's sister, Kristie, is such a lovely young lady. She's the best thing that ever happened to Thomas. So young... and with all the responsibilities of running the family's big company on her shoulders."

CHAPTER 7

EVIDENCE UNCOVERED BY ISLAMIC SCHOLARS suggests that Muslim immigration to the New World may have predated the historic voyages of Christopher Columbus. A more recognized source of Muslim growth in our fledgling nation resulted from the slave trade. Approximately ten percent of the Africans brought to this country had religious roots in Islam. Following the end of the Civil War, a series of unrelated worldwide events contributed to additional influxes of Muslims from all parts of the globe.

Close to three million Muslims reside in the United States. African Americans make up the largest block of this Muslim population. Although the African American community is fragmented in this regard, a sizeable portion leans toward the orthodox Sunni sect in its fundamental acceptance of the first four caliphs.

In the mostly Caucasian population making up the base of Morris County, New Jersey, the African American community represents a scarce five percent of the total. This is two-thirds less than the average African American population in the rest of the Garden State.

While the odds of finding a female African American teenager of the Islamic faith attending George Washington Regional High School in Morris County were better than winning the New Jersey Powerball lottery, finding one who had a crush on a specific science teacher in that same school dramatically worsened those odds.

Most of this data was of no particular importance to Marty Calebrese. His only need was to identify this unsuspecting female Muslim as the seventeen-year-old senior named Leilah Harris, whose heart ached for the opportunity to be with her science teacher.

During several surveillance episodes at the George Washington Regional High School, Marty had made an interesting observation. This specific science teacher was popular and well-liked. On most days, packs of students surrounded him after school as he made his way to his car.

Marty observed that one particular student always placed herself in a prominent position next to her teacher. Even more telling was the longing expression on her face when she had faded into the background, staring at him from a safe, unobtrusive distance. In the shadows, she stood alone with her emotions, unaware of being monitored.

On one occasion, as the girl sat on a bench watching her science teacher drive out of the lot, Marty watched her writing in a notebook. After the teacher's car disappeared around the corner, the girl tore the sheet from the pad and kissed it. She crumpled it up and deposited it into a nearby trashcan before heading to her own car.

Marty remained patient; he waited for the area to clear out before strolling over and throwing his empty coffee container into the same trashcan. As he did this, he picked up the discarded paper. He returned to his car and flattened it out on the center console, smiling at the beautifully written words. Finding out the girl's identity would be child's play for Marty.

Most people misjudged Marty Calebrese. They never underrated his physical prowess or the danger emanating from his presence. Everybody saw the image of a thug; but Marty was much more than that. His electronics and computer skills gave him a decided edge; one he kept hidden from his enemies, but his current employer found advantageous.

* * * * * *

Several days later Leilah Harris left school and climbed into her car. After pulling out of the parking lot onto Saddleback Road, the ten-year-old faded red Honda Civic hatchback diverted into the delivery entrance behind the local Shoprite. Leilah Harris's heart pounded with such intensity; she swore it would burst free from her chest.

She had seen the envelope sitting on the driver's seat the second she opened the door. Her whole life changed after sliding out the single sheet of paper, along with a credit card-sized plastic item, from the sealed white envelope. Leilah had imagined the world glaring at her as she read the letter before starting her car. Even now she glanced around expecting someone to spring forward and call her a whore, or worse, for considering such a thing. Finally convinced she was alone, Leilah picked up the letter again and cherished the words one more time. She hoped she wasn't dreaming. At the same time, she prayed not to be sent straight to Hell for what she was about to do.

Leilah Harris, seventeen, was a senior at George Washington Regional High School in Morris County. Two months ago, she had passed the test for her driver's license. Three days a week after school and all day on Saturday, Leilah worked at this particular Shoprite to earn enough money to pay for insurance, gas, and any necessary repairs on the Honda. Her father had signed the title over to her. That was the deal. The car was hers if she took on the responsibility for taking care of it.

As far as any social life for the teenager, Leilah Harris kept to herself. For the most part, the boys ignored her. As one of the scarce black students in the school, her uniqueness should have been an advantage. However, her features, although not unattractive, were forgettable.

Her grades were near perfect, and she engaged in two after school activities: swimming and debating. Leilah did well in swimming but was self-conscious and embarrassed in a bathing suit where everyone stared at the boyish-like figure still plaguing her. On the other hand, as captain of the debating team she felt confident in her abilities to compete with anyone, on any level.

Her sole dalliance into anything of a sexual nature came late in her junior year. One of the other top performers on the debating team was an awkward, geeky looking senior, Todd Benson. None of the girls in school cared he even existed. One day after the debating team had wrapped up their session, Todd and Leilah somehow ended up alone behind the closed door of one of the library's private reading rooms. The rest of the library was deserted.

To this day Leilah failed to comprehend how things had gotten so out of hand. They wound up naked on the grayish-green carpet. Todd's scrawny, naked body kneeling between her legs. She barely noticed his shaking hands or the beads of sweat forming on his forehead as he struggled to tear open the condom from its sealed package.

She vaguely recalled thinking it a bit odd for him to be carrying a condom around in his wallet. Did all the boys do that? Did everybody have sex in school? And on this same carpet? Her nose instinctively sniffed for any telltale signs.

In contrast to Todd's diminutive stature, Leilah scrutinized this colossal throbbing penis staring her right in the face. At least she supposed it was huge. But it was the first one she had ever seen; up close and personal. What did she know? That almost made her laugh. Without considering the consequences, she reached out with her right hand and gave it a slight tug. And a little twist too.

Todd moaned and let out a stifled gasp. His hand still gripped the unused condom. Leilah found her tiny breasts covered in the thick milky substance. Closing her eyes she imagined trace scents of her damp swimsuit after a practice session in the school's heavily chlorinated indoor pool.

Todd looked away sobbing, his face on fire. In a panic, he shoved on his clothes and ran out of the room. She lay motionless on the floor for several minutes, trying to will away the guilt and the embarrassment. They never spoke another word to each other about the incident.

Leilah looked up from the letter as she clutched it to her chest. She dreamed how things would be different with her science teacher, Mr. Thomas Pauling. Every day in class she fantasized about being with him. She realized it was wrong but couldn't stop the biting sensations coursing through her young body. Until now, she never once dreamed Thomas Pauling felt the same way about her. He always treated her with respect and kindness, but he did the same to all the other students in class. She understood from his words in the note; they needed to be discreet. She must tell no one and meticulously follow his instructions. Soon they would be together. The rendezvous set, her desires turned to guilt. No longer a fantasy, her shame rose, but she still couldn't stop herself.

Leilah glanced at her reflection in the rearview mirror, seeing for the first time that in someone else's eyes her copper-toned, heart-shaped face with its wide upturned nose was beautiful. She managed a small smile as she primped her medium length, kinky-styled hair.

CHAPTER 8

NANA USHERED EVERYONE OUT OF the house and Sampson Pauling got behind the wheel. They waved goodbye to Nana and drove away in relative silence. Sampson, Steve, and Edie headed out of Newton and into the more rural part of Sussex County. The rolling farmlands and countryside provided a serene backdrop for their thoughts. After passing through the quaint town of Stillwater, they were again surrounded by thick stands of towering oaks, expansive pasturelands, and meadows on fire with vivid splashes of wildflowers.

Steve remembered that the guidebook Edie gave him had referred to New Jersey as the Garden State. Until now, recalling the expanses of oil refineries and petroleum tank fields plaguing the urban landscape surrounding the airport they had earlier flown into, he reckoned the book's author had never even set foot in New Jersey.

Those words sounded mean-spirited, he conceded. He actually did remember less industrial parts of the state from previous excursions. When he'd driven his motorhome cross-country to surprise Edie with an unexpected visit, he'd encountered lots of beautiful scenery in the Garden State. And right now, the engagement ring he'd carried with him on that long journey fit perfectly on Edie's finger. Even though the job didn't get done during that particular trip. He recalled the task had been easier said than done.

"We'll be there in a minute," Sampson said, turning left.

The car slowed and swung onto a paved driveway. Stopping at the black wrought-iron gate, Sampson smiled into the surveillance camera and hit the intercom button announcing their arrival. They emerged from a length of dark, marshy terrain and headed up a steep grade. This brought them to a landscaped plateau framing the Griffin family retreat.

Steve stepped out of the car and spoke first. "Wow. This is something. You guys been here before?"

Sampson nodded as he pointed to the black Dodge Durango parked in the pullout area adjacent to the four-car garage. "I drove that SUV up here last night. But technically I haven't been any further than the foyer. By the way. That's your new rental car. In case you were wondering."

Steve gave Sampson a questioning look but said nothing. Amber romped around the expansive lawn; then bee-lined to the more interesting prospects of the adjacent wooded areas.

Edie responded to Steve's question. "Nope. First time for me."

They stood gazing at the panoramic views of the Kittatinny Mountains. The dotted lakes that punctuated the meandering valleys and the almost limitless southern rolling landscape gave them the sense of standing on top of their own little world. In fact, they were standing at an elevation of less than twelve hundred feet. About six hundred feet shy of the highest peak of the Kittatinnys in New Jersey where they sliced across the far northwest corner of the state. Not exactly the Rockies; but impressive for the Garden State.

"You guys coming inside? Or are you waiting for Nana to appear out of the mountains to give you a sign?"

At the sound of the voice, they turned to see Vice President Tyler Griffin standing in the front doorway of the two-story stone colonial house. Amber, not impressed by the sight of the vice president, continued to scour the underbrush. The rabbit she'd been sniffing out had a much greater appeal.

The vice president turned, and they followed him into a spacious sunroom that spanned the entire south-facing front of the house. Once inside, they gazed at the sunroom's stunning rear wall: a coppery red metamorphic slate rising to the full height of the second story. Individual stones cleaved at varying widths and heights formed a rustic storage sink which captured the heat from the low-angled winter sun. A red porcelain energy-efficient woodstove, centered on this wall, served as a focal point.

Edie walked over to Tyler Griffin and planted a friendly peck on the cheek. "I'm impressed by what you're doing to save the planet. Wait till Al Gore sees this set-up," she said, her eyes taking in the striking surroundings. "Don't tell me you've been cozying up to the D.C. liberals, being shackled so close to a democrat staff and cabinet?"

"What? What the hell are you—I don't... Oh." The vice president nodded and waved his arms dismissively. "You mean this solar set-up? First of all, you of all people should recall that as president, Alice has made unpopular decisions from the perspective of the more liberal elements of her party. In particular, those pertaining to energy regulations." He placed his hands solidly on his hips. "And she garnered enough votes to repeal inane legislation that had stifled our ability to explore domestic fossil fuels." A smile arose as his brows hiked. "And thanks to that little incident you were involved with in the Idaho panhandle, Alice has put forward great strides in reeling in the powers of the EPA. Fixing the new healthcare debacle may take a bit more time." He winked.

Steve couldn't resist. "You seem to be dodging Edie's question, Mr. Vice President. Not that there's anything wrong with it, but why all your interest in solar energy?"

"Enough with the Mr. V.P. stuff. You're almost family now. But the truth?" Tyler Griffin's smile widened. "The story goes that before breaking ground for the foundation, the original owner of the property stood here and agonized for hours about the positioning of the front of the house. He wanted to make sure the sunroom faced exactly south. Not magnetic south; but *true* south. Whatever the hell that means." He shrugged before continuing. "One of the locals told me the excavator almost buried him with a backhoe. And then later, while the mason poured cement to fill in the hollow concrete blocks behind these stones…."

The vice president walked over to the stone wall and pounded his fist against it. "This wall is twenty inches thick. And it's solid. It has to be; they tell me. So it can capture the heat from the sun and release it back into the house at night."

Edie smiled and said, "Mind if I take notes? I might want to do a documentary. Would you be chopping your own wood for this stove?" She tapped her fingertips across the glistening red surface. "Imagine what could be done with the photo ops."

Griffin grumbled something and continued, "As a matter of fact, I'm proficient with the splitting maul. I find chopping wood keeps me from doing the same to certain members of congress. But where was I? Yeah. As I was saying…."

He pointed a finger at the stone wall. "When the contractor began filling in the hollow gaps in this wall, the owner threatened to use sonar equipment to check for voids. Told the mason he wouldn't get paid unless he did it right. They say the mason had an even better solution for this guy than the excavator."

His guests held their gaze on the beautiful, hand-crafted stone wall.

"And you should see the rest of the set-up we've got here. R-whatever insulation values in the walls and ceiling. Airtight construction. Special heat exchange circulation system. Solar panels on the roof for hot water. And probably a couple of other things I forgot about."

Steve said, "That's impressive, sir. This place must be remarkably energy efficient."

"Yeah. I guess. Anyway," Griffin said and looked around with a conspiratorial expression. "I bought the place because of the damn views. Try to get up here as much as I can; but hell, I never tire of looking out these windows."

He led them into a great room large enough to accommodate a much larger group than the current number of guests. Not counting the vice president's secret service detail, no one else was in the house. After Griffin finished playing host, insisting it appropriate to serve something stronger than coffee or tea, the three guests relaxed on the oversized tan leather sofa. Griffin sat facing them in one of the matching armchairs. Amber settled down in a tiny, shaded corner of the sunroom after padding back out carrying the piece of antler Griffin gave her.

"I'm sorry about shaking up your original plans," the vice president said to Steve and Edie. "And thanks, Sampson, for stepping in at the last minute and getting these guys up here today. I wanted to keep their arrival low key. I'm sure you can understand that sending my security detail out to the airport would've resulted in a major commotion...."

The former attentive expressions on the faces of his three guests changed into looks of amusement. "Is there something funny about what I said?"

"Nope," Edie said. "We were just a little surprised seeing Sampson standing by the... ah... carousel. It was good to have extra help with our luggage. With having to retrieve Amber from the luggage compartment, it could've been a little hectic. It was nice to have Sampson show up and smooth things out."

Steve watched Griffin search Edie's face with his deep-set black eyes—but only for an instant. He usually reserved anything longer for his adversaries.

Running fingers through his dark brown hair, Griffin leaned back and moved on, holding a somber expression. "I understand Nana filled you in on Alice's health. Her doctors just confirmed everything, but she's suspected as much for a while."

The vice president paused and shook his head. "In fact, we've had several frank discussions about when and how she should make the announcement. She's more concerned about what her stepping away from the presidency would do to the progress made since she inherited this fiasco from her former boss than worrying about her own health."

Steve glanced at Edie and reached for her hand. Sampson gazed at his shoes.

"And now on top of that," Griffin continued, "we have reason to believe there might be a leak. Alice doesn't want any rumors creating a panic and train-wreck the economy. It's barely on the right track to begin with. So she's being forced to move out in front and address the nation as soon as possible."

The vice president took a deep breath. "We've also discussed one other thing. I've decided to seek the nomination and run for president. And Alice is going to endorse me."

The room grew quiet enough to hear the crunching antler sounds emanating from Amber's teeth in the sunroom.

The three guests exchanged glances, but before anyone spoke, Griffin said, "The point being, Steve, there's good reason to anticipate that what I've asked you to look into might escalate into something much bigger. There's a hell of a lot more at stake than somebody just screwing with my family's business and my sister's own political aspirations. I'm sure my enemies have already been discussing how to make things even more difficult."

The intensity of his eyes assured that Steve grasped the gravity of his words. Without realizing it, Steve had placed a hand on Edie's shoulder; his mind racing with images from the vice president's words.

After a quick glance at Edie, Steve gave the vice president a slight nod. "Anything specific you have in mind?"

Griffin's face tightened and he aimed his words at Steve, but Steve noticed the vice president's eyes occasionally darted in Edie's direction. He sensed her being drawn closer into the picture.

"I realize you're meeting with Kristie tomorrow," Griffin said, "and if I know my sister, she'll have her own take on this. Which she should, being the CEO of the company. But for now, I wanted to give you a heads-up on these new developments with the president and the upcoming election."

He handed Steve a folder. "This is everything we've got on the specific fire incidents and a few other suspicious events. Kristie figured since I rearranged your schedule, I might as well give you this information now. Once you've had a chance to check things out, talk to Kristie about the details and the other disturbances at the facilities."

This time he turned toward Edie, his face softening. "And Edie, if you don't mind a little extra work, I'd appreciate your help and input on this too." He handed Edie an additional folder. "Please share this information with each other. I hope it doesn't cause any personal animosity between you two. I understand you have differing opinions on labor unions."

Steve glanced at the folder in Edie's hands. It looked a lot thicker than his folder. He then recalled Nana's earlier remarks about New Jersey labor relations. Why did he feel like an outsider, and everyone else had things already figured out?

The vice president said, "I appreciate you guys coming out here." He finished filling them in on a few more details.

* * * * * *

Behind her supportive nod, Edie visualized one thing. If Tyler Griffin ran for president, he'd be assured of having enemies coming at him from all sides. Since earlier learning of his request for Steve to investigate the suspicious fires described in that folder, Edie had decided this might be a good excuse to put together a story on labor and union tactics in her home state of New Jersey. Adjusting to the vice president's new request shouldn't be much of a stretch.

Edie was also interested in learning more about Kristie's recent ambitions to run for the state legislature. Politics could become a Griffin family tradition. She guessed this might have been the spark that prompted the union's initial ramping up the pressure on Griffin's employees to join the union. From what she recalled about Kristie's political platform and her efforts to fight for new right to work laws in the Garden State, she assumed the unions would do everything in their power to keep her from being successful. Kristie already wielded a lot of power as the CEO of one the state's most successful non-union companies. Not to mention being the vice president's sister. The fact that she was also the wife of Edie's brother, Thomas Pauling, made this fight personal.

CHAPTER 9

KRISTIE PAULING LISTENED TO THE metallic clanking of the trash receptacle's lid slamming shut as her husband opened the bathroom door in their hotel suite. "Mr. T," she called out, using her post-coital term of endearment. "You certainly are a creature of habit."

Thomas Pauling looked over his shoulder and smiled. "You want the ecological picture of where it would go and what it would do…?"

He took a step forward and extended his index finger. "But septic system or not, no one should ever—"

"Jesus. Come back to bed and snuggle up while we still got time. My flight leaves in two and a half hours and I want to make the most of these last few minutes."

Thomas nodded and ran a finger across his neatly trimmed goatee. A touch longer than his buzz cut hair. Compared to his brother, Sampson, Thomas was considered the runt, although a tad over six feet and close to two hundred pounds. His skin tone and facial features, however, were closer to that of his sister, Edie. The first time Edie saw his new goatee she had laughed and said at least now people could tell the two of them apart. That would never be a problem unless she stood on a stool and put on another hundred pounds.

Fulfilling Kristie's request, he tucked his body under the sheets and pulled her close. As she turned, her long blond hair cascaded over bare breasts. With a loving expression, Thomas stared into her hazel eyes.

Kristie sighed, but said, "Let's not get frisky; I'm just looking for a little cuddling. After I fly to Albany, I'll be on my feet for the rest of the day. I'm supposed to inspect the facility before we finalize the new contracts. Then I need to run over to our downtown offices for a board meeting."

Kristie changed her mind about the cuddling, but less than an hour later they were hurrying through the ornate lobby of the Liberty Suites International Hotel in Philadelphia. Thomas kissed her goodbye as he closed the door to the brown and white Crown Vic PHL cab. He watched the driver smoothly merge into the traffic and disappear as it turned onto Vine, headed for the southbound interstate. Traffic was light and Kristie should have no problems catching her US Airways flight to Albany. They wouldn't see each other until after the convention when he got back to Morristown.

This year's conference for the National Science Teachers Association would keep Thomas busy. Checking his watch, he shook off the last images of Kristie and walked briskly toward the Pennsylvania Convention Center. The Bioethics Workshop was getting under way in about ten minutes. He'd catch a bite to eat after the workshop and run through the exhibit hall before heading back to his hotel suite. The rest of the evening would be spent preparing for tomorrow's keynote address. Thomas was scheduled to deliver the speech at the conference's annual banquet dinner in the Grand Ballroom at six o'clock. There wouldn't be any time to work on it tomorrow since he'd be at an all-day symposium on the human genome. He knew by the time he returned to his suite tomorrow night, he'd be thoroughly exhausted. It was still too bad Kristie wouldn't be there waiting for him. No matter how tired, he rarely missed any opportunity to spend time with his bride. Although they were technically no longer newlyweds, he couldn't imagine his fervor waning.

Thomas Pauling and Kristie Griffin had met at the campaign election headquarters for her brother, Senator Tyler Griffin. Tyler Griffin had previously won the senate seat by beating his democrat opponent during a special election following the premature death of the incumbent New Jersey senator, Lawrence Hardy.

At the time, Thomas Pauling was still trying to come to grips with his own sister's involvement in the dramatic episode that took place in Spokane. A group of conspirators led by people from the White House, including the former president himself, had attempted to assassinate the vice president, Alice Andersen.

In the aftermath, Edie coaxed Thomas into joining the campaign staff for Senator Griffin's bid for reelection. She became an ardent supporter of the senator who had emerged from the political turmoil as one of the leading proponents for the Restraint in Government Alliance. The RGA was the grassroots movement that had almost been squashed by the incipient actions of the then incumbent president, John Connor, and his staff. Their bold plan was aimed at discrediting the fledgling group before they had the chance to become a dominant faction in mainstream politics.

On day one, when Thomas Pauling walked into the old Wells Fargo building which housed the senator's campaign staff, he became transfixed with Kristie Griffin, the beautiful, youngest sister of Tyler Griffin and the CEO of her family's business. From that point on, political strategies paled at his quest to win the heart of Kristie Griffin. As he later found out, she had a similar strategy, complementing his to a T.

CHAPTER 10

THE VANISHING SUN'S SPIDERY RAYS failed to penetrate the graying spaces between the oak trees lining the western corners of the Griffin family property at the eastern base of the Kittatinny Mountains. Steve slammed down the rear hatch of the rented Durango. The cargo area packed with luggage; Amber found a vacant spot on the rear passenger seat. Steve and Edie rode in a comfortable silence, finally getting a chance to reflect on the events of a long and tiring day.

Most of the trip to Edie's condo was a backtracking of their earlier ride following Sampson's surprise appearance. After bypassing the exit that would have completed a circuit back to the airport, Steve took the downtown Morristown exit off the interstate. While Edie dozed, Steve got himself disoriented but refused to nudge her until the third time around the Morristown Green. Groggy, she mumbled and pointed him in the right direction.

* * * * * *

Steve listened to the jetted bubbles from Edie's bath. After taking a quick shower, he walked around the condo admiring the changes Edie had made. Although he figured she'd be in the steaming tub for a while, he sidestepped the folder given to him by the vice president. It conspicuously stared back at him from the foyer table. Plenty of time for work tomorrow.

Recalling the final conversation between the vice president and Edie, and his comments on labor unions, Steve smiled at the idea of her now taking an active role in this investigation. Did he ever really think she was just along for the ride?

The condo tour didn't take long. He headed back to the bedroom. Tired from the long day, he crashed onto the king-sized bed, pulling up the soft down comforter. Thoroughly relaxed, Steve drifted into a semi-conscious state devoid of the issues that loomed on the horizon. His senses were awakened by Edie sliding her warm, moist body against his back. He turned his body over to blanket Edie's. They both opened their eyes together and stared into each other's souls. Beat for beat, their hearts kept time to the gentle rhythm of their entwined bodies.

CHAPTER 11

MARTY CALEBRESE LOOKED OUT THE café's large plate glass window in downtown Philadelphia. The Liberty Suites International Hotel was directly across the street. He hadn't eaten all day and the greasy cooking smells from behind the counter made his stomach growl from anticipation of the cheeseburger platter he planned on ordering. Something caught his eye as he turned back to talk to his partner, Tony Funetti.

"Jesus, Tony. Will you get that damn thing off the table before somebody gets a look at it?"

With a crooked smile spreading over his plump face, Tony slid the plastic bag across the table, shaking it in front of Marty. Marty barely had brushed it onto his lap before the redheaded waitress appeared at the booth to take their orders. Both men gazed hard at the swaying hips as she left with the order pad stuck in her apron, pen tucked behind her ear.

Tony leaned across the table. "What's a matter? You don't think she's ever seen one of those before? Did you check out those long red curls bouncing like tiny springs all over her breasts? And those sexy full lips? I tell ya, with an ass like that, I'm betting—"

"Put a lid on it, Tony." Marty interrupted with his normal response but was too pumped to be taken in by Tony's antics. After assuring himself it was sealed, he wrapped the plastic bag in several paper napkins and deposited it into the pocket of his windbreaker, zippering it shut.

Carrying a tray piled with dirty dishes, the redheaded waitress bumped her ass on the swinging doors, her twirling image disappearing into the kitchen. Tony's eyes remained fixed until the doors' hinges ratcheted several times, finally obliterating his view.

He turned back to Marty and nodded. "Careful you don't rip the bag with your zipper. You wouldn't want a big wet spot on your jacket."

A dangerous remark with Marty's hand so close to his holstered Glock.

Two days ago, Tony had been waiting in the hotel lobby when Thomas and Kristie Pauling arrived at the front desk to check into their room. After beating the couple into the empty elevator for the ride to their twentieth-floor corner suite, it was a simple matter for him to slip a hand into Thomas's coat pocket. Thomas had been momentarily distracted by the sudden coughing fit of the well-dressed, overweight gentleman in the rear of the car. Tony's coughing stopped as soon as the elevator arrived at the twentieth floor.

He held open the doors while Thomas and Kristie Pauling made a hasty exit. Either to run away from the potential germs spewing from the mouth of the stranger or to jump into the sack before the door to their room swung shut. From the distracted looks on their faces, Tony imagined the latter.

His next task proceeded as planned. Good thing for Tony. Marty had spent hours preparing for him to operate the electronic device. If the tiny instrument hadn't been so expensive and difficult to procure, Marty might have followed up with his threat to shove it up Tony's ass. Tony enjoyed trying Marty's patience before finally convincing him he could pull this off.

In less than five seconds and with no mistakes, Tony inserted the picked key card into the cloning device and recorded the necessary data. He breathed a sigh of relief, and he called out to the retreating couple. Tony waved the key card in his extended hand, asking them if they dropped something.

Yesterday, Marty included one of the hotel key cards cloned from the data read off the device along with the letter into the envelope they stashed in Leilah Harris's car in the Morristown Regional High School's parking lot. The second cloned key card now sat in Marty's shirt pocket. Earlier today, after watching the young couple say their goodbyes at the taxi stand, they used the key card to enter Thomas Pauling's hotel suite to give it a final sweep before setting the trap.

Using another one of his handy skills, Marty had hacked into the Paulings' electronic calendars. Knowing their schedules, he was confident of having plenty of time to get everything in place. Marty also thanked his lucky stars for the bonus items discovered in the metal waste receptacle in the hotel suite's bathroom. They were now sealed in the plastic bag inside his coat pocket. He envisioned that with a few minor supply purchases this evening, tomorrow's plan would have an even greater chance for success.

Marty experienced a slight twinge at introducing this new part of the puzzle but presumed he could handle the task with discretion. After all, he'd done a lot worse things. He wondered if Tony could deal with this. Tony was somewhat of a slimeball, but even he had his limits.

In a quiet, restrained tone, Marty outlined the modified plan to Tony.

"Oh fuck, Marty, she's just a kid. I didn't think we were gonna—"

"Look. She won't even remember what's happened. When she wakes up, she'll think it's a good thing. Well, at least till the cops grab Pauling and throw the poor bastard in jail."

CHAPTER 12

EDIE HAD BEEN WORKING AT HER desk for about an hour. The morning sun which had earlier cast long shadows through the lacy curtains of the living room window in her condo had become hidden by the increasing cloud cover. Hearing footsteps dragging toward her, Edie hit the screensaver button on her laptop and turned to face Steve. She was surprised to see him fully dressed, yet half asleep.

"You're up early." Steve arched his back and yawned. "Looks like you're now a part of this investigation too."

"Yep, but apparently you got an earlier start. I guessed that was what you were up to last night after slipping out of bed." She stared at the folder Steve got from the vice president. When Edie woke up this morning, she'd found its contents spread over the coffee table.

"I tried to wake you, but you were snoring so loud—" Steve ducked as a box of tissues sailed over his head.

"If you weren't sleepy afterwards, why didn't you to talk to me? We could've talked before, but something got in the way." Edie smiled at Steve who probably preferred a direct hit by the tissue box, or even a more deadly object. She was well aware that personal talks never ranked high on his to-do list. Maybe because she worked hard at getting him to open up to things he'd rather leave unsaid.

Steve said, "I guess I'll learn more details when I talk to Kristie later, but first I'm checking out the initial fire at the Cedar Knolls mill. That'll give me the best chance of finding any real clues to what's going on. My plan is to go in cold and do it by the book."

He nodded toward the files on the coffee table. "That's why I only scanned those papers from the vice president, just to get the dates and locations straight. Once my initial assessment at Cedar Knolls is done, I'll let Amber have a go at it too. After I'm satisfied, I'll talk to Kristie. You wanna join us? We're meeting in her office here in Morristown."

After a quick glance at the laptop's screensaver, Edie said, "Depends. I need to finish going over this background package first. Tyler asked me to take a fresh look at the union's potential involvement in orchestrating these little antics. See if I can put things in perspective."

"So," Steve said, nodding and raising his eyebrows. "Does that mean the vice president has not only decided the fires were deliberately set, but he's already indicted the culprits? I don't think I should be listening to this."

"Tyler's just being proactive. I've got a list of those same timelines too. And in that other folder he gave me there was a complete chronology of the events sponsored by the union. Seems they've been busy educating Kristie's employees on the benefits of unionizing. I need to check out the history of this particular union and how they've approached other open shops in the state. See how all this other nasty business fits their usual tactics."

Edie said this while avoiding eye contact with Steve.

Her eyes became unfocused, but then she blinked and continued. "I also want to hear Kristie's input on her campaign strategy. The union won't appreciate her platform regarding right to work legislation in the state."

She paused, recalling yesterday's discussion with the vice president. "The other concern is they might already know what's going on in the White House. Remember

Tyler was convinced about there being a leak? Once the union leaders in D.C. find out he plans to run for president, that'll be a more serious issue than any local political activities in New Jersey. Big labor will be really pissed at the Griffins."

Steve shrugged. "Not that I'm trying to criticize your investigation, but none of this sounds openminded to me."

"Where have I heard that warning before?" Edie said.

Steve cleared his throat. "You wouldn't be talking about your little EPA investigation, would you? And how did that turn out for you?"

"I doubt the EPA director pulled out her gun because I asked tough questions." Edie raised her chin, but then shrugged. "On the other hand, if the Consolidated Brotherhood of Tradesmen is run by the kind of people I'm thinking about, you just might have a valid point."

Edie smiled, eyes flirting. "But I'm sure the top union leader from firefighter's Local 7890 in San Francisco could straighten things out for poor little me."

Edie stood and pressed up against Steve. "Don't ya think?"

Steve held his ground. "Is this the conversation you had in mind for last night?"

A brief smile disappeared, and he continued with more of an edge in his voice. "But you wanna talk about unions? I've seen the hype about right to work laws. I consider my union dues a tax. You can't have some people paying, while others opt out, but still reap all the benefits."

As Edie pressed closer, his voice cracked. "What would happen to fire departments if paying taxes in the community were optional?"

Edie wrapped her arms around Steve and whispered in his ear. "That argument doesn't even make any sense. If you really want to discuss it, we can work on it later. But now you and Amber have a job to do. Maybe you'll be more successful keeping her in line."

Steve picked up the folder he had started reading late last night. He gave Edie a quick kiss and patted her on the backside as he walked out the door, Amber close by his side.

"You both respond well to treats though," he said right before the door closed.

Edie was coming to the understanding that their fantasies about this task being a simple look-see operation were vanishing faster than a slice of liver in Amber's food bowl.

CHAPTER 13

THE FORECAST FOR A THIRTY percent chance of rain and intermittent showers became the reality of a persistent, nagging drizzle, teasing the patience of the most sophisticated rain-sensing variable speed windshield wiper technology. To the aged and brittle blades on the old Honda, the erratic motion across the grime-sprayed windshield did a better job of drowning out the soft sounds coming from the radio than in providing any serious improvements to view the traffic ahead.

None of this penetrated into Leilah Harris's deeper reflections as she sat behind the wheel driving westward toward the Delaware River. Exuberant, frightened, nervous, embarrassed, and most of all guilty; but in her mind, no rain clouds existed. She visualized the warmth of the hidden sun, giving her the strength to go forward, ignoring the consequences.

The note had been burned as per Thomas's wishes. Leilah took care of that yesterday in the parking lot behind the Shoprite. She had placed the torn note, piece-by-piece, into the ashtray and gazed at the flames engulfing his gentle words. She then flicked the cooled ashes into one of the green dumpsters next to the loading platform. The scent of the burned paper lingered in her memory. The key card to Thomas's hotel room sat hidden behind her driver's license in the clear plastic slot of her wallet.

Although the rendezvous with her science teacher, Thomas Pauling, was not until later in the afternoon, she left the house this morning at her regular time for school. She wasn't expected home until late evening, scheduled to work at her part-time Shoprite job after debating team practice. Dressed in her usual non-descript school attire, she had packed a more alluring outfit for when she met up with Thomas. She prayed her wardrobe choices didn't just make her look silly. Last night while her family cleared the dinner dishes and filled the dishwasher, she slipped out and stashed the carryall containing those garments in the Honda's trunk.

Leilah had tried to work up the courage for a quick detour to the Victoria Secrets at the Bridgewater Commons Mall but was too embarrassed to even touch such revealing garments, let alone walking up to the provocative and sexy shop clerks to make a purchase. She imagined them sneering behind her back and speculating why someone like her would believe such adornments could make a difference. They would probably ask her if she needed any extra tissue paper to stuff into the pointless push-up cups of the skimpy lingerie. Those images almost made her lose all resolve, but the words in Thomas Pauling's note kept her on course.

After a slow and circuitous route, Leilah plucked a ticket from the parking garage's automatic kiosk, and the red and white gate sprung upward. After cozying up in one of the stalls of the hotel's third floor ladies' restroom, she removed her drab, fashionless garb. Looking at her plain white panties and bra, she chastised herself for allowing her shyness to overtake her longing for more desirability. She drove back the recurring notion of not even needing a bra. With a trembling fingertip, she applied dabs of perfume to places she'd never touched with such feminine scents. Leilah had selected a white ruffled and pleated spring dress to masquerade her boyish figure and small breasts. She slipped it over her head and emerged from the ladies' restroom feeling insecure, but none the less, a little more feminine.

With time to kill, she took a brief walk outside the hotel before returning to the lobby and heading for the elevator to transport her up to Thomas's suite.

CHAPTER 14

THE OLD MILL IN CEDAR KNOLLS was located
on an expanse of land behind one of the newest retail
stores of the Griffin Mills and Home Center, or GMHC,
chain. The mill operation itself was housed in several
older buildings, part of the first expansions made to the
fledgling company after the death of Edward Griffin,
Tyler's father.

As a boy, Edward Griffin dreamed of owning such a
mill. He often recounted the stories of sitting on his
grandfather's lap, listening to the colorful tales of his
family in Ireland and their struggles to save enough
money to come to this country. To his own family,
Edward Griffin described the passed down images from
his grandfather, who as a child, fought with his sister and
brother for the chance to peer through one of the tiny
portholes and see the Statue of Liberty and the bustling
New York Harbor. It signaled the end of their grueling
journey from Ireland, confined in the bowels of the
crowded ocean steamer.

This iconic statue had represented a new life to the
weary travelers disembarking at the new port of entry on
Ellis Island. A life that each ensuing generation of the
Griffin family would add to, making their mark, so those
who followed would have a better chance; never
forgetting to give back to a nation that provided such
endless opportunities.

High school complete, Tyler Griffin was ready for fall
classes at college when the crushing news befell the
family: his father's unexpected death from a coronary
episode while seated in his office overlooking the
millworks. With the help of his mother, Tyler stepped up

to take over the family business. As his siblings came of age, a ll worked together to turn the small operation into a successful, expanding business. Today it boasted twenty-six stores in New Jersey, New York, and Pennsylvania.

The three original millworks located in Cedar Knolls, Morristown, and Lakewood remained functional, but now served as boutique operations to supply high-end specialty trims, moldings, and doors for local building contractors. The bulk of the commercial millwork operations were now housed in upstate New York, closer to the vast New England lumber industry. Distribution centers served the needs of the GMHC retail operations as they expanded across the eastern seaboard. The remarkable success of the boutique millwork operations led to the corporate decision to integrate those fabrication services into as many retail centers as was feasible.

None of the mill workers in any of the GMHC operations were unionized. Nor were any of the employees in the retail stores. Keeping with the original traditions of the Griffin business model, the family worked hard to maintain a safe workplace culture that provided good paying jobs to all their employees. To the Griffin family, this made sense from both an ethical and a business point of view.

CBT union leaders recently concluded that the Griffin operation had been ignored for too long. They formulated their own initiative to correct this negligence and source of a major labor force. This coincided with another pivotal event. Last spring, a leading labor supporter in the New Jersey state legislature had been removed from office after being convicted of campaign finance fraud. The governor had scheduled a special election to take place in two months. When the union learned that Kristie Pauling, the CEO of GMHC, and the sister of Vice President Tyler Griffin, was throwing her hat into the ring, they dramatically stepped up their actions. Her campaign strategy was crystal clear. She was determined to fight for new, and what the union considered, anti-labor legislation. The leaders of the CBT could not let that happen in their state.

On top of that, with the latest rumor of the president stepping aside, and Tyler Griffin vying for that office, the union's fears about losing popularity and being subjected to greater scrutiny significantly escalated. Not only for their local efforts in New Jersey—but rising to the national level.

CHAPTER 15

EDIE PULLED ASIDE ONE OF the frilly, laced curtains, a gift from Nana, and watched as Amber scrambled into the Durango and Steve drove off. She walked back to her desk and ran her finger across the laptop's touchpad. The page she'd been viewing when Steve had earlier walked into the room reappeared on the screen.

One of her priorities this morning, besides what she'd told Steve about researching the CBT union for the vice president, was to dig into the possibility of finding out if Steve had any unknown surviving relatives. Steve rarely talked about his past, but she recalled hearing his father had grown up in central New Jersey. She also remembered seeing his father's high school diploma when they were combing through family papers at his house in Coeur d'Alene. That was issued from a school in the Garden State.

Why did everyone want to leave New Jersey? That was a different matter. Having even less knowledge about Steve's mother, she had to start somewhere, so investigating the Casella family seemed the logical choice.

The problem Edie faced was that Casella was a common family name and there were boatloads of possibilities sailing in the vast sea of people she had come across. Edie considered putting her newly developed covert computer skills to work but opted to allow someone else's expertise to do the dirty work. She didn't want to take advantage of her high-level connections for personal activities. At least not yet. If she were going to get caught, she'd need a better reason than this. Choosing one of the more popular dot com options, Edie followed the simple on-screen instructions for opening an account. After a flurry of keystrokes, she witnessed the unrelated Casellas sink to the bottom faster than cement shoes in the Hudson River. She printed out several pages of genealogies and family tree diagrams. Since the dot com genies had done all the work, Edie paid little attention to any of the mundane details of the complicated Casella family tree.

Edie returned from the kitchen and popped open a can of Pepsi. She grabbed the papers from the printer as she settled onto her new chocolate brown suede sofa. What the hell was she thinking when she bought this piece of furniture? In less than twelve hours, with Amber spending most of the time in the bedroom, fine white dog hairs already blanketed the sofa's cushions. She smiled at the recollection of looking in the mirror this morning and brushing her straight black hair free of those same white hairs.

Remembering how Steve reacted to Nana's blonde references, maybe she should consider lightening her hair. Nah. To be honest though, Edie was the one who responded by placing her hand on... anyway, things could get weird if that turned Steve on. She was never into hairdressers and beauty salons all that much anyway.

She read over the pages, jotting down names and other key information. Edie was not one to play a passive role in anything she came across, or in this case, had actively sought out. On a whim, she picked up her phone and called one of the names from the list. The contact information was almost as easy to find as the first part of her quest. Did she remember to thank Al Gore today for inventing the internet? She usually saved that jibe for when Steve was around.

After a pleasant chat with a person named Dominick Casella, who turned out to be an accountant with an office in Short Hills, New Jersey, Edie wrote down the directions and time they had set up to meet. Pleased with herself for taking this next step, she hoped Steve would be surprised and happy at the news of her discovering one of his relatives.

Dominick Casella came across as an open and well-mannered person. Even more interesting, he confirmed Edie's assumption that someone named Vincent Casella might be a close relative to Steve's dad. For some reason that name sounded familiar to Edie. When she pressed Dominick for more specific information on the person he called his Uncle Vinnie, he became subdued. Was he being evasive? No. Probably busy, but too polite to hang up on her.

Edie, excited about all the progress she'd managed in such a short time, looked forward to breaking the good news to Steve and the chance to meet one of his new relatives. She almost grabbed the phone to call him. But no, he needed to concentrate on his work for the vice president. She'd have plenty of time when he got home. Lay it all out for him. She imagined seeing his appreciative expression.

For now, she would put all that aside and work on filling in the gaps for the background information she needed on the labor unions.

Edie had difficulty transitioning.

Gradually at first, and then like a sudden leg cramp pulling her to the bottom of a dark and cold lake: Or was it those cement shoes again? Her innocent inquiry into Steve's family took on a distinctly different tone. A slight shadow evolved into a dark and foreboding eclipse.

Before hitting bottom, Edie lunged at her laptop, and her fingers flew across the keyboard. Her multitasking skills resurfaced, and at the same time she sifted through the notes she'd been working on earlier in the day for Tyler Griffin.

Everything she did. No matter how she looked at what she uncovered. The distinct outcome emerging produced a pounding, throbbing pain that spread across the previously contented topography of her consciousness.

Edie slipped out of a trance-like posture, her eyes flitting across the words still glaring back from the screen. She tested out her 'firm' voice. The one she relied on when countering the talking heads she confronted on one of her many cable TV guest appearances.

"Vincent Casella, or Uncle Vinnie as Dominick called him, is an accomplished, high-profile attorney. Steve's gonna want to speak to him." Her eyes pressed closed, and her face crinkled. "And I can't imagine he'll have any problems making an appointment. Uncle Vinnie's calendar appears wide open."

CHAPTER 16

THE LOBBY OF THE LIBERTY Suites International Hotel bustled with activity. In a far corner away from the flowing crowds of people, but with a good vantage point to take in the entire scene, two men had been sitting for most of the morning.

"There she is, Marty." Tony Funetti rustled the newspaper around for a better look.

"Keep it down, you moron."

"Shit. Dressed up in that outfit, she looks even younger," Tony whispered, lips pressed together.

"Get that damn paper out of my face. Why don't you just stand up and wave your fat arms around. That'll get more attention on us. You're acting like a fucking amateur."

Although Marty Calebrese agreed with Tony's observation, he needed to erase those images from his head. The newspaper crackled in his ear while Tony worked to fold it up. At least he wasn't peeking his head through the fake ficus tree next to his chair.

"Look, asshole," Marty said in a polite, measured tone; a smile fixed on his face. "We got a job to do. Let's concentrate on getting it done. Then we're outta here. Remember, we still need to return to our day job and crank up the pressure on the GMHC's employees."

Marty checked his watch. "Let's give her about a half hour. Then we go to work."

* * * * * *

Hands wringing, shoulders tight, Leilah Harris walked across the hotel lobby, envisioning all eyes focused on her, condemning her for what she was about to do. For a brief moment, her eyes locked on the two men seated in the far corner, partially obscured by a newspaper that thrashed about as they appeared to argue.

As she walked, Leilah swore the distance to the elevator grew longer. With a final effort she reached her destination and, after a slight hesitation, pressed the button, leaving a sweaty imprint. Leilah almost jumped out of her shoes as the doors to the closest elevator popped open.

She tried to smile at the elderly man with shaky arms who shuffled out of the elevator, positioned his wheeled walker over the grooved threshold, and inched across the polished blue marble floor of the lobby. At the last second Leilah heard the doors swooshing shut. She stopped the closure with her left knee. Luckily, she didn't tear her brand-new nylon pantyhose. Without tripping, she scooted into the elevator, grateful to ride alone to the twentieth floor with no stops on the way. Leilah feared if the doors opened before reaching Thomas's floor, she might panic, abandon her quest, and head for the nearest stairway to the parking garage and regain her sanity.

On the twentieth floor, Leilah stood in the quiet alcove as the elevator doors shut behind her. She checked the room numbers and directional arrows on the wall. Reaching into her purse, she pulled the key card out of her wallet and headed left down the corridor.

Right into the path of a hotel service cart being maneuvered by a short, overweight Hispanic woman in a crisp black and white uniform.

"S... sorry...," Leilah blurted out from her new position. Flat on her ass with an ugly rip in her pantyhose. Thankful for little things, towels and bed linens covered her spread-eagled legs. Several hotel guests walking by tried not to laugh at her predicament.

"Nooo... NoNoNo... Miss... It all mine fault. Please, I help you. You be okay, Miss?" The flustered hotel employee pushed, pulled, and grabbed at Leilah, attempting to help her to her feet.

"I'm fine. Don't worry. I'll just be on my way." Leilah rose as quickly as she dared and tried to place one foot in front of the other, heading in her original direction.

She had advanced about twenty steps down the corridor when—

"Wait right there, Miss!"

Leilah Harris froze in place. Convinced she'd been found out and about to face more embarrassment than she had experienced from that sticky little incident with Todd Benson in the library reading room. She felt like her torn pantyhose had opened a window exposing her brazen attempt to seduce a married man. Seduce? Who the hell was she kidding?

"Miss. You drop this. Your room key. Here. I find under towels."

Leilah stood motionless for a good thirty seconds after the clinking sounds of the cart faded away around the corner. She got a whiff of a harsh cleaning solution that must have dripped from one of the bottles knocked off the cart onto her dress as she lay on the floor. This new fragrance mingled with the applied perfumes in the hidden crevices on her body. Her eyes flicked down to assess the damage to her pantyhose, then darted about to make sure she was alone. She shivered at the icy conditioned air streaming across the clammy skin exposed by the expanding rip. And then, without realizing how she got there, she stood in front of the door with the key card shaking in her hand.

Leilah took a deep breath and pushed the card into the slot, succeeding on the third try. Although the process, silent and swift, resulted in the rapid flashing of the green LED light, Leilah swore a dagger had penetrated her heart. She imagined thunderous alarm bells reverberating throughout the entire hotel.

Once inside Thomas Pauling's corner suite, she kept reminding herself to breathe. She looked around, relieved to find the drapes—deep, rich, and floral-patterned— pulled tightly shut. Recessed overhead lights were on but dimmed. In spite of this, she pictured herself on center stage; spotlights following her every move. She wiped a bead of sweat off her brow.

Leilah noticed the bouquet of roses on the coffee table; a card hanging from the vase. She plucked the card and bent over, inhaling the sweet fragrance and ignoring the encroaching sanitizing aromas still wafting up from her dress.

According to Thomas's brief note, he would return to the room within the hour. After reading the message twice, she placed the card back in the envelope. Next to the flowers, a bottle of wine cooled in an ornate sterling silver ice bucket. An Anderson Valley cabernet sauvignon, that Leilah vaguely thought shouldn't have been cooling down. A single glass sat in front of the bucket.

A little disappointed, especially after agonizing about selecting this particular dress, but not wanting to spoil the moment, Leilah submitted to Thomas's latest series of instructions. After all, the last sentence made it all sound romantic and seductive. Her face grew hot from the words, accompanied by an unsettling tingling sensation deep within her womb—long after she had placed the card back in the envelope. She stood still, eyes closed, absorbing the intimate heat. Shivering, she blinked several times.

Thomas had thoughtfully opened the bottle of wine, so Leilah didn't need to fuss with the cork. It still took both hands to pour the wine into the waiting glass. She had tasted wine and even something stronger on previous occasions but tried to adhere to her family's religious beliefs as much as possible. Needing to block any religious notions from her mind, Leilah again closed her eyes and drank the entire glass. The wine spread a calming effect over her body, playing and intermingling with the lingering sensations from reading Thomas's words. Leilah refilled her glass to summon up the courage to approach the bedroom door. After another quick gulp, the glass was again half empty. Before heading toward the bedroom, she topped it off again with another healthy portion of the wine.

She arched her body back and tapped the door open with her foot. Her eyes gazed at the bed: the glaring centerpiece of the room. Leilah stepped out of her clogs and circumvented the bed, pulling back the covers. She half expected to be swallowed up into the mattress. Her fingers touched the naked sheets, perceiving an electric charge course up her arm. The linens smelled fresh, as Thomas's card had promised.

Leilah understood what Thomas wrote on the card, suggesting to make herself comfortable while waiting for his return. Taking another slug of the wine, she placed the glass on the edge of the nightstand. Several drops dribbled down her chin and splattered on her white dress, leaving a spreading red circle.

Regardless of what she did next, the torn pantyhose needed to go. That task completed, Leilah closed her eyes and tried to yank her dress up and over her head. That simple maneuver turned out to be more difficult than normal as Leilah stumbled and almost lost her balance. Remembering she hadn't eaten since breakfast, she guessed the wine was making her lightheaded and woozy. She also experienced a resolving calm that slowly washed away all anxiety. Leilah turned and stared at herself in the dressing mirror on the far wall. That sight made her laugh. Some temptress. Her body swayed as the giggles accelerated. The whole encounter somehow encouraged her to finish the job. So off came the shapeless cotton panties and bra.

Silly ideas paraded through her head. Should she have removed her white panties before putting on the pantyhose? Should they have gone on over the pantyhose? Would Thomas care about those things? She was grateful he wasn't standing here now to find out how naïve she was.

Not capable of standing up with any degree of certainty, Leilah's legs became useless, and she crashed onto the soft satin sheets, snugging the covers up to her neck. As her eyes blurred, she stole a final glance at the half-empty wine glass on the nightstand. Just before her eyelids shut and her mind eased into a semi-conscious state, she visualized being loved and caressed; treated like the woman she always wanted to be.

She murmured, "Please, Thomas. I need you now. I'm waiting."

CHAPTER 17

AFTER CHECKING IN WITH THE GMHC manager in Cedar Knolls and picking up the key to the fire damaged building, Steve hustled back to the Durango and grabbed his equipment bag. He looked up into the rainy skies. The earlier downpour had lessened, and Steve noticed brightening to the east. Being used to the more arid climate in California, he had trouble adapting to this damn humidity clinging to his skin and making him feel like a soggy, overcooked piece of pasta.

"Okay, Amber. Relax, girl," Steve said, roughing up her coat. "For now, you gotta stay here. Your turn will come after I finish my initial inspection."

Besides Amber's prior training in scent discrimination, bomb detection, and search and rescue work, she had recently completed an extensive training course as an accelerant detection canine. Amber was well on her way to becoming the most educated member of the Casella family. That forced Steve into last place, with his acceptance of being the only other surviving member in the family.

While a canine's ability to detect common reagents used as accelerants represented an important aid to the fire scene investigator, the presence of such highly flammable substances did not necessarily indicate malicious intent. Nor did it lead to the conclusion that the fire was deliberately set. Canines were used to help guide the investigator and streamline the gathering of evidence at the scene.

Steve headed to the site of the fire at the mill's processing building. He selected to investigate this location over the more recent fire in the Lakewood facility since the extent of damage to this building in Cedar Knolls had been limited. The fire sprinkler system had activated properly, confining the spread of the fire. In the Lakewood facility, the fire had burned unchecked following the apparent failure of the sprinklers. The entire building had been destroyed following a devastating flashover, complicating the investigation into the analysis of any potential incendiary areas of origin.

According to Tyler Griffin, there were indications that the sprinkler system in Lakewood had been tampered with prior to the fire. Since the system itself was an older design, with failures common, the findings were inconclusive. The maintenance records on the system had disappeared, and the county investigators provided no corroboration regarding the required inspections. Officials deemed the fire accidental, with supporting statements of potential negligence by the company. Tyler Griffin vehemently disagreed. He was convinced the alleged arsonists had learned their lesson from their first attempt here in Cedar Knolls.

There had been no serious investigations into this first fire and Tyler Griffin had done his best to keep the building closed off. Once the second fire occurred, Griffin wanted his own investigator looking into the evidence; someone he trusted to be both thorough and discreet. Union influences on the public sector administrators in the county and state offices tended to be overreaching, especially in light of the mounting campaign for unionization of the GMHC employees. Before making any public gestures, Tyler Griffin demanded answers.

Regardless of the personal concerns of the vice president, Steve wanted to start with the more straightforward investigation. The evidence found at the Cedar Knolls site had the potential to clarify the confusing information surrounding the second fire in Lakewood. Assuming the events were related. Griffin had also given him the official reports from the Lakewood fire, but Steve wanted to complete his investigation here in Cedar Knolls before tackling any in-depth reviews of those documents. Needing a clear head to avoid any premature conclusions, he did his best to put Griffin's personal opinions aside.

Although Steve's arson experience was not extensive, he remained confident in his ability to do a thorough job. He had taken the recommended courses based on the latest National Fire Protection Association guidelines as part of an assignment for his department. During that same time, while on a six-month leave in the Idaho panhandle, he had enrolled in advanced chemistry and physics classes at the Panhandle Institute of Technology and Sciences. Before embarking on a career in firefighting, he had completed basic college level chemistry classes at Santa Rosa Junior College in the San Francisco Bay Area.

It was possible he inherited the Casella science gene from his father, a tenured professor in the Biology Department at U.C. Davis for many years. At any rate, he was trying hard, but Amber still maintained the educational lead.

Although Steve's career choice shifted him away from the academic world, his father had always been proud of his accomplishments and kept a close eye on his firefighting profession. Steve didn't learn this until after the dramatic death of his father.

After his mother was killed trying to break up a fight between two of her students, Steve and his father never reconciled a growing strained relationship. Edie had shown up two years after the events leading to his father's death and helped him resolve a long list of haunting issues.

Steve approached the processing building and glanced around at the cluster of the three attached wooden structures. According to the documents he skimmed over last night, they were close to seventy-five years old, but looked to be in good condition. The leftmost structure housed the processing setup. The other two attached structures held the milling and sanding operations. Steve unlocked the steel entry door to the processing unit, flipping on the light switch as he stepped inside. Since the interior damage had been minimal, the electrical power had been turned back on.

He was hit with the damp, smoky remnants of the fire and the aftermath of the sprinklers. Tyler Griffin was true to his word regarding his efforts at keeping the building closed off. Exhaust system still shut down; windows and doors secured. Adjusting his senses, Steve slipped into this familiar element as easily as one would absorb the welcoming scent of bacon frying in the skillet. He let the swirling currents surround him and engaged the odiferous symphony of ashes and blackened timbers.

The inside construction materials included a concrete floor with several floor drains, fire resistant sheetrock covering the walls and ceiling, and an identical steel door on the opposite wall. Bright yellow steel cabinets labeled for flammable liquid storage lined the entire left wall. He opened up each one and examined the containers, noting their contents and condition. The cabinets were double-walled and outfitted with flame retardant vents ducted to the exterior. They conformed to the latest code requirements, and the different containers were stored and separated according to their classifications. The remainder of the room housed worktables and several steel rack units holding wood trim boards and custom designed doors. There were also three steel-framed, wheeled disposal bins with steel meshed sides and bottoms.

Steve spotted the one he was looking for, but first checked out the central exhaust system, verifying the high-temp cut-off switch. Knowing the fire sprinklers had functioned properly and suppressed the fire before any significant damage occurred, he gave them only a cursory examination. He shuddered at the consequences if the flammable liquids had reached ignition temperature. The whole complex would've been destroyed.

"This is why I'm paid the big bucks," Steve said, walking over to the disposal bin closest to one of the loaded racks. "Don't need no stinkin' dog for this."

This was the obvious origin of the fire. The items in the bin were charred, with a mucky ash pile spread over the concrete floor beneath it; a dried-up charcoal river snaking toward one of the floor drains. Steve first gazed at the sooty, charred inverted cone pattern outlined on the racked lumber next to and above the bin. The sprinklers had triggered before any of the formidable fuel supply figured into the potential devastation. He snapped photos from every possible angle, documenting the remains of the bin contents. Pulling on a pair of work gloves, he was about to initiate the task of picking up, examining, and removing the individual pieces of debris, when he observed something lodged against the wheel at the bottom of the bin. After a brief hesitation, Steve reached for his phone.

Satisfied with the explanation, he ended the call and got back to work. He removed a small plastic bag from his equipment case and snapped another photo. After placing the discarded item inside, Steve recorded data on the outside of the bag. He remembered the prominent signs posted at the building's entrance and in conspicuous locations throughout the interior. Steve made a note to ask Kristie Pauling if the company enforced those restrictions.

Piece by piece, he placed the debris found in the bin on the floor, trying to maintain the approximate original positioning for all the items. He jotted down notes as he proceeded. Steve's heartbeat momentarily notched up, sensing something materializing in the pattern, but at this point the dots didn't connect. Various sizes, shapes, and lengths of scrap wood, plus what looked like remnants of cardboard and paper were spread out on the floor. All exhibiting different degrees of charring. He reached the final layer in the bin and paused, staring at one of the remaining items. Before attempting to remove it, he snapped several more photos.

The object was a steel-framed box—about the size of a shoe box—with burned wood inset panels making up the surfaces. Like handling a newborn baby, with two hands, he lifted it from the bin and placed it on the floor. While appearing paralyzed for several minutes, his brain worked to piece together important bits of information.

"Son... of... a... bitch," Steve said, grabbing his camera.

Ten minutes later, he was leaning up against the Durango reading the investigation reports for the second fire at the Lakewood location. He contemplated whether it was even necessary to bring Amber into the building. Shrugging, he erred on being cautious and allowed Amber to check things out for herself.

* * * * * *

Steve pulled the Durango into the front parking lot, wanting to have a look around the inside of the GMHC retail storefront before driving over to see Kristie Pauling in her Morristown office. He snapped on Amber's leash and headed into the mega home improvement store. Inside the main entrance, a beaming young lady greeted Steve, offering him a shopping cart and a store directory with an attached sales flyer.

"Welcome to GMHC," she said. "Can I direct you to any particular department or help you find anything?"

Before Steve answered, she got down on her knees and greeted Amber to the pet friendly environment, offering her a doggie treat and pointing to a water bowl. She handed Steve a small bag of extra treats; to be used at his own discretion. She pointed to a coffee and donut counter in the corner of the reception area, but he would have to help himself. She must've thought Amber held the credit cards. As he pushed the cart down the aisle, he noticed an extra bounce in Amber's step and a wolfish grin on her face.

Steve didn't know what he'd hoped to accomplish, but he wanted to probe the working conditions of the operation and try to read the general attitudes of the employees. He acknowledged that Edie was more adept at getting people to open up, but he'd give it a shot and see what he could find out.

Throughout the store, diligent employees approached and offered assistance before he could open his mouth. Although made comfortable by the helpful, service-oriented staff, Steve gained little insight as to the internal working atmosphere. He felt like an outsider at a private club or organization.

As he drove away from the complex, he came up with an idea to run by Kristie Pauling.

He shook his head and smiled at the package sitting next to him on the front seat. At the checkout counter, he had been tempted to pull out his firefighter credentials and ask for a professional courtesy union discount, but remembered GMHC was a non-union shop.

What prompted him to purchase the deluxe GMHC branded cordless power tool kit complete with its own green and white molded carrying case? Since he hadn't gotten around to buying Edie a personal housewarming gift; this might work instead. A lot more practical than a bouquet of flowers.

While he imagined the genius of this decision, a distinct chuffing sound came from the rear seat. He checked the rearview mirror. Amber appeared to be resting with her eyes shut, but Steve wasn't convinced.

Earlier, observing from next to one of the supply kiosks under the loading portico, the man had reached inside his green and white GMHC apron and punched in a number on his personal cell phone. Steve had spent several minutes talking to this same employee while browsing through the specialty trim section in the lumber department. The name Curtis was imprinted on the man's apron. If he'd been paying a little more attention, he might've realized Curtis had learned a great deal about him from their seemingly casual discussion.

CHAPTER 18

ON THE TWENTIETH FLOOR OF the Liberty Suites International Hotel, Marty Calebrese inserted the other key card into the door lock on Thomas Pauling's suite. The two men slowly opened the door and slipped inside.

"Shhhhhhhhhhhhhh," Tony Funetti whispered, grabbing Marty's arm. "You hear that? I think there's someone else in bed with her."

"Don't be an ass. How the hell could anybody else be in there? We've been watching the whole time. It's just the sedative taking effect. You make a hell of a lot more noise when you're sleeping."

"You tiptoe around my room when I'm in bed? Should I be locking my door?"

"Fuck you. I can hear you snoring from downstairs with the TV on."

Marty peered around the door jamb to the bedroom. Leilah Harris's head lay nestled on the oversized pillow, with the down comforter pulled to her chin. A few more mumbled words rolled off her tongue, but he could see she had succumbed to the drug cocktail mixed in with the wine. Marty's homebrew concoction: a tried and true formulation, usually a lot more dependable than counting on his own charms to woo the ladies. The next course in the treatment would allow him to perform his distasteful task with no worries of Leilah feeling, or better yet, remembering a thing.

He nudged Tony and signaled to him it was time. They entered the darkened bedroom and Marty turned on the bedside lamp. He checked his watch, placing the small leather case on the floor next to the nightstand.

Looking back up, he said, "So we got Pauling back here—in three, three and a half hours."

Marty glanced at the nightstand. "She didn't even finish the whole glass of wine. I'm going to give her the full dose. That way she'll still be out cold when Pauling gets here. He'll be so shaken we'll have him eating out of the palms of our hands. Do you want to bet on who he'll be most afraid of? Even though we, as dedicated union representatives, aren't the most cordial guys he'd be dealing with, my money goes on his feisty little wife. Once she sees her stallion has been dipping his stick in this little black box, not to mention the age thing, it'll be one hell of a show."

Marty reached into the case and pulled out the first syringe. Plucking off the safety cap, he inserted the needle through the rubber seal in the glass vial and withdrew the drug up just past the desired mark. He flicked the barrel and then pushed a bit on the plunger. Tiny air bubbles spit from the tip of the needle.

"Gimme a hand here, Tony."

Tony grabbed the covers and pulled them back. "Oh God, she actually did it."

He dropped the covers back over the slim, naked figure on the bed. "Oh Christ, Marty, I can't do this. Did you see her? Jesus! She looks like a little—"

"Will you get a grip?" Marty said. He twisted Leilah's covered body on its side and peeled backed a small section of the comforter, exposing her butt.

"Can you at least hold this up? I gotta stick her with the needle here. There's no meat on her arms. Come on, let's do this."

Tony reached out to hold up the comforter, twisting his head away. "I can't look at this. I'm not having any part of what you're gonna do next."

"Just hold the damn blanket and shut up."

"I told you, it's sick. And I'm not squeamish. I'll cut off somebody's dick if I have to, but this… I don't care what the hell you say about putting the nail in the coffin. She's a baby! Where the hell did you come up with this idea anyway?"

"Fine. The injection's done. So shut up and stay outta my way. I'll be done in a minute."

Marty got to work trying to reposition Leilah's body, but to accomplish his goal it was necessary to remove a substantial portion of the covers. He slipped part of the covers up and over her head and tried not to fixate on the image of the sleeping young girl any longer than needed. The lower half of her body was exposed by peeling the covers back from the foot of the bed and tucking the bottom edge of the comforter just above her navel. He spread out her legs and attempted to bend her knees to keep them propped up, but they kept flopping back down.

Frowning, Marty said, "Tony. You're gonna have to hold her legs like this for me. No excuses, there's no other way to do this."

This time Tony cursed under his breath but obeyed. Marty grabbed the other syringe from the case and removed it from the plastic bag. It was already filled with the contents from Thomas Pauling's used condoms salvaged from the bathroom's waste receptacle yesterday. He squeezed out and spread lubricating gel onto the syringe. As gently as possible, he inserted it into Leilah's vagina, emptying the contents deep inside. Marty gathered up his stuff, throwing it all back in the case while Tony straightened out Leilah's legs and repositioned the comforter, tucking it back under her chin.

Tony froze.

"Hey, Marty. Something's not right."

Tony stared at Leilah's face and backed away.

Marty clicked on the bright overhead lights and panic took hold.

"She's not breathing right, Marty."

Marty yanked the covers off Leilah and began a desperate attempt at CPR. His old army training kicked in and he cycled through the steps, over and over, to revive the still figure beneath him. This went on for almost fifteen minutes. There were no signs that Leilah's heart would beat on its own, or her lungs would ever draw a natural breath again.

Finally, Tony grabbed the sweating and trembling Marty away from Leilah's lifeless body.

Marty rubbed his face, wringing his hands, pacing fiercely about the lavish suite like a caged animal. In the sitting room, he noted the bottle of wine was over two-thirds gone and realized the poor girl must've drank a lot more than he'd thought. Another vision flashed across his frenzied mind. The tiny girl in the next room weighed a lot less than he calculated.

"Shit. Shit. Shit."

Marty had killed before—many times. But not a child. He didn't stop to think of the other perverted acts he'd just fostered on this young girl—that was just business. Now, he'd crossed his own line. He could do nothing to change that, so he needed to focus on the job at hand. How could he make this work?

Tony stayed silent as Marty slumped onto the sofa. They didn't have much time. On the outside, Marty's face remained blank, but his gut wrenched and his head spun, trying to figure out what the hell to do.

CHAPTER 19

FROM OUTSIDE, THE BUILDING LOOKED like many of the other storefronts along Broad Street in the heart of the business district in downtown Newark. An unassuming sign stenciled on the glass door welcomed people to the Carter Community Prayer Center. A crowd had gathered in the meeting room. The usual number of poker games at this time of night had been preempted, the tables stacked against the wall. Rows of folding chairs now lined the room, and the occupants listened to the booming voice coming from the figure standing at the podium.

"I mean… this is for real, people." His dull watery eyes focused on the supporters seated in the room. Ribbons of tobacco smoke swirled above their heads like ghostly snakes dancing to a familiar tune.

"I've toyed with this idea since my last run." His mind had effectively erased everything relating to that failed debacle.

The man at the podium looked around the room and continued, "But this news, well it's not news yet, but I got it from one of my best sources."

A young woman standing to his right bobbed her head and body so hard her huge breasts undulated in rhythm to the man's words.

Momentarily distracted by this sight, the man at the podium slowly turned back to the crowd. "Let me just tell you all like it is. President Alice Andersen won't be seeking the nomination for our party."

Several voices in the crowd murmured a host of acrimonious words.

"What?" The man's eyes popped wide open. He grabbed the podium tighter with both hands and responded. "No. Doesn't matter why. But this time it's in the cards. The job is finally going to be mine. I can feel it in my bones. Andersen believes she paved the way. But hell, she wasn't even elected. This time we're pulling out all the stops. You can all see it, right? I got the cards in front of me. And I'm playing them till every last pathetic, guilty white voter is begging for a real black president. They'll be flocking to the polls to show the world America is at last colorblind."

He dismissed the transient notion that if America was colorblind, he wouldn't stand a chance in hell of attracting enough votes to be a dogcatcher in Queens, where he grew up in a middle-class family. A safe distance from the plight spreading in nearby ghettos.

His standby group of community activists was about to be transformed into the campaign staff for the soon-to-be-announced presidential candidate, Reverend Jefferson B. Carter. A shadow of the man he used to be during his youthful days of rebel-rousing his way through the disenfranchised communities of every major city.

Reverend Jefferson B. Carter pushed back from the podium and stretched his short lanky frame and pumpkin head back, strutting in front of the room, looking like a grotesque creature oblivious to the axe about to fall.

Eight years ago, the long-time civil rights advocate had made a perfunctory bid at the top job but was trampled before his campaign took hold. In the interim, the reverend maintained his racially toned antics to boost his public persona, biding his time and sharpening his nails to ready himself for the next opportunity. As long as Reverend Carter was alive and kicking, civil rights issues would not be dying. His attempts at schmoozing up to the current president, Alice Andersen, had been dispelled faster than water off a duck's back: not that a little thing like that could quell his self-imposed inflated self-image.

The reverend was good at one thing. If this nation could become divided in the absence of division, Reverend Carter was the one to slice it in half. His cultivated activism kept him in the public eye, while making him a rich man. Ironically, he never considered his rampages against greedy capitalists to be inconsistent with his own means of success. Or that he had used and abused the suffrage of the impoverished black and minority communities as much as, or even more than, those he pointed his holy finger in undisguised accusatory rhetoric.

* * * * * *

In his customary, self-indulgent, pulpit-like postural pose, Reverend Carter placed both clenched fists back on the makeshift podium in the front of his community center meeting room. The casual supporters had been dismissed. All that remained in the previously packed room was his select core group of close advisors, but nonetheless, a show is always a show, and the stage would soon be set.

"What we need to get this campaign going," the reverend said, "is a cause. One where we can invade, overtake, and sink our teeth into—like a rattlesnake holding on to a lamb's butt."

The small, dedicated group understood you never questioned the reverend's choice of words. He prided himself on his mastery of speech.

"And the sooner the better."

The reverend paused for effect. "I mean… I want my face in front of the cameras from the day I announce my candidacy to the day I give my first inaugural address to a grateful nation. We need something to demonstrate my power to lift the spirits of the downtrodden communities across this nation and point out the social injustices that keep a stranglehold on our brothers and sisters."

Making sure everyone was on board, he finished. "This time we shall not fail. Praise our Lord, Almighty God."

That last phrase never failed to stir the reverend to new heights of grandeur.

This handpicked team didn't need specific guidelines from the reverend; they'd worked those particular muscles before, and they were well-oiled. With their marching orders in place, the race was on.

After the room had emptied, Reverend Jefferson B. Carter stood motionless at the podium for several long minutes. A sharp click sounded—the room went black. The reverend waved his arms about and the motion sensors reenergized the lights.

"Goddamned energy Nazis," the reverend hissed. "But every vote counts. Sometimes more than once."

His laughter turned into a coughing fit, echoing throughout the empty room as he reached into his coat pocket and lit up another cigarette.

CHAPTER 20

EDIE SAT ACROSS FROM HER sister-in-law, Kristie Pauling, at the round conference table in the CEO's third floor office. The red brick, colonial-styled administrative building was located at the GMHC headquarters in Morristown, a short drive from Edie's condo. After a brief episode of small talk, the two got to work. Kristie brought Edie up to date on her political plans and campaign platform for the upcoming special election for the New Jersey state legislature. She chronicled the troublesome union tactics and their stepped-up actions since she announced her candidacy.

Up until the vice president's request for her to help, Edie had not spent a great deal of time researching either the labor laws or the colorful union history in her home state. She'd had a few interesting discussions with her brother, Thomas, regarding the teachers' union, but other than that she'd never given those topics any real justice. That was about to change, and Edie was primed for the fight.

Edie pushed the conversation toward the possible connection of organized crime to the alleged strong-armed tactics blamed on several powerful labor unions in the state. Not sure where to go from there, she teetered on confessing to Kristie about her activities to locate Steve's long forgotten relatives, when….

There was a quiet knock on the door. Kristie's assistant led Steve and Amber into the office, closing the door behind her. After a quick wave and smile to Edie, Steve headed directly toward Kristie, and Amber padded over to Edie.

"Hi Kristie, good to see you again," Steve said.

She stood up and gave Steve a brief hug. Amber gave Edie several nips on her ear.

"You don't seem surprised to see me here," Edie said to Steve.

Steve turned to Edie and gave her a warm smile. Raising his eyebrows, he said, "Four door, forest green sedan; late model Toyota Corolla?"

Her eyes narrowed, mouth opening. Edie then shifted her attention to Amber and smiled. "Did you find my new rental car, Amber? That's a good girl."

Stone-faced, Steve responded, "By the way, did you sign up for the extra insurance to cover comprehensive damages?"

Not waiting for an answer, he walked to the window and looked down at the parking lot. "Ah, never mind. I'm sure those scratches can be buffed out. Right, Amber?"

Amber slunk down behind Edie, small well-honed whimpering sounds emanating from closed jaws; until Edie turned and gave her a fake menacing look. Amber scooted over and sat by Kristie's side, lifting a limp paw onto the CEO's lap.

Steve walked around the table and kissed Edie on the cheek. He slid a chair up to the table as Kristie's assistant returned with a tray of sandwiches and drinks. She was now Amber's new best friend.

Steve pulled the evidence bag from the Cedar Knolls site out of his pocket and tossed it onto the table. Kristie looked questionably at Steve, waiting for an explanation, but Edie couldn't help herself.

While biting her tongue, she said, "Wow, is that a real evidence bag? What happened? You run out of poop bags?"

"That's not all I keep in my pocket."

"Anything I might be interested in?"

"Wanna check it out for yourself?"

"Wouldn't that be tampering with the evidence?"

Kristie's neck twisted back and forth in sync to the bantering.

Satisfied for the moment, Edie moved the conversation forward. "I see you've recorded the information on the bag. But why did—"

"The vice president is not concerned about any evidentiary chain of—"

Edie threw her head back. "You called Joe, didn't you?"

A retired attorney, Joe Wilton was a good friend to Steve and Edie. He had helped them out after they got caught up in a number of terrifying experiences in northern Idaho. Today wouldn't have been the first time he'd given Steve his legal opinion on collecting evidence.

Steve shrugged. "I laid out the situation at the Cedar Knolls processing facility for him. Explained what I—"

"From experience, he probably assumed you'd do it your way regardless," Edie said.

Kristie jumped in. She rubbed her neck and tapped the bag. "Steve? Are you saying this caused the fire?"

He took a deep breath and slowly exhaled. He then held a steady gaze on Kristie. "Can I ask you something first?"

Kristie spread her palms.

"The entire area—inside and outside the building—had numerous *No Smoking* signs posted. Are they there just to comply with the regulations, or are they strictly enforced?"

With a forceful nod of her head, Kristie said, "You better believe we're serious about those signs. We make sure it's drilled into every one of our employees. They must follow the rules. If someone gets caught anywhere near those areas trying to light up, they'd be dealt with right on the spot. In most cases, they'd be reassigned to a warehouse position and sent to a refresher course on our safety guidelines. After that, they're given a second chance. We rarely need to fire anyone once they understand the necessity for adhering to those policies."

"So, tossing this into one of the disposal bins inside the building wouldn't be something you'd expect from any of your employees? At least not by accident?"

"You're saying this cigarette caused the fire?" Kristie stood up, still staring at the contents of the bag. "If that's the case, then someone must've done it on purpose."

Steve ran his fingers through his hair and leaned forward. "Whoever's responsible for this fire wanted the authorities to blame it on the careless toss of a lit cigarette. Most likely to provide evidence the company doesn't enforce those safety regulations. That you're lax about getting the employees to follow the rules."

Steve's eyes pointed toward the bag. "But this didn't cause the fire."

CHAPTER 21

LEILAH HARRIS'S LIFELESS BODY REMAINED on the king-sized bed in the bedroom. Tony Funetti repeatedly glanced at his watch as Marty Calebrese sat frozen on the sofa in the sitting room of Thomas Pauling's hotel suite. Coming out of his trance, Marty stood up and sprang into action.

"Okay, Tony, listen-up. Run down to the Lexus and bring back the two packages of coveralls from the trunk. And grab a few extra trash bags too. I still got enough latex gloves in my case. But don't forget to remove yours before traipsing through the lobby. If you still got any duct tape in the trunk, bring that too."

Tony stood motionless with his jaw dropped, so Marty ratcheted up his voice. "Will you get the hell going? Now! Hurry it up. I'll explain when you get back. I'll get things moving up here. Now! Go—Go—Go."

Ten minutes later Marty opened the door and handed Tony another pair of gloves. He barked orders, but Tony remained staring at the rolled-up area rug in the sitting room. Marty didn't expect him to ask any questions.

"Come on," Marty said, pointing again at the items he'd thrown onto the coffee table. "Everything goes in the bag—except my leather case. I'll hang on to that. Give me the duct tape. We don't want the damn rug unrolling before we make it to the car."

The two men got to work. They acted in a quick and efficient manner, always checking the time. They had at least forty-five minutes but didn't want to cut things too close. Marty flushed the remaining wine down the toilet, throwing the empty bottle and glass into the trash bag along with the flowers and card. Tony grabbed Leilah's clothes, poised to drop them into the bag, but Marty looked up and stopped him.

"Hold on. Toss over those panties."

Marty caught them and headed for the bedroom closet where he pulled out Thomas Pauling's suitcase and peeled back the silky lining material from one of the side pockets. After tucking the panties inside, he refit the material back in place. It would take more than a casual glance to notice anything amiss.

Tony smacked the side of his head. "Oh shit, Marty. I almost forgot. When I lifted the key card from Pauling, this came along for the ride."

He held up a conference attendee badge with the name Thomas Pauling and his photo imprinted on it.

"I don't know why," Tony said, eyebrows raised, "but I never considered giving it back."

Marty smiled and slowly nodded his head, more than a little surprised at Tony's initiative. "Good work. Wipe it clean and take it with us."

They were satisfied that everything in the room looked okay. Marty left a note for Pauling from the housekeeping department, apologizing for the removal of the area rug for cleaning. He figured that should keep him from asking too many questions before he checked out.

Attired in the crisp, laundered coveralls, Marty and Tony passed unnoticed through the corridor and down the hotel's service elevator to the parking garage. They looked the part, and no one paid them any attention. Without being observed, they dumped the rolled-up carpet with Leilah Harris's body inside, along with the filled plastic trash bag, into the trunk of Tony's Lexus. Marty placed his leather case in the side pocket storage compartment in the trunk and they drove out onto the streets of Philadelphia, headed toward the Benjamin Franklin Bridge and points east in New Jersey.

CHAPTER 22

STEVE STOOD UP FROM THE conference table in Kristie Pauling's office. He leaned over the table and picked up the evidence bag, waving it in the air. "I'm sure leaving this cigarette butt behind was done for misdirection. And whoever's responsible must be knowledgeable about the science of combustive processes."

Kristie's face scrunched up, and she asked, "Why is that? How difficult would it be to start a fire in such an incendiary location? I'm amazed the sprinkler system stopped it from destroying everything. My God, I still cringe at the thought of all those flammable solvents and chemicals."

"Maybe they underestimated those sprinklers too." Steve contemplated how things proceeded in a much different manner at the Lakewood location where someone had most likely tampered with the sprinkler system.

He sat back down and toyed with the half-eaten donut on his plate. Finding no answers, he took a quick swig of coffee. "In my opinion, the game was to point everyone in the direction of negligence—make the company look lax in enforcing the safety guidelines. They were careful not to use accelerants which would cause any serious investigators to suspect arson."

"I see what you mean. In the second fire, they took an even more proactive approach. Tampering with the sprinkler system. And they succeeded in producing a whole lot more damage." Kristie shook her head. "Thank God nobody got hurt."

"Yeah, I didn't look at the photos until after I finished in Cedar Knolls. But before heading here I opened up the file the vice president gave me with all the reports of the fires. Things could've gotten nasty. The fire department did a hell of a job fighting it. Even though it was too late to save the millworks, the fire could've easily spread to adjacent structures. The whole facility would've been destroyed."

Edie joined in. "Okay, a discarded cigarette didn't cause the fire, and you found no evidence of any accelerant use. And with that, I'm sure Amber played an important role. So what evidence is there to make you think someone deliberately set this first fire?"

Steve clicked on his digital camera and rotated the screen around for Kristie and Edie to see. "When I was going through one of the disposal bins—the one where the fire originated—I came across this box. See this?" His finger pointed to an object on the tiny screen. "Near the bottom of the bin, close to the metal mesh? I didn't bring it with me. Damn thing almost fell apart when I took it from the bin, so I left it in the building."

"Looks like the rest of the burned-up stuff all around it," Kristie said, Edie nodding in agreement.

"Okay, here's a better look." He scrolled to a photo of the box after he had placed it on the floor.

"This is what I want you to see." He zoomed in on the box as much as possible on the camera's small screen. "Look at the burn pattern on the lid. Can you see the inside of the box? It has a larger burn radius than the outside."

Steve got no response. "It means the flames penetrated the lid from the inside out—not the other way around—the way it would've done if the box was just caught up in the spreading fire like the rest of the debris in the bin."

Edie and Kristie looked at him like he was speaking in tongues.

Steve took a deep breath and tried again. "This was the incendiary device responsible for the fire. It's almost foolproof, not to mention sophisticated, in its simplicity. It leaves no suspicious elements or residue because nothing unusual was used in making it. The genius lies in the knowledge needed to make this work."

Kristie and Edie looked at each other and shrugged but remained silent.

Steve's eyes drifted to Amber, scooched behind Kristie's desk, apparently not interested in the conversation.

He glanced back at the screen on the digital camera. "It's a timer. If you look here, you can still make out a number of holes drilled through the sides of the box. Those are for ventilation. Inside, on the bottom, there're melted fragments of plastic stuck to the wood. Also charred shreds of aluminum foil. See it?"

"We're not stupid, Steve," Edie said. "We get what you're saying. But it's difficult to see any details on the tiny screen."

Kristie pointed to the whiteboard on the far side of the office.

Nodding, and finally recognizing his misstep, Steve walked to the whiteboard and began to draw the device he had been trying to describe. He explained as he drew.

"Okay, so we have this metal-framed box with wood panels, about the size of a shoe box. There are a number of holes drilled through each of the panels. The melted plastic bits I showed you in one of the photos are what's left of one of those re-useable freezer packs. The things you stick in ice coolers? Instead of ice cubes?"

This time both Edie and Kristie tilted their heads slightly and leaned forward.

He drew in a rectangular object resting on the inside bottom of the box. "On top of the ice pack they used a layer of aluminum foil to keep the ice pack intact; that is to assure this…."

Pausing, he sketched a jagged-edged object with swirls and smudges sprouting from its surface. It rested on top of the squiggly lines he used to represent the foil.

"…smoldering piece of wood-fibered block didn't melt away the plastic too soon. Using the right combination of temperature, airflow, and fuel you could set this device inside the bin and have it ignite into an open flame several hours after planting it. This was then covered with layers of combustible materials. The kind you would use to light a fire in a fireplace—paper and twigs or small wood scraps near the smoldering source, followed by larger and larger pieces of materials."

Steve stopped to see if Kristie and Edie were still on board. They both nodded.

"The flames would then erupt and spread to the nearby wood storage rack, eventually igniting enough combustibles and heating the room to its flashover point. And bam! All the flammable solvents and chemicals would ignite, and soon the entire structure would become engulfed. But fortunately, before the open flames in the bin had the chance to spread, the sprinkler system triggered and did its job."

Edie asked, "Why wouldn't the whole thing just burst into flames as soon as the smoldering wood block was set into the box?"

"Good question," Steve said with no hint of sarcasm. "That was the purpose of the ice pack. It kept the temperature inside the box below the flash point of the smoldering block. Once the substance inside the ice pack melted, then the temperature inside the box gradually increased until the whole thing ignited."

"Incredible," Kristie observed, looking amazed at Steve's analysis of the incident. "I can't believe you determined that from a charred and burned, harmless looking piece of debris."

"The point is," Steve said, "whoever did this was no amateur, and this was no harmless prank. These guys mean business."

The last remark was unnecessary given the recent occurrence of the far more destructive fire at the Lakewood location.

For the next hour, Steve and Edie grilled Kristie on a broad range of topics, trying to better understand the company's cultural philosophy regarding employee relations, her current political aspirations, and any previous run-ins with the local labor unions.

All these issues now needed to be put into the context of Tyler Griffin's potential presidential candidacy and how not only the local unions, but the national organizations viewed this as a serious threat to the strength of labor forces in the country.

Steve still tried to keep an open mind regarding the union's potential role in what he definitely considered arson, but the circumstantial evidence kept getting in the way.

Before they left Kristie Pauling's office, Steve remembered to ask her for a job at GMHC. He wanted a better opportunity to interact with the employees. Steve guessed the employees in Cedar Knolls had been wary to speak with him earlier today due to possible experiences in dealing with union strong-arm tactics. After pulling a few strings, he walked back to his SUV with a new, laminated photo ID employee badge hanging around his neck.

Steve Casella, the new specialty wood buyer for GMHC, turned to Edie. "I'll see you at home tonight. It's my first day on the job, and I want to make a good impression with the boss. I'm going to introduce myself to the people at the Lakewood site and see if anyone has any useful information."

She leaned up, gave him a kiss on the cheek and laughed. "It's about time you got a real job. Remember, you'll be paid for performance. No union representatives to bail you out."

Before Steve countered her words, she continued, "Should I take Amber home with me?"

"Yeah, why don't you take—" He abruptly stopped, remembering how Amber had been accepted by the helpful employees in Cedar Knolls.

"Never mind, I'm going to keep Amber with me. She's good at breaking the ice. People tend to open up when they're distracted by such a friendly pooch."

Steve was right about his decision to bring Amber, but dead wrong on his reasoning.

Chapter 23

THE PINE BARRENS HAS A long and colorful history as an integral part of the region's culture, starting with the appearance of the Paleo-Indian tribes almost twelve thousand years ago, to the more recent contribution of episode thirty-seven of the HBO original series, *The Sopranos*.

The early Native Americans were the first to impact the original landscape and ecosystem of the Pine Barrens. Later, influxes of Europeans had an even greater influence as a direct result of their search for a better life, freedom of religion, and a means to accumulate land and wealth.

Even during those early quests of the Europeans to escape from the entanglements of an impoverished lifestyle in their homelands, colonial New Jersey had its share of detractors. The Dutch decided to suffer the tribulations back home rather than endure the stigma of residing in the lands to the west of the Hudson River. The English and several other European settlers had different standards, and those colonists became the first dominant class of rural land developers. They fostered crafty land deals and procured vast tracts of properties from an unsuspecting indigenous population. That trend endures to this day.

If the environmental movement existed when the Lenni Lenape tribe had first settled in the region and had successfully shackled the Native American use of fire to transform the primal forests, today's task confronting Marty Calebrese and Tony Funetti would have been a lot more difficult.

Tony's Lexus traveled east on the Atlantic City Expressway. From time to time he glanced at Marty, who appeared lost in a blank stare out the windshield. Wise enough not to strike up an idle conversation, Tony drove in silence and refrained from queueing up his Frank Sinatra, *A Voice in Time* collection, on his state-of-the-art Bose audio system.

"Turn off at the next exit," Marty said, speaking for the first time in almost an hour.

Tony nodded and slowed onto the exit ramp, crossing over onto Blue Anchor Fireline Road. He now ran on autopilot, leaving the main roads and maneuvering over less traveled and more rutted paths. Tony swallowed back his usual complaints as the Lexus became spattered with mud. The undercarriage endured a barrage of scrapes, while the traction control system protested, proffering a chorus of agonizing grinds and chatters.

Marty raised his hand for Tony to stop. "This is good."

Tony did as he was told but didn't say a word.

They got out of the Lexus. Their heads became ensnared by invigorating resinous scents which would conjure up yuletide memories in most people. For Marty and Tony, this fragrance defined a more menacing agenda.

Marty pointed to the left where the pine needle blanketed terrain worked its way down to a trickling stream meandering through the lower lying, boggy ground. On the other side of the stream, the embankment rose in a steep grade to a grove of knurly looking pine trees. Craggy barberry outgrowths studded parts of the hillside. A well-traversed hiking trail lay beyond the rows of pines. It wove its way through one of the popular parks in the Pine Barrens. Marty and Tony had taken a more clandestine route to get here.

With their rubber overshoes in place, they lugged the rolled-up rug, first across the easy to negotiate bed of pine needles; then the more slippery and muddy bog and streambed. They headed east, sloshing through the shallow stream, concealing their tracks. Finally, after traveling a safe distance from the Lexus, they looked around, not seeing anyone in sight. They changed direction and maneuvered the duct-taped rug up the steep embankment, lodging it between several prickly branches of a nasty looking barberry bush near the edge of the pine grove. It lay barely within sight of the hiking path. Tony withdrew the small plastic bag from his pocket and Marty nodded for him to dump out Thomas Pauling's attendee badge and room key card on the ground next to the rug. They returned to the car and tossed the muddy overshoes into one of the plastic trash bags containing the items taken from the hotel suite. Later, they'd dispose of it where no one would ever find it again.

As they approached the signs for the Atlantic City Expressway, Tony said, "So you gonna give Big Al a call? Fill the boss in on what happened?"

After a slight hesitation, Marty responded, "Get on the Expressway to the A.C. We're gonna take care of business first. Then I'll speak to the man."

* * * * * *

It felt like being submerged in the putrid mud at the bottom of the Passaic River. From above, flashes of light and sounds drifted down through the murky waters of an urban cesspool. The images became stronger and then receded into the background. More compelling than the images, layers of pungent smells swirled, lingering in his sinuses. With an exaggerated effort, Marty Calebrese worked his way to the surface and rubbed his burning eyes to clear away the remaining sticky layers.

He lay anchored in a bed, not remembering where he was. His stinging eyes landed on a scattered pile of empty booze bottles. They then focused on a second bed on the other side of the room. In that bed, he recognized the shape of someone who looked a lot like Tony Funetti, although the guy's face was pushed deep into the pillow. Grotesque snoring sounds escaped around the edges.

As his eyes cleared, Marty was stirred by the sight of two naked women seated on a sofa in the far corner of the room. Coming into focus, he saw their splayed legs resting on a wobbly looking coffee table. The women blew smoke rings above their heads. Either they were twins, or his eyes were playing tricks on him.

The vision of the swirling smoke rings made his head throb. The women pointed and shook their heads at the flat screen TV on the wall. At first, he ignored the images on the TV and remained focused on the more enticing view. His eyes walked their way up between the almost endless legs of twin number one.

And then.

Something on the screen caught his attention. And all pretenses of unbridled debauchery disappeared.

CHAPTER 24

HUNCHED OVER IN THE REAR seat, Reverend Jefferson B. Carter tapped the tiny electronic screen, consumed by his obsessive social media rhetoric. As usual, oblivious to where his black Lincoln Town Car headed. Samantha Cleveland, his longtime assistant, knew they would soon arrive at their destination. It was time to interrupt the reverend. She hit the button and lowered his window halfway down. As the smoke-filled interior cleared, the reverend looked up, but before he spoke, a coughing fit took over. His hand reached for another cigarette. After lighting up, he closed out the fresh air intrusion and, for the first time, glanced at his surroundings.

"Samantha! Where in the hell are we? What happened to the press conference and rally for this poor missing girl. I mean... we're in the middle of white suburban heaven."

Samantha sighed, rubbing her irritated eyes, and suppressed a cough. "Relax Jefferson, we'll be at her high school in a—"

"School? Why aren't we going to her apartment or tenement? And you haven't answered my question." He waved his hand, pointing a finger against the glass. "What the hell kind of neighborhood is this?"

"Okay. Right now, we're just south of Morristown." Samantha handed the reverend the notes he'd be using for the press conference. "This is where the girl, Leilah Harris, lives. And we're going to hold the press conference at her high school because her father didn't want us anywhere near—"

"Her father? What the hell does he have to do—"

"Listen, Jefferson, we don't have time to discuss these things now. You should read up on your talking points. Everyone is in place behind the podium. The signs you asked for have been handed out. You just need to get the rest of the crowd riled up and chanting."

"Yeah, yeah, I get it. So, tell me about this girl and where she's from."

"It doesn't matter. She's black. Just do what you do. Don't worry about anything else. We'll make sure her mother and father are—"

"She's from a regular family? Don't tell me they're not poor. Damn, she's probably got a dog too." Carter waved his hands about. "No—don't tell me any more. Please."

"Look, Jefferson. You said you wanted to be out in the public eye as soon as possible. And this is all we've got. We can make this work. *You* can make this work. As I said, just do what you do."

The Lincoln pulled into the parking lot of the George Washington Regional High School. The brigade of news vans with satellite uplinks lined the streets; the reporters in formation and primed for a story. Samantha knew that by the time Reverend Carter reached the podium in front of the steps to the high school's main entrance he would've put aside his prior concerns and pumped himself up for the orchestrated crowd and the press core in the audience.

Samantha Cleveland looked on as the reverend's body took on an aggressive posture. His face transformed into his familiar enraged trademark profile as he positioned himself behind the podium. She relaxed and watched the crowd absorb his fervor.

"How long can we stand by while our children are forgotten? Another black child leaves home to go to school. She never makes it. Never shows up at work where the poor girl labors to earn a few dollars so she can afford to drive her car. Now the car and... ah... Leilah... ah... Harris... are gone. Do the police in this town care about another poor missing black girl?"

The crowd chanted in reply.

"What are we here for?" the reverend shouted.

"Justice!" the crowd replied. Everything now in sync.

"Why isn't anybody doing anything to find her? If poor little Leilah Harris was a white child who'd gone missing...."

* * * * * *

The hookers departed the stale and stuffy hotel room. After consuming two pots of black coffee, Tony Funetti still struggled with consciousness.

He looked at Marty Calebrese. "What the hell day is it?" He glanced around the large but disordered Atlantic City boardwalk hotel room. Fortunate his sense of smell had been wiped out by the unknown number of hours spent in this ostentatious ossuary without coming up for air.

Without taking his eyes off the TV screen, Marty pointed a finger at the close-up image of the speaker poised behind the podium and said, "Shut the fuck up. Who the hell is this guy?"

Tony rubbed his eyes and leaned closer to the screen. "It's that civil rights activist. Calls himself a reverend. He's always sticking his nose in everybody's business. Gets people all riled up and makes them do things they shouldn't be doing. Promises them shit and never delivers."

Marty turned away from the screen and stared at Tony. "Sounds similar to your job description, Tony. He could be a useful addition. Add a little color to our team."

"Ah, Marty?" Tony's voice cracked as he rubbed his hands over several days' worth of stubble. "Didn't you make that anonymous call to the cops?"

When Marty didn't answer, he repeated the question.

"Christ, Tony. Apparently, that part of the plan slipped my mind. And I guess the narcissistic joggers are too into themselves to see a rolled-up rug and dead body within arm's reach of the trail."

"The rug wasn't that close to—"

"What difference does it make?" Marty hissed. "Besides, you didn't happen to think of reminding me about any of this while you were drinking yourself into a drunken stupor and fucking your pathetic brains out. Did you? No, don't bother to answer. Let me just think here."

Marty stood up and opened the slider, tripping onto the balcony. He yanked on a pair of boxer shorts following Tony's advice not to expose his shriveled-up dick to patrons sunning themselves by the pool ten floors below. After lighting up another cigarette, he walked back inside.

Tony remained quiet as he watched Marty focus on the TV screen. After three long drags and an extended exhale, Marty shrugged, a tiny smirk replacing his scowl. He marched closer to the TV screen where Reverend Jefferson B. Carter pontificated his righteous racial rhetoric and jabbed his finger against the screen.

"You see that, Tony? Looky here behind that blathering asshole. Isn't that our favorite science teacher? Certainly looks like Thomas Pauling. And he's looking so sad, or even a little guilty. It's time to make that phone call now. I'll say I was watching the news and saw his face. The same guy who acted suspicious when I bumped into him during my daily jog in the Pine Barrens. This is even better than what I had planned. See, Tony? That's why I'm the one calling all the shots around here."

"Just make sure you put your pants on before running out to find a pay phone." That kind of remark usually had Marty reaching for his gun; Tony was thankful it was nowhere in sight.

"By the way," Tony said. "Do you think Big Al will buy your story? I'm assuming you neglected to fill him in on this minor change of plans. Why don't you ask the good reverend to explain it to the boss. That loudmouth could sell a Christmas tree to a Muslim."

The resounding voice and waving arms of Reverend Carter knocked them both back to reality. Two days of drunken denial washed away in an instant as the brunt of their actions hit home. Not to mention the prospect of having to convince Big Al everything was premeditated, and they were on top of the situation.

Before Marty pulled on his pants, his phone bleeped. Checking the caller ID, he took a deep breath and tried out his bullshit story on Big Al Rozano. The cops would have to wait a while longer.

On the TV screen, Reverend Jefferson B. Carter stood at his pulpit, arms raised, fists clenched, and jaw set. His racial rant transitioned into a platform of divisiveness and political expediency. His usual script.

* * * * * *

Not far from the action at Leilah's high school, in a respectable home in an upper middle-class community of Morris County, Theodore Harris, his wife, and youngest daughter viewed the painful theatrics of the self-proclaimed guru of the racial grievance industry. At one point Mr. Harris stood up shaking his fist at the screen.

"The nerve of that hate-mongering son of a bitch to make a political folly of our Leilah. Somebody should silence that bastard. He has no right to make a mockery of our lives."

His wife and daughter pulled him back onto the sofa where he buried his head and sobbed uncontrollably into his shaking hands. After a while his body slackened. Inside his heart, the fear for his missing daughter burned out of control.

The local police had hit this hard from the moment they reported the girl missing. This was a close-knit community and things like this were not the norm. Despite their efforts, the local authorities didn't have any leads and were hoping to catch a break before the trail went cold.

CHAPTER 25

STEVE HAD NO NEED TO comb through the wreckage of the more recent and devastating fire at the Lakewood millworks. Before leaving Kristie Pauling's office in Morristown, he had scrutinized all the photos and reports issued by the county agency in charge of fire investigation. He then shared his own views with Kristie.

In one of the Lakewood photos, Steve identified the remnants of an object, similar in all aspects to the wood-sided, metal-framed box he discovered in the waste bin of the processing structure at Cedar Knolls. What Steve had determined to be the timing device responsible for starting the first fire. The significance of this article had gone unnoticed, or perhaps deliberately ignored, as no one had singled it out in any of the official Lakewood reports. The lack of professionalism exhibited by the people running the investigation appalled him. He questioned if there had been something even more sinister involved in how this whole thing had been handled.

Now convinced the same person or persons deliberately set both fires, Steve also agreed with the vice president that the sprinkler system in the Lakewood fire had most likely been tampered with prior to the event. Either the perpetrators had learned their lesson from the first fire, or they chose to ramp up the pressure to convince people that GMHC was not a safe, employee friendly place to work.

Steve arrived at the Lakewood retail facility wearing his new employee ID badge. He hated misleading the other employees at GMHC but needed to hear their honest views about the company and their take on the escalating problems. He tried to learn as much as possible about what the employees thought of the fires, how much they blamed GMHC management, and what kinds of pressures or temptations they were up against from the CBT union activists. With no legal evidence that the union itself had been responsible for either of the fires, he considered second-guessing his decision of already tampering with potential evidence of a crime. Been there; done that, he reasoned. Besides, Tyler Griffin had no interest in the fine legalities. He just needed answers, and he needed them now. With each passing day, the vice president became more concerned about the safety of all the employees working at GMHC.

Steve struggled with his own mixed opinions regarding unionization and the rights of workers to choose for themselves. He accepted that by this point Edie would have armed the workforce into a militia poised to eradicate the evil union thugs with a show of deadly force.

* * * * * *

"Welcome to GMHC."

Steve turned from a conversation with several other workers in the Lakewood facility's employee breakroom to see a slim woman with graying, curly hair extending her hand. Amber's lead tightened and he heard several sharp sounds escaping the dog's jaws. Before responding, Steve backed Amber away and placed her in a down position, perplexed by Amber's antics. Until now, Amber had enthusiastically greeted the other employees. Maybe she'd had enough stimulation after putting in a long day.

"Thank you," Steve said returning his attention to the woman and shaking her hand. "I'm Steve. Steve Casella." He glanced at Amber who had quieted down after his command; but her ears remained alert and her eyes focused on the newcomer to the room.

"Nice to meet you. I'm Phyllis Sheridan." She smiled while her eyes flashed on the dog at Steve's side. "I work in customer service."

Phyllis slowly pushed into the circle gathered to welcome Steve into the GMHC family.

"As I was saying." Steve nodded toward the others in the group. "This is my first day and the boss suggested I visit a few of the local company sites and get a feel for the operations and introduce myself." Several people he'd been speaking with had taken a step back. One or two had turned away and left the room after waving a quick goodbye.

Steve noticed that Phyllis ignored those reactions. "If you really want to meet a lot of our employees, Steve—is it okay to call you Steve?"

Steve smiled and nodded.

"And please, call me Phyllis," she said. "Your timing couldn't be better." She looked around and winked at him. "This may not be popular with our management, but the CBT union is sponsoring a promotional event this evening and all GMHC employees in the state are invited. It would be a great way for you to get acquainted with a lot of people."

Phyllis gave Steve the details of the union gathering being held that evening at the amusement park called Great Adventure—otherwise known as Six Flags by outsiders to the state—in nearby Jackson Township.

"I won't be going," Phyllis said and lowered her voice. "Not that I necessarily disapprove of the union's plans." She returned to her normal speaking voice. "But these events are geared for the younger crowd, and I'm much too old for any wild parties. Besides, I need to go and check in on my father. He lives alone and depends on me to help him out in the evenings."

She turned to go but looked back before reaching the door. She nodded. "Really, Steve. You shouldn't miss out on this great opportunity."

Phyllis left the room.

Steve glanced down at Amber and then stared at the empty doorway. He shrugged and walked over to the coffee machine. Amber kept a keen eye on the door.

* * * * * *

Like Curtis in the GMHC retail facility in Cedar Knolls, Phyllis was not only a GMHC employee, but was also on the CBT union payroll. Before approaching Steve, Phyllis had taken a discreet photo of him and sent it to Marty Calebrese.

Although Phyllis realized the importance of checking this guy out, the anxiety heard in Marty's voice after receiving the photo and confirming the name *Casella* still surprised her. Marty suggested that Phyllis do her best to persuade Casella to go to this evening's event at Great Adventure.

Within minutes of receiving the message from Phyllis, Marty alerted Big Al Rozano to the troubling news.

CHAPTER 26

SIX MONTHS AGO, THE NEW JERSEY governor's office in Trenton initiated a controversial pilot program. The directive was limited to Morris County and required all public school employees, including teachers, to provide a biological sample for establishing a DNA profile for inclusion in a new database administered by the Special Investigations Section of the New Jersey State Police. This database is also linked to the FBI's Combined DNA Index System, or CODIS. The purported purpose of this expanded database, which now included a growing list of non-criminal profiles, was to serve as a basis for a crackdown on organized crime operations in the Garden State. Some viewed this act as part of the retaliation for the lack of union support during the governor's last election campaign.

The state's teachers' union was currently challenging the new mandate. There was strong public support to end this program as the citizens of New Jersey had seen too many of their rights to privacy eroded in recent years. A federal judge in Trenton ordered a temporary stay on any further requirements for the public school workers in Morris County to provide biological samples for DNA profiling but allowed the current database to remain intact until a permanent ruling was filed within the next ninety days.

At a quarter to eight in the morning, an immaculate black Ford Focus ST pulled into one of the far spaces in the parking lot of the State of New Jersey's Office of Forensic Sciences newest DNA Laboratory in Cedar Knolls. Although the lot was almost empty at this hour, the driver chose this isolated space to avoid any potential dings from careless drivers. It was also situated away from any overhanging tree branches to eliminate the possibility of sap marring the mirror-like finish of the car.

The driver's door opened, and a slim, attractive young woman with close-cropped curly black hair stepped out while grasping an attaché case off the white leather passenger seat. After closing the door, Sally Dreyfus took one final glance to assess the amount of accumulated driving dust deposited on the car's gleaming metallic finish and headed toward the building.

Sally Dreyfus would be changed into her sanitized scrubs and sitting at her lab station desk in plenty of time before her scheduled shift. Ms. Dreyfus was the head technician in charge of processing DNA evidence. She specialized in DNA collected as part of rape investigations.

She often teased her colleagues about being well-suited for this task because of the unlikely possibility of her contributing any contaminating male DNA. Her longtime committed partner, Denise, didn't appreciate her humor regarding this topic.

Ms. Dreyfus's behavior should not be taken as a diminution of the serious nature of her work. She used it as a way to cope with the vile aspects of the crimes she worked so hard to solve. It was imperative for her to maintain objectivity and focus on the intricate details of the sensitive processing employed in profiling evidentiary DNA samples.

This morning, Ms. Dreyfus signed the transfer forms and logged a new case number into her ledger. Her first indication of this particular case being different was the special prefix added to the coding label. This alerted her to the fact that the state's attorney general had flagged this with the highest priority level, making it her duty to focus continual attention on this case and reassign all other cases to her staff. The clock started ticking before the ink dried on her signature.

She gave pause to what this meant, since priority requests usually were submitted with a known suspect's court ordered DNA specimen so the evidentiary DNA sample could be immediately profiled against the suspected perpetrator. Submitting the test results profile from the evidentiary DNA into the CODIS database was a shot in the dark unless the investigators reasoned the possible offender's profile was already entered. That meant this was a high-profile case, and the investigators needed to proceed with caution.

Sally Dreyfus analyzed these prospects without interrupting the initiating steps for the differential extraction methods to separate and purify sperms cells from the vaginal sample obtained from the victim. Before opening up the sample itself, she followed a rigorous series of procedures to minimize any potential contamination from tainting the test results.

After lysing the purified sperm samples, Ms. Dreyfus prepared the exposed genomic DNA for loading into the thermal cyclers to allow the polymerase chain reaction step, or PCR, to amplify the number of DNA molecules to a sufficient quantity to be subjected to the short tandem repeat, or STR, analysis. This provided the investigator with a series of base pair repeat sequences at specific locations or loci along the DNA strand. The FBI had chosen a standard set of STR loci. The more of these loci present in the test sample, the greater the accuracy of the profiling. If all loci were present in the test sample, the likelihood that the comparable DNA from a suspect with the same profile was not a match would be greater than a billion to one. Remarkably, over ninety-nine-point-nine percent of human DNA was conserved throughout the human population. That still left approximately three million base pairs that specified a unique individual.

After forty-one consecutive hours of combined prep, run time, and analyses, Ms. Dreyfus signed off on her data and logged out of the case file. She was secure in the technology, which although transitioning through different iterations, had been around since 1985. At that time, she was just a toddler.

And while she was also confident in her skills and professionalism, she kept herself humble by frequent glances at the plaque posted on the wall above her desk. It read in bright, bold letters: *If it doesn't fit, you must acquit.*

Hanging from that same frame, a number of black leather gloves dangled from short strands of nylon monofilament suture.

Not that it mattered to Ms. Dreyfus, but by the time her analyses of the samples were completed, the jurisdiction of this particular case had been shifted to the FBI and brought to the attention of the US Attorney's office in the Eastern District of Pennsylvania.

CHAPTER 27

BEFORE LEAVING THE GMHC FACILITY in Lakewood, Steve called Edie and discussed the possibility of her joining him at Great Adventure and adding her input to the mix. The potential gains didn't justify her making the long drive. Steve was still intent on attending the event and seeing for himself if any quasi-ethical tactics were being used by the union.

Although Great Adventure's main parking lot was less than half-filled, Steve drove to the far northeast corner near the entrance to the overflow lot. He picked a shaded spot afforded by one of the larger maple trees lining the fence. Not an official parking space, but Steve figured Amber could convince anyone coming near the SUV she had every right to be there. Steve glanced around. He wasn't the only one who wanted to avoid parking a vehicle in the hot but waning late afternoon New Jersey sun. He guessed the white parking lines were only a suggestion in this state.

Map in hand, Steve entered the park and strolled down Main Street, losing himself in the ambience of the crowd. The shrieks of thrill-seeking riders being electrified, jarred, scared, and exhilarated, along with getting a little queasy on many of the park's attractions, assaulted his head. As he approached the Boardwalk section, he spotted the union sponsored GMHC event.

The area reserved by the union was hyped-up for the occasion. Large and brightly colored banners hung from the biggest and best-equipped pavilion available for rent. Instead of utilizing one of the park's all-in-one package catering plans, the union, although paying for that service, brought in their own food, chefs, rock band, and staff.

They did their best to serve up unending supplies of gourmet food and top-notch entertainment. The tantalizing aromas of grilled steaks, roasted prime ribs, and honey-basted hams captured Steve's senses, making his empty stomach growl in anticipation. Malty wafts of locally brewed kegs of beer steered him to a thirst-quenching pit stop.

Plenty of union staffers stood ready to schmooze up to the attendees. They held discreet meetings in several of the park's indoor show venues that the union officials rented for the sake of privacy for any employee who wished it when discussing their union options.

Steve concluded that the whole event was over the top, but not out of the realm of typical union tactics for prodding and promotion. He caught nothing overtly threatening from the entire undertaking.

Unknown to Steve, Marty Calebrese and Tony Funetti were also in attendance, but not part of the union staff intermingling with the employees. They stood in the shadows observing Steve. What they had learned about his identity in the short time since discovering his presence at several of the GMHC locations, got Marty and Tony scrambling for a way to nip this thing in the bud.

The band started its next set, and the party gave all appearances of rocking well into the night. Tired from the long day, Steve made his departure after pleasant, but unproductive discussions with many of the other employees. He'd also spoken to several union staffers but learned little to help him with his investigation.

Amber remained cooped up for too long in the Durango, but more important was the chance that Edie would still be awake by the time he got home. That was squarely on Steve's mind as he strolled out of the park. Bright lights, whiffs of cotton candy and greasy fried foods, and echoes of the screaming riders on the Green Lantern and the Superman Ultimate Flight faded behind him.

Steve crossed the lot and the density of cars decreased as he approached the Durango in the darker shadows of the trees outlining the perimeter. The not-so-friendly resonance of his name being shouted out knocked Steve from his reverie.

"Hey! Casella!" the voice said. "What's your hurry? Don't got time to say hello to two old friends?"

Steve stopped, still facing away from the ominous sounding voice. It grew louder and more hostile with each word.

Steve started to turn and face this potential threat, trying to fathom what in the hell this was all about.

"Gee, Casella," the voice said. "I'd hate to make you late for your check-in call to Vinnie, but at this time of day, it wouldn't go through anyway. What say we take a little ride and have a nice chat about you guys not going along with the program."

Steve continued to turn around, slowly to the left. With his right hand hidden from whoever was behind him, he reached into his pocket holster for his Ruger.

But instead, he came up with the key fob for the Durango.

Son of a bitch!

That's when he remembered his decision to abide by the non-reciprocating concealed carry law in New Jersey.

"Look at that," another voice said. "He doesn't wanna join us. You shoulda told him we'd be taking my car, so he wouldn't be needing his keys."

Steve looked impotently at the useless object in his hand.

Well, not so useless, he considered. Steve talked as his thumb inched over the key fob, trying to find the right button.

"I'm sorry, gentlemen, but you must be confused. I have no idea what you're talking about. And I never heard of anybody named, who did you say? Vinnie?"

His thumb hovered over what he hoped was the correct button. He tried to gauge the distance to the Durango.

The two men stood in the shadows about twenty feet from Steve. He made out only vague outlines of their images.

The one man shook his head. After a quick glance at his partner, he turned back and said, "So you got the balls to bullshit me like the rest of your has-been family? You don't look familiar, but I can see that same stupid Casella 'deer caught in the headlights' look on your face. I gotta admit, Big Al was right all along. He said just because Vinnie Casella's doing time doesn't mean he still won't be trying to run things from inside the joint. But let's put that aside for now, and we can go have a nice little talk. It's time to remind the Casella family who's running this show."

The headlights of a passing car reflected briefly from the man's face. His less talkative partner still lay hidden in the shadows. Steve kept coming up blank, scrambling for a logical answer to what the hell this guy was talking about. They obviously knew his name. The damn employee ID badge hanging down his neck felt like one of the larger patio stones from the well-stocked outdoor and garden department of his new employer. It was beginning to look like the vice president's idea to keep a low profile on things had just gone to hell.

But what's with this Casella family crap? Somehow, they must have tagged him as working for Griffin. How did they manage that so quickly? But Vinnie Casella? What the hell was that about? He realized taking a ride with these two assholes wouldn't be the best way to solve the problem, at least from his prospective.

Without drawing attention to the act, Steve pressed the button on the key fob.

Still talking, the man never caught the two subtle beeps coming from about forty feet behind Steve. Before he finished his last sentence, a series of sharp screeches escalated across the pavement as Steve issued a command.

The two men froze at the sight of a large white dog materializing several feet in front of them. The dog halted, poised on its haunches and growling, piercing eyes swinging back and forth between them.

Neither of them moved a muscle.

Steve swallowed and took a step closer to the two men who remained cloaked in darkness. The words hung in his throat when the sound of running footsteps and a child's voice shouting out intervened.

"Oh look! See that nice puppy, Mommy? I'm gonna go pet her. Can I please, mister? She's so pretty. Isn't she, Mommy?"

Without waiting for anyone to answer, the child charged ahead.

The frantic mother pushing a stroller and surrounded by three other kids failed to corral her five-year-old daughter. With Steve looking on in alarm, the child reached out, wrapping her arms around Amber.

In the commotion, the two men gave a quick salute to Steve and eased themselves out of the picture. Steve focused on making sure Amber stayed put and made no hostile moves toward the young girl and the approaching family members. The mother apologized to Steve for such a foolish act by her daughter. Steve was thankful Amber's training had become solid. If this happened a year or so earlier, Amber might've lost control and attacked the child.

As the woman babbled on, Steve tried to spot the fleeing assailants. He caught a glimpse of the disappearing taillights on a late model Lexus, possibly carrying the two men. It sped away down the exit lane, spitting gravel in its wake. He made a mental note of the two numbers he'd picked out from the mud-encrusted license plate.

As they skidded onto the county road, Tony said, "Jesus, Marty. That coulda gotten real ugly back there. And just a reminder. I don't kill animals. Especially dogs. It'd break my heart. I just can't do it."

Marty gave his supposed macho partner an incredulous look. "You'd be talking a little different if that mutt had gotten a hold of your balls. Then again, the dog probably wouldn't be able to find them. Because you musta lost them when your pathetic dick withered away."

"Fuck you, Marty. And I don't recall you making any overt moves toward that nice little puppy."

CHAPTER 28

LOCAL AUTHORITIES SCRAMBLED INTO OVERDRIVE. An anonymous tip led to the discovery of Leilah Harris's body close to a hiking trail in the New Jersey Pine Barrens. Her remains wrapped in a rug found clinging to a tangled bush on a steep embankment. An expedited autopsy indicated evidence of sexual activity. Alcohol and several drugs found in her system. Preliminary cause of death cited as drug overdose.

DNA samples retrieved from Leilah Harris's body had been immediately transferred to the state's forensic science laboratory. At the request of the lead investigator, the state's attorney general had placed a high priority code designation on the samples, assuring they would rise to the top of the list.

Specific evidence found at the recovery site red-flagged this as a high-profile case. The investigators wanted the evidence to be foolproof before issuing any public statements prior to making an arrest. But they were determined to move swiftly. The heightened racial animosities kindled by the sudden appearance of Reverend Jefferson B. Carter had law enforcement officials antsy to do this right before his antics incited the community. He had the habit of carnivalizing any situation he chose as his cause of the week. His daily radio program had recently been syndicated, so his bully pulpit now had the momentum to thrust him back into the national limelight once again.

The subsequent identification of Leilah Harris's missing Honda in an underground parking garage in Philadelphia prompted the swift involvement of federal law enforcement and the demand to surrender jurisdiction to the FBI. Although the girl had been found inside a rolled-up rug taken from a hotel suite, they never determined if Leilah Harris was alive or dead when brought to the Pine Barrens. The FBI used this as an added justification for taking on the role as primary lead investigators in the case. As usual, this did not sit well with either the state or local officials. The original lead investigator chose not to take this in stride.

Following the dismissal of local law enforcement involvement in the case, the FBI deployed a team from their Behavioral Analysis Unit, or BAU, to the scene where the body was found, as well as to locations of interest in the Morristown area and Philadelphia. This elite team worked at a feverish pace to assemble the pieces of this dreadful puzzle. Even before all the evidence had been turned over and reviewed by the FBI, the analysts compiled a hypothetical profile of the perpetrator. The agents of the BAU addressed the main core of investigators assembled in the FBI's briefing room.

"We are looking for a male between the ages of twenty and thirty-nine," Agent Carlotti stated.

"We deem the unsub to be highly intelligent and consider him socially and sexually competent. Most likely he is in a heterosexual relationship, living with an unsuspecting partner. There's a good chance he is in what would appear to be a normal and healthy traditional marriage," Agent Cromwell added.

Taking over, Agent Pittman said, "We would psychologically profile the unsub to be an organized, nonsocial offender. It is probable he works in a professional field, meaning—"

Pittman was handed a folder. Pausing, he opened and read the contents. He stared at the folder for an extended period as his normally pale face turned the color of a shiny red fire engine. His ears gave the effect of transitioning into a pair of Knockout roses in the dead of summer. Steadying himself with one hand, he dropped the folder on the table and reached for his bottled water. After gulping down half the bottle in one shot, he gave a quick glance to the rest of the BAU team and grabbed the folder off the table. He then resumed his profiling description.

"To be more precise," Agent Pittman said, his voice straining, lips compressed, "the unsub is an African American male, age thirty-three. He is employed as a science teacher at the George Washington Regional High School. He attended a recent conference in Philadelphia. The unsub's name is Thomas Pauling."

Much of this information was obtained from the convention badge found near Leilah Harris's body. It had been bagged at the scene by the detective who expedited the DNA profile request. This important line of investigation was either overlooked or lost in the jurisdictional mire when the transfer of the case to the FBI took place.

The name of the identified suspect provided by the convention badge was confirmed from the DNA database following the rapid analyses of the samples taken from Leilah Harris's body. This prompted the new FBI investigators to contact the US attorney's office in Philadelphia to file a complaint with the US District Court and obtain the appropriate search and arrest warrants.

Once Agent Pittman recovered from his initial shock and embarrassment, he initiated his own investigation into the detective who neglected to pass along these critical pieces of information, although he adamantly denied calling in a favor from a personal friend in the Internal Revenue Service to utilize the power of the federal government to exact punishment on a smart-ass local official.

* * * * * *

Thomas and Kristie Pauling sipped glasses of a Sonoma Valley cabernet sauvignon on the patio of their Morris County home, gazing at the waning daylight reflecting off the kidney-shaped swimming pool's mirror-like surface. They were barely aware of the crying tires and slamming doors. The splintering front door and commanding voices echoing through the house did get their attention, overriding the peaceful shadows set to cloak the cultivated landscape surrounding the patio.

The intrusion would have come earlier, but for the jurisdictional blustering between the local authorities, state police, and the federal government. The primary team members poised for action at the Pauling residence sported windbreakers with the letters 'FBI' stenciled across their backs. The local and state authorities made up the rear. Pittman had made certain the original lead detective was left off the roster.

The first team whisked Thomas Pauling away, handcuffed and unceremoniously tossed into the black sedan. As Kristie tried to catch up, she listened to one of the agents reciting from a card held in his hand. "You have the right to…."

An agent pulled her back from the car.

Horrified, Kristie Pauling stood in the driveway, surrounded by federal agents and other law enforcement officers, until her husband disappeared around the corner. She glanced down at the warrants and complaints forms in her hands, even as the second team had already begun the intensive and invasive search of their home.

Chapter 29

Steve had at least been right about one thing this evening. When he walked through the door to Edie's condo, he found her awake.

"Don't you remember me telling you union activities could be a little more, let's say, proactive here in the Garden State?" Edie said in response to Steve's watered-down version of the incident at Great Adventure.

"What makes you think those two guys had anything to do with the union?" Steve asked.

Edie rolled her eyes. "Should I ask Tyler to pull a few strings and see about getting you a concealed carry permit? Either that or I'll try to stay closer to you while we're here."

Steve shrugged. "Would this be a good time to suggest the Flash-Bang holster again?"

Edie pointed at her concealed carry purse on the foyer table and smiled. "Nah, I'm good."

They were sitting on the sofa in her living room. Pleased, but surprised to find Edie still awake, Steve saw no indications she was ready to call it a day. A bottle of red wine on the coffee table had been opened and breathing when he'd gotten home. Although the fresh scent of his favorite perfume shrouded her frame, the slight dampness of her hair and lingering aromatherapy scents suggested she'd just bathed. Yet she still wore a snug-fitting one-piece yellow summer dress.

Enjoying the moment, they clinked glasses and sipped their wine. He leaned closer, stretching an arm around Edie's shoulder and reeled her in for a warm, wine-tainted kiss. His ordeal in the parking lot at Great Adventure; a fading memory.

"How much do you love me, Steve?"

His arm froze at the same time his lips stopped, making him look like a fish about to be set onto one sharp and ugly hook.

Where the hell was this going? He needed real direction, or he'd be saying the wrong things. Who was he kidding? Even if he knew where she was going, he'd still take the wrong road.

"I love you more than I could ever put into words."

That just popped out of his mouth.

"You mean everything to me, babe," he added.

"And I love you too, Steve." Edie snuggled against Steve's shoulder. "You remember what we talked about at that fantastic surprise engagement party?"

"Ah, sure. You told me your family didn't care if you married a liberal white guy."

"Well, that's true, they don't. And I'm also coming around to accept that."

"*You're* coming around? You got me carrying guns— well, unfortunately not tonight. And I'm snooping around for one of the most conservative right-wing families in the state. Not to mention spying on one of the nation's most powerful and influential unions."

"It's all in the way you look at it, but I'm bending to your little ideologies too."

"Oh? Care to—"

"But Steve. That's not what I'm talking about. I've got my family, but…." Edie swallowed hard and closed her eyes. "I didn't want you to feel cheated with not having your own family around on our wedding day."

Steve sighed. "We've gone over this, Edie. I'm just grateful to share our happiness with your family. Besides, there's nothing you or anybody else can do about it. Right?"

As soon as those words left his lips, he felt the subtle shift of Edie's body against the satiny softness of her dress.

He listened to an almost incoherent string of words.

"You're busy, but tomorrow morning I'd like you to meet one of those relatives you didn't think existed. I located him by searching through online databases. And he's anxious to meet you. We're going to see him at his office in Short Hills. He's a certified public accountant. His name is Dominick Casella and he's about your age. Isn't it unbelievable that I found him? Ain't the internet just great?"

Edie had a strange expression on her face that had Steve wondering if she'd imparted the entire story. And maybe he'd been wrong about never being surprised by whatever spouted out of her mouth. With a slight shake of his head and a small smile on his closed lips, he stared into Edie's eyes.

"I thank God every day for the things you do for me," Steve whispered. "Sometimes I don't think I deserve all this." Al Gore's name surfaced in his head, but he let it sink back down.

Edie stood up and cocked her head, probably trying to gauge the sincerity of his remarks. She extended her hand and tugged on his arm. "What about the nights? If you're ready for some more things I can do for you, I'm sure we can find a few activities you'll be thankful for."

Like a slamming door, the immediate discussion disappeared from his consciousness, and he followed her into the bedroom. Much later, as her gentle rhythmic breathing lulled him into a blissful, comfortable sleep, he jolted back awake with a single, unrecognizable image—and a name—no, not Al Gore: Vinnie. Vinnie Casella. How did that name fit into this whole equation? Then the moment passed and soon his own breathing paralleled that of the girl nestled at his side. From the opposite side of the bed, Amber's sporadic leg shimmies served to push him closer to Edie.

Chapter 30

Imam Rashid Kamal typed the last sentence and hit the save button. Clasping his hands behind his head and allowing himself a small, but rare smile, Kamal reviewed the document on the screen. Brief, but powerful. The truth immutable; and no one argued with the truth.

In his mind, and unfortunately for too many others of our time, the United States Constitution was considered a poorly written and outdated document in need of a major overhaul. Or even better, just discarded. In particular, he deemed the first amendment's sole purpose was to denigrate the peaceful religion of Islam and demonize all true believers of the only real faith.

Kamal knew of only one law to follow: Sharia law.

The main topic for Kamal's treatise focused on the breaking news story about the missing young Muslim girl whose body had just been found. The media reported that the girl had been sexually assaulted and murdered, her body discarded in the Pine Barrens. A suspect already in custody.

According to the imam, in Sharia law, the only recognized punishment for a rapist is death. Rape is defined as a male forcing himself on a female. Clear and simple, but how does one determine this is the case?

By a thorough evaluation of the evidence.

There must be at least four male Muslim witnesses to the supposed rape. Females need not be counted, since they have an insufficient capacity for memory, as well as a lack of understanding of how the act took place. If the accused were so inclined, he could confess to the rape, and he would be put to death. But the more likely scenario would be a complete denial with a swearing on the Koran.

In a more modern application of Sharia law, DNA evidence would not be considered admissible. That leaves the victim as the lone responsible element for the crime of sex outside the bonds of matrimony. And the fitting punishments for that crime come down to flogging, death, or exile.

The learned Imam Kamal prided himself on being tough, but just.

His punishment of choice: death.

After one last review of the document, he uploaded it to his weekly blog site.

* * * * * *

Reverend Jefferson Carter exited his Lincoln Town Car in a coned-off parking space across from the Morristown Green. The location for today's scheduled press conference and rally for Leilah Harris. He was due to address the crowd in five minutes, in a continuing effort to gather public support for his role as a leader and savior of the black community.

Before Carter straightened his tie and walked over to the podium, his assistant, Samantha Cleveland, charged across the street waving an armful of papers. She narrowly avoided being run down by at least two, ready-for-blood, New Jersey motorists. Samantha took the blaring horns and squealing brakes in stride as she shoved the papers into Carter's hands.

Slightly out of breath, Samantha said, "Jefferson. What the hell took you so long to get here?" Before he responded, she waved her arms and continued, "Never mind. We got breaking news on Leilah Harris. Her body's been found. They've made an arrest."

Samantha Cleveland looked around at the spectators who were eager for the rally to get under way. "Come on. Let's go back to the car. We need a little privacy to talk. See what we should do with this."

Once inside the Lincoln, Samantha jabbed a finger at the papers she'd placed in Carter's hands. "Start reading these notes while I fill you in."

Carter held up a hand and scanned the papers. "Just give me a minute."

Samantha looked at her watch and folded her arms, her foot tapping on the floorboards.

Not waiting for Reverend Carter to finish, she blurted out, "We should cancel your speech and back away from this whole mess. We don't have time to change your talking points and prepare you for any new remarks."

Carter finished reading. He turned and smiled at Samantha. "Hey. I don't see that happening." He pointed out the window. "I mean… look at this crowd. They're all waiting for me to walk up to the podium. Anyway, I've already been spotted. I can't just hightail it out of here."

Samantha tried to interrupt, but Carter persisted. "I can handle this. These are my people. And I'm confident about how to work with this new information. Grabbing this black guy right away for murder and possible kidnapping and sexual assault charges? This could be even better than the police not doing a damn thing to find that poor missing girl. Don't you see? They're trying to blame it on black-on-black crime. Like they always do, ignoring the oppression and despair ingrained in the poor black communities. They did this to hide the fact the investigation was going nowhere."

Samantha Cleveland considered mentioning that the investigation had been proceeding quite well, the pile of evidence against the prime suspect mounting, and neither the victim nor the alleged perpetrator lived in any ghetto. But Carter spoke first.

"Come on, Samantha. Let me show you how I do this. Remember? That's exactly what you always say. I'll have the crowd so riled up, it'll look like the police tarred and feathered this guy."

Before she could stop him, he opened the door and headed for the podium.

After a brief hesitation, trying to remove the not-so-positive images from her mind, Samantha Cleveland grabbed for the door handle and ran to catch up with Carter, shouting, "You did see the FBI is involved with this now, didn't you?"

Carter waved his hand in a dismissive fashion and stepped up to the podium.

Reverend Carter waited for the din to subside as the crowd responded to his presence. Like an outgoing tide, a hush spread out from where Carter stood, fist raised to his supporters, both paid and authentic alike. Samantha had made sure the on-site media crews were prepared and satellite uplinks secured.

As he got ready to speak, Samantha noticed Reverend Carter glancing at a man dressed in distinctly different garb sitting in the front row. The reverend tapped the mike, and his familiar voice rang out.

"I have just been informed that our efforts to rattle local law enforcement to take the disappearance of poor

Leilah Harris seriously have stirred them into a belated action. And we've succeeded in getting the federal authorities to investigate this too. There is a clear civil rights issue that needs to be addressed. That's why I prodded the Department of Justice to take charge of the investigation."

The cheers from the crowd spurred him on.

"It is unfortunate, but the disinterest shown by the local authorities during the early stages of her disappearance played a role in the tragic conclusion to another forgotten black child. They discovered Leilah Harris's body in an isolated area in the Pine Barrens. Her young life tossed aside. Leilah was kidnapped, sexually assaulted, and then murdered."

Samantha Cleveland watched Carter's rhythm falter. He appeared distracted by the man seated in the front row. Samantha focused her attention on this man, observing a gangly looking individual with a full, jet black, bushy beard. His head was covered by a white, tight-fitting headgear, and he wore a long, flowing one-piece coat with a collar that zipped up and embraced his long and slender neck.

Reverend Carter carried on, appearing to regain his momentum. "And the shameful behavior of our law enforcement personnel gets even worse, if you can believe it. I keep hearing our nation no longer has a race problem. That we are united as one. But I point to the fact: blacks are still being profiled. The authorities, as usual, jumped on the first poor black man they found. They immediately took him into custody and charged him with the kidnapping, sexual assault, and murder of this young girl. I'm surprised they took him alive. I'm sure if we weren't involved from the beginning, the man wouldn't be so lucky. So, now we have the same old excuse of another black-on-black—"

"The man is innocent!" The shout came from the bearded man in the front row. He now stood, his coat billowing in the light breeze.

"Ah, now we have," Carter stuttered, "a way for the authorities to sweep this whole thing under the rug. All we got is another black-on-black crime. What do they care? Black lives are not important. Nobody cares if—"

"The man is innocent! The evidence is false! The man is innocent!" The man in front had moved two steps toward the podium, his voice taking on a lyrical chant.

Unnerved by this action, Samantha jumped to the podium and whispered to the reverend. Carter shook his head, but instead of continuing his speech he grabbed Samantha's arm and spoke into her ear. Her expression should've caused Carter to reconsider his plan. Samantha pleaded for him to call in their security detail, but Carter turned back to the mike.

"As you all know… this story isn't about me. I am not here just to listen to myself speak or to have my face spread all over the evening news."

Hearing those words, Samantha had to check to see if Carter had been replaced by an imposter.

"We are all here to make sure justice is done. And the voice of this community is heard by everyone. We are here to work together and support the effort to make sure the life of another innocent black man isn't ruined. So, sir…."

Carter pointed to the man in the long billowing coat. "Your voice is as important as mine. I want you to join me up here and talk to these people. I mean… together we will see justice done. Because without justice… there can be no peace."

Samantha Cleveland's jaw dropped. What the hell was he trying to do? There was no script for any of this. Why the hell didn't she lock him in the freakin' car before he crossed the damn street? She was ready to call security and get Reverend Carter the hell out of here. Shit. She was ready to pull him away from the podium herself. Not for the first time, she questioned her own sanity in working for the reverend.

Carter extended a hand to the man and guided him up to the platform, giving him room at the mike.

Nodding his head, first at Carter, and then at the crowd, the man spoke with a clear, booming voice. The lyrical chanting disappeared. "Thank you, *my friend*,… *Reverend Carter.*"

Maybe Samantha imagined it, but she didn't like the sound of how the man just pronounced her boss's name.

"If we work together, we will assure that justice indeed will be done. I am Imam Rashid Kamal. I am here to tell you that this man who they have arrested, Thomas Pauling, is innocent of all charges. The charges should be dropped, and he should be released. The evidence the authorities say they have gathered is false. I repeat. They must let him go at once."

In a smug sounding voice, Carter whispered to Samantha, "See. I know what I'm doing. This guy is gonna reinforce everything I said." He turned to the crowd, leaning into the mike. "The ah… the imam speaks the truth. Let's all listen to the voice of reason."

Kamal continued, "Yes. According to the laws of the one true faith, the young Muslim girl, Leilah Harris, got exactly the correct punishment for her sins."

Carter spun back to Samantha and said, "I mean... what in the hell is he talking about?"

"There is no evidence of rape," Kamal said. "This so-called DNA profiling should not be admissible. It is not recognized in a true court of Sharia law. The real issue is that this sinful woman engaged in a sexual act outside the bonds of marriage. According to Sharia law, there is no evidence of rape. None of the required four witnesses have come forward to attest to this charge. Thomas Pauling imparted the correct punishment on this disgraceful woman—an outcome dictated by her sins. It is about time that everyone in this nation recognizes Sharia law. Mr. Pauling should be commended for his actions. I understand he has already denied any sexual contact with this girl. I assure you his actions were guided by the desire to exact punishment. It is rare to see a non-believer act in such a noble fashion. I demand he be released. And then we will see to it he converts to the one true faith—Islam."

Kamal turned to where Reverend Carter had been standing. "Reverend... join me in rallying for the release of this innocent man."

He was speaking to the back of the retreating reverend being hastily whisked away by two very large members of his security detail. Samantha Cleveland had stopped listening to any of Reverend Carter's pleads to respond to the imam. Free speech was one thing, but the hole Carter had already dug for himself didn't need another shovel to the ground.

CHAPTER 31

LITTLE TIME FOR SMALL TALK on the short drive southeast of Morristown. From Edie's perspective—a good thing. She still hadn't told Steve any of the troubling details she'd picked up regarding his family.

Steve's eyes stayed focused on the road. Though Edie's head tilted down, her eyes didn't register the words in the notebook on her lap. Their earlier conversation had been stilted. For an instant, Edie second-guessed the wisdom of diving into the internet and digging up Steve's family tree. Even that wasn't as bad as taking the next step—contacting Dominick Casella.

Not one to falter at her own actions, she shrugged it off but remained nervous as to the consequences. Not her fault the Casellas were… were what? There could've been another explanation. She really didn't believe that.

Steve didn't know what to think. He'd never seen Edie this quiet. Possibly, he'd been a little harsh. He knew she was only trying to make the broken pieces of his life whole again. What the hell. This little distraction may not be all bad. After recent events, it might be fun to meet one of his new-found relatives. Get to know the guy. Dominick. Yeah. Couldn't hurt. But then—the fleeting name *Vinnie Casella* tripped his consciousness—causing the slight tightening of cranial muscles, instigating the first phase of an impending headache.

After the Columbia Turnpike changed to South Orange Avenue, Steve hazarded a glance at Edie. "So, Dominick's a regular guy?" The words sounded more stupid hearing them out loud.

"Ah, yeah. We had a great talk. You're gonna like him." Her voice flat, Edie glanced at the GPS unit on the dash and unnecessarily repeated the computer voice prompts. "His Short Hills office is coming up in about a mile—on the right."

"Short Hills? Not according to that sign we just passed."

"Short Hills isn't a town. It's an unincorporated part of Millburn Township."

He peered out the side window thinking: what the hell is a township?

But instead, he said, "There's the sign: *Short Hills Piazza.*"

Edie nodded as Steve turned onto a narrow, tree-lined drive. It opened into a parking area with reddish-brown cobblestones lined with flowering shrubbery and huge shade trees to provide respite from the hot New Jersey sun. The image of the office building added to their amazement. Edie imagined being transported back in time, and swore she was gazing at one of the Italian villas she'd toured on a long-ago trip to Naples.

As they walked toward the grand entranceway, Steve pointed to the decorative aged bronze placard identifying the specific businesses housed in the building. In addition to the accounting office, there were two additional establishments: a beauty parlor and a beauty supply store.

He nudged Edie's arm. "Why don't you get a bit of work done while we're here and then bring home the necessary sundries for the required maintenance treatments?" Visions of blond tresses replacing Edie's straight black hair danced across his Sicilian brain; more intense than usual, fitting in with these new classic Italian surroundings.

Before Edie responded to Steve's suggestion, the two large wood entry doors swung open, and a slim figure burst through and bounded down the stairs. He shouted out Steve's name. Not the first time Steve had been recognized when approaching a supposed stranger. However, this usually occurred with members of the opposite sex. Steve attempted a smile as he recalled several instances when these kinds of greetings hadn't gone so well. On the other hand, Edie had used a similar advantage when they'd first met. And if not for that occasion, he wouldn't be here today.

His cranial muscles gave a more definite twitch.

Steve's eyes bulged. If this was Dominick, the Casella family must also harbor the Woody Allen gene. The young man wore a charcoal gray, vested pinstriped suit. He stood about five foot five. The vertical stripes minimized an already shockingly skeletal frame. His straight black hair, plastered down, sported a precise part on the left. Maybe he spent his spare time allowing the new beauticians in the building to practice their skills.

A pair of wire-rimmed Marshwood-styled glasses, which framed small black eyes, represented a noticeable exception to the Woody Allen gene pool. Perhaps a smidgen of the John Lennon phenotype also fit into the Casella mix. Although Dominick was close to Steve's age, he appeared freeze-framed into the body of a gangly teenager still fighting the onset of puberty-driven, hormone-induced transformations.

Dominick's face glowed as he introduced himself and pumped Steve's hand. In an awkward move, he turned to Edie and froze. Edie embraced him. Images of shimmying up telephone poles danced across her brain as her arms encircled the slight frame.

From a thin-lipped mouth came a slightly squeaky, cracking, but nevertheless, pleasant sounding voice, confirming Dominick's puberty-anchoring status.

"Steve. Oh my God. All this time. I never knew we were related. And those stories. I never connected the dots. Our name, Casella, is so common. Whoa, this is so cool."

Dominick looked over at Edie. "I can't believe it. Shooting terrorists. Finding those nuclear weapons. And before that you guys helped put those White House hacks, including the president himself, in prison."

Dominick lowered his voice, which conspicuously squeaked at a higher rate. "Just between us, there were people, close to the family? Well, actually a few in the family who were not as thrilled with how things turned out in Washington. I'm talking D.C., not the state. Except for the—"

"What're you talking about, Dominick?" Steve interrupted, eyes narrowing. Edie glanced away, casually taking in their new surroundings.

"Well," Dominick said, with a lame attempt at a wink, "a few important people here in Jersey were involved in some, let's say, lucrative projects that got the bottoms knocked out when the shake-up took place in the White House."

Steve remained quiet and stared. Dominick shifted his body and turned his head around. It made him look like he was trying to get a bead on a sniper.

"You've got a really pretty garden out here, Dominick, and some very nice trees too," Edie said.

Steve glared back and forth between the two, thinking: nice trees? Who the hell has nice trees?

"Come on," Dominick stammered, "let's go to my office. We can talk there. I cleared the rest of my morning, so we've got plenty of time. And Barb has already brought in refreshments."

Dominick led his guests inside.

If the exterior of the building seemed daunting, as they entered the reception area they were in awe of the over-the-top interior, including an elegant circular reception desk with inlaid marble tiles. Near the window at the far end of the space was a young lady, probably the receptionist, bending over and watering potted plants on a tiered planter.

Steve forgot all about the nice trees outside. He leaned over to Edie and whispered in her ear, "She could be Melissa's sister. She's got all the same—"

Steve knew it was coming but failed to stop Edie's elbow from exerting a healthy blow to his kidney. Rubbing his side, he maintained sufficient focus on the girl as she finished watering the plants closest to the floor.

"You think she's carrying?" Steve whispered.

This time Edie went with the program. "With that painted on, slim bandage dress she's wearing, I'm sure you'd see the telltale outline."

"I've been looking for it, but so far I'm not seeing—"

Dominick, obviously catching part of the exchange, interrupted. "Ah, excuse me guys. Who's Melissa? I'm pretty sure Barb doesn't have any sisters."

Edie smiled and turned to Steve with both hands extended. "I never tire of hearing you tell this story."

In a practiced performance, he rattled off the merits of the Flash-Bang holster and the convincing demonstration of its attributes by a dedicated, talented salesperson named Melissa.

Edie watched Dominick's glasses fog up as Steve spun his tale.

When Dominick brought Barb over for introductions, his face burned and droplets of sweat formed on his temples. Speaking to Barb made his face grow even hotter. Edie rarely noticed those particular genetic traits displayed on Steve; except perhaps when Nana was around.

Always up for a challenge, she contemplated a plan to help poor Dominick.

Barb turned out to be a sweet, shy young girl who had begun working at the Short Hills Piazza three weeks ago. Enrolled in college courses in the evening, she majored in accounting. Edie concluded Barb had noted Dominick's hesitating displays in her presence and appreciated the attention. Maybe she'd let Barb take care of things on her own. If it turned out they were both too shy to move things along, Edie would be waiting in the wings, ready to stoke the flames.

Steve watched the way Edie sized up the situation. He smiled at her, took her hand, and gave it a slight but definite pop with his wrist.

Under his breath, he said, "Leave it, Edie. Leave it." He pulled her body to the left, to break the stare. That trick sometimes worked with Amber.

Barb waved a quick goodbye and returned to her seat at the receptionist's desk. Dominick ushered them down the center corridor on the far side of the reception area.

On the way, they passed offices with employees working at their computer stations. Other workers viewed a high-tech PowerPoint presentation in a cram-filled conference room.

Dominick opened the intricately carved door to his office.

"Holy crap!" Edie couldn't pull back the words, grasping the extravagance of Dominick's private enclave. She gazed about the room as she strolled across the plush forest green carpeting, tempted to kick off her shoes. Her eyes wandered to the French doors framing a cozy outside patio with an aged bronze Florentine fountain surrounded by curved white marble benches.

Refocusing her attention, Edie turned to Dominick. "Jeez, Dominick, I'm impressed. I never realized how lucrative accounting could be. Can't imagine what the rent would be for a set-up like this."

Dominick mumbled something in reply. Steve stood back trying to comprehend Edie's bizarre behavior and comments. His cranial muscles resumed ratcheting their way toward a major headache after the brief, but pleasant distraction with Barb.

"I'm sorry, you said you don't what?" Edie said, taking a step toward Dominick.

"Ah, there's no rent. The building is owned by the… ah… we own the building. The family built it. The beauty shop and supply store are owned by the family too. The place is modeled after a villa in Italy."

He shrugged and pointed to a large oval coffee table flanked by a leather sofa and two Queen Anne high-back leather armchairs. "Come on, let's sit down. I'll pour the coffee. Help yourselves to the goodies."

Steve gave Edie a look, and they both sat on the sofa. Dominick dropped into one of the facing armchairs, speaking casually about the Casella family, which he explained was scattered around the state. Some had left the area, but most Casellas still considered New Jersey their home turf.

Dominick filled in a few missing details about how Steve's father fit into the family tree and recounted personal stories he'd picked up from the older family members. Edie concluded that Dominick had wasted no time spreading the news about meeting with Steve today. That explained how he had all the info about Steve's dad at his fingertips.

The names of these relatives meant nothing to Steve. Listening closely, he realized that one name in particular remained absent.

Dominick mentioned that the family owned a chain of beauty parlors and beauty supply shops throughout the state. The family was also involved in waste management operations. The main interest of his accounting firm was based on those particular businesses.

Edie asked several specific questions about the Casellas, but Dominick always turned the conversation back to Steve and Edie's escapades. He seemed genuinely entranced, craving the details of their accomplishments.

Edie became concerned with Steve's increasingly subdued posture and tried prodding him to open up. But in the back of her mind, she couldn't shake the idea that she was in part, well not in part, fully responsible for the imminent opening of Pandora's Box.

With all her journalistic talents, she remained stymied in how to lead Dominick down the path to open the correct doors without slamming Steve in the face. With her guilt building, she wondered why she hadn't prepared Steve for the inevitable. What little hope she'd held out about her first conclusions being wrong had dissipated. She turned her attention back on the two men and realized she'd missed part of the conversation but was pleased to see Steve becoming more of an active participant.

Dominick was saying, "...that can be arranged. I'm sure they'd be eager to sit down and reminisce about the old days."

"Yeah. Too bad I'll be leaving in about a week. Probably won't get the chance to talk to all of Dad's relatives. But Dominick, there's one guy I'd be interested in talking to. I don't believe you mentioned his name though."

Dominick looked puzzled, shrugging his shoulders. "Can't think of anybody I forgot. And by the way, most of 'em live close by, so if you're still here this weekend, I'd be glad to arrange a little something and bring the family all together."

Steve cleared his throat, leaned forward and stared, his eyes piercing directly through Dominick's Marshwood glasses. "So, do you think they would give Vinnie a weekend pass, or should I make arrangements to visit him in prison? Is it somewhere local? Or was he one of the family members who left the state? Perhaps not on his own accord."

Edie shrunk into the sofa as a sheen of sweat formed on Dominick's forehead. Before Dominick responded, Steve swiveled his head toward Edie, gave it a slight tilt and formed a tight smile.

"So, it seems," Steve said, turning back to Dominick, "two old friends of this *Vinnie Casella*—"

"Everybody in the family calls him Uncle Vinnie," Dominick mumbled, wiping droplets of sweat off his brow with the embroidered white linen napkin.

"Fine. Like I was saying—these two guys assumed *Uncle Vinnie* had sent me to—let me see—how did they put it? Oh yeah, we weren't going along with the program," he said, using his fingers as quotation marks. "They got the impression Uncle Vinnie wanted to interfere with whatever the hell they were doing."

Steve edged in a little closer to Dominick. Edie latched onto his arm. She almost said, 'leave it'.

Speaking a little slower, Steve continued, "So, could they've been hairdressers not happy with how the Casella family took over the beauty trade in New Jersey? It's almost too stereotypical, but could they've been taking issue with the Casella family's management of the trash-recycling program? Not to mention the possibility of dabbling in union activities?"

Edie acted quicker than Dominick. She grabbed Steve's other arm and swung him around to face her. "You mean those guys who tried to grab you last night? They mentioned Vinnie Casella?"

"Why do I think this doesn't surprise you?" Steve responded.

"You should've told me they referred specifically to Vinnie Casella." She folded her arms.

"Yeah?" Steve said, smiling tightly. "And why would that name mean anything to you?"

Oops.

"Well, I did come across several suspicious stories when I researched the history of union corruption and tactics for Tyler."

She turned to Dominick, who appeared content to not be a part of this conversation. "This was after I talked to you, Dominick."

To both of them, she said, "Never anything concrete. Nothing anybody ever made stick. Just a lot of accusations and innuendos. From what I understand, Uncle Vinnie is doing time for tax evasion and other...."

Edie's voice drifted off. She tried putting on a smile and flashed her eyes at Steve. "And Steve, he's still in New Jersey from what I understand."

She turned to Dominick. "How far would you say the Federal Correctional Institution in Fairton is from here?"

"About two hours, depending on traffic." A safe question to answer.

Steve patted Edie's hand. "Edie, I don't say this often enough, but I thank God every day for the things you do for me. Sometimes I don't think I deserve all this."

She took a deep breath and exhaled. This time she didn't have to guess if he was sincere. She gave him a quick kiss on the cheek and turned to Dominick.

"So, Dominick. Care to expand on the family business? Steve's got a lot to catch up on."

Getting serious, she turned her head. "I'm sorry, Steve, this isn't the way I anticipated hooking you up with your family."

Again, she turned. "Look, Dominick. There're some nasty things going on with the Griffin Mills and Home Center. It has to do with the union and what they might be up to. With what Steve has found out, and after what happened last night, things might get a lot worse, real quick. So now's not the time to hold out. If you've got anything you think can help—we need to hear it."

"Look, guys. There's a lot of truth to a sordid history with my...." Dominick looked at Steve with a sheepish smile. "I mean, our family. But it's all in the past. I swear. Part of what we're doing here is to clean up the businesses and—"

"Money laundering?" Edie asked.

"No. Well, at one time maybe, but what I'm trying to tell you is I'm part of the new generation of Casellas."

Steve leaned forward, bit his lower lip and raised his palms in surrender.

Dominick pulled himself back in the chair and continued. "We're dead set on turning the family around. Uncle Vinnie is the past. Even he's getting the point. At least he's got plenty of time to ponder it."

Steve interrupted. "Did anybody consider mentioning this to those two thugs I ran into last night?"

This time Dominick inched forward, holding his ground. "Look, Steve. I'm sorry that happened. But if what Edie just said is true, you stumbled on something that has gotten somebody pissed-off. And I don't see what that has to do with whatever my... your... the family... was involved with in the past."

Reluctantly, Steve had to agree, and nodded his acknowledgement to Dominick.

CHAPTER 32

STEVE PLACED AN ARM AROUND Edie's waist as they walked down the steps of the Short Hills Piazza. Before getting into the Durango, they engaged in a tender embrace.

Edie whispered, "So you're not mad at me?"

"Uh-uh. It was sweet. What you did. I guess you just forgot to mention a few particular details last night. And in no time at all, I'll be ready for your next good deed."

Edie shrugged. "I guess for a while I should concentrate on what we came out here to do."

Steve took in a deep breath and focused his eyes on the grand façade of the building, trying to comprehend what any of this meant.

"It appears the New Jersey branch of the Casella family might have interesting connections to that puzzle."

"Hi, Sampson," Edie said as the phone call interrupted their conversation. "Whoa… whoa… slow down. No, I haven't seen the news. Thomas—arrested? Slow down, Sampson. Take a breath. Okay, now why— What? A student? Jesus Christ. Are you kidding? Oh my God! The hearing's already over? The arraignment's tomorrow? How in the hell did they corral a grand jury to… Okay, okay, so he's out on bail? Where? Gottcha. We're on our way."

Steve grabbed the door handle and helped Edie inside the Durango. Rushing around to the driver's side and jumping in, Steve started the engine and turned to Edie, his eyes forming the unspoken question.

"Stillwater. The Griffin place. Oh my God, Steve! What in the hell is going on? This is bullshit! Not

Thomas. No. Never. My God! Nana's gonna die when she hears this. I didn't even ask Sampson if he'd told her yet. Oh God."

Tires squealed and the Durango spun down the long driveway, threading into the traffic on South Orange Avenue. Steve reached over and massaged Edie's neck.

"Whatever's going on, Edie, we'll get to the bottom of it. If anybody can fix this, she's sitting right here next to me. And we're going to do this together. We're a team, remember? And a damn good one."

Edie's eyes remained shut tight, but Steve sensed a slight loosening of her tense neck muscles. Sighing, her eyes fluttered open as she looked over to Steve. Her knuckles knocked away several tears as she crooked her head back to nestle against Steve's comforting hand.

"Thanks, babe. Let's go do this."

* * * * * *

"I told Tyler to stay away from this, but I got the impression he wasn't listening. He's coming as soon as he can break away from a cabinet meeting. Said he needed to get a handle on a few things too." Kristie Pauling related the message while her hands rested on Thomas's shoulders.

She walked around and sat next to him in the matching armchair. Across from Kristie and Thomas—Sampson, Steve, and Edie all leaned forward on the leather sofa in the same room they had recently met with the vice president at his family retreat in Stillwater.

Edie spoke first. "Thomas. Tell me what the hell is going on. I know damn well you had nothing to do with this poor girl's death, but what does the FBI got to charge you so fast? Sampson told me you're being arraigned in the federal district court in Philadelphia tomorrow. The feds usually hold off until a grand jury gets the chance to wade through the evidence before they issue the warrants."

Thomas pursed his lips. "I shouldn't be talking about this. I don't want to put you guys in an awkward position. My attorney said if I talk to anyone, they could be forced to testify in—"

Sampson jumped to his feet and leaned over the cut-log rustic coffee table, both hands clenched. His face rigid. "Thomas. What the hell you talking about? I'm sure I speak for everybody here. If anybody's gonna help you, you're looking at 'em right now. When you're with the feds or in court—you listen to your lawyer. But when you're with family, we're gonna do this our way."

Sampson pounded his fist on the coffee table. "Whatever the hell it takes to get through this. Understand? You gotta talk to us."

Sampson turned to Edie and pointed a finger. "And you, sis. I'm counting on you to ask your brother the right questions. That's what you do on those fancy cable shows. So, let's put it to some good use right here."

All eyes turned to Thomas as Kristie reached across and grasped both his hands.

Thomas chuffed. "Well, Sampson, I wish I were still in kindergarten with you fighting my battles, but this one may be a little different."

Thomas Pauling's bright, penetrating eyes welled up and receded below a shimmering pool of darkness. "Let me tell you what they're saying happened to Leilah Harris, and why they think I'm involved."

His voice cracked. "From their prospective, I'm guilty as hell. They say they got enough evidence to put me away for life."

He shook his head, trying to blink back the tears. "Hell. Instead of worrying about me, I should be grieving for that poor girl. Talking to her family, trying to console them. Leilah Harris sat in my classes for two years. What a bright, sensitive kid. Her whole life ahead of her. And now she's dead. I can't even go to her parents and talk to them. Christ. I'm accused of raping and murdering their daughter."

"Thomas," Edie said, "right now we need to find out what's going on. We all want to make this right for Leilah's family too. But we can't do that till we get to the truth. So, what evidence does the FBI have?"

"Short version? They say I enticed Leilah into my hotel suite. I got her drunk, knocked her out with drugs, and then had sex with her."

He looked right at Kristie when he said this.

He turned to Edie and shrugged. "They're a little fuzzy about the details, but they say I gave her a drug overdose. That killed her, or at least left her unconscious. Then I wrapped her up in a rug from the hotel suite and drove to the Pine Barrens and dumped off her body."

Thomas's voice had been almost monotone as he recited this. But as he finished, his body shook and his voice broke again. "But you want to hear the good part? If I were them, looking at all this fucking evidence? I'd have to agree with them."

"What are you talking about?" Edie said, voice quivering.

Steve had never heard Thomas use that kind of language before.

Thomas stared straight ahead. "Okay. You guys might as well be my jury."

Pausing, Thomas shut his eyes for several seconds and then looked around at his family. "First, the local authorities found Leilah's car in the underground parking garage of my hotel. Several people remembered seeing her walking through the lobby. Even better, a maid talked to her on my floor. Claims Leilah had a room key."

"She saw her going into your hotel suite?" Edie asked.

Thomas shook his head. "No. Just heading in the general direction. But that doesn't matter since they placed Leilah in my suite from trace evidence on the carpets and the bed. Oh, and not to mention the rug they found wrapped around her when they discovered the body in the Pine Barrens. There happened to be a room number tag sewn into the bottom of the rug. And on the ground next to the rolled-up rug? They found the key card to my suite, as well as a photo ID convention badge with my name on it, along with my signature."

Thomas paused and swallowed hard with a quick glance at Kristie. His voice grew shakier and quieter as he continued. "When they examined Leilah's body, they... ah... they identified my semen in... inside her. And the DNA profile was as good as it gets. Then last night, searching our house, they discovered Leilah's panties in a hidden compartment in my suitcase."

Covering his face, he rubbed his hands over his cheeks, smearing away the tears. In a more forceful voice, Thomas said, "Damn. Damn. Damn. What the hell happened to her? My God. Poor Leilah. That girl was an angel. Why the hell would anybody want to hurt that little girl? I can't imagine what her family is going through right now. Christ. I wouldn't blame her father if he wanted to kill me. When I looked at him in the courtroom today, I felt their pain. But also the hatred. It pierced my heart and I wanted to die right there."

Thomas turned to Kristie, his voice small and faltering. "You remember? We talked about this several times. Figuring out how to handle it. I tried to do the things we discussed. Did I do something wrong?"

To the rest of the group, Thomas clarified what he said to Kristie. "You see, Leilah had a crush on me. I've known it for a while. But I didn't know what in the world to do. She was such a sweet, delicate girl. I didn't want to encourage her, but at the same time I didn't want to hurt her feelings. Kristie and I talked about it. We agreed not to treat her any differently from the rest of my students. I tried to be friendly, but also professional. She was one of the best students in my class, and I felt a responsibility to encourage her to excel. I knew she had great potential."

His fists tightened, his breathing labored. "Jesus. It was a fine line. I must've screwed things up. Gave her the wrong impression. But even if she somehow snuck into my hotel suite, why would someone want to kill her? None of this makes any sense. Christ. Even if it made sense—look at the evidence against me. I would have to judge myself guilty."

Edie stood, walked around the coffee table, and kneeled in front of her brother. She swallowed and cleared her throat.

"Tommy," she said.

Steve knew that was the name she first called Thomas when she was a toddler.

"I'm only your little sister. But listen to me. Never in a million years would I consider you capable of doing anything like this."

Edie's face softened. "And if you recall. I hardly ever blush, but we both have the same light skin tone, so we can see it on our faces, right?"

She stared into Thomas's eyes. "So, look at me. I'm damn sure I'm blushing now. But I gotta ask you, Tommy, how did your semen wind up inside Leilah? Everything else can be explained. Evidence can be fabricated. But that one thing. How?"

Sampson chimed in. "I for one am glad I refused to bring Nana here tonight. This talk is even too much for me to handle."

For the first time, a faint shadow of a smile appeared on Thomas's face. He turned to Kristie, and she mirrored the gesture.

"You may be wrong about that, Sampson. What do you think, Kristie?" Thomas said.

Kristie slowly nodded. "I don't know why we didn't put it together till now. But I can't come up with any other explanation. Thomas. Why don't you remind your brother of one of Nana's little stories?"

Steve looked back and forth at Edie and Sampson to see if they had any clue as to what in the hell was going on. He knew Nana was a unique and mysterious person, but it was impossible to understand how she played a role in this situation. From the spreading blush and look of confusion on Edie's face, she didn't seem to have the answer. Steve couldn't imagine Sampson capable of blushing, and not only because of his dark complexion. But now he looked even more confused than Edie.

"So as not to embarrass my little sister any more than necessary," Thomas began, "I'll try to give the shortened version. This should ring a bell with you, Sampson. Edie, you were too young to remember any of these stories."

Kristie stood and walked over to the L-shaped bar, placed several glasses on an oval pewter tray, and grabbed a chilled bottle of vodka from an undercounter freezer. Returning, she set the tray down onto the coffee table and poured everyone drinks as Thomas began his story.

"I'm sure Nana would have a whole lot more flair in telling this, but here goes." Thomas paused and gulped down the shot. "When Nana was a little girl, she lived on a farm. And her daddy complained all the time about how the kids would flush the damnedest...."

By the time Thomas got around to how Nana's childhood experiences led to his obsession, or as he put it, sensible habits regarding the proper procedures for maintaining a functioning septic system, the group had made considerable progress in emptying the vodka bottle.

Everyone stared at Steve, who'd lived most of his life dealing with septic systems, when he said, "It all makes perfect sense, Thomas. In an effort not to embarrass your sister, I've never made a big deal about that particular topic."

"Hey, Sampson," Edie replied, "you gonna let a white boy talk to your little sister like that?"

Perhaps that was the vodka talking.

Edie stood up and paced, pausing to stare out the large expansive windows of the great room. Steve gazed at her profile as the distant lights of an airliner arched across the horizon.

When Edie turned back to face the others, her face reflected a renewed strength. With clasped hands and a quick nod, without a hint of blush remaining, she said, "Okay, we can make a case for how someone got hold of a used condom out of the trash, but we've got no proof or motive or opportunity. So the feds will brush that explanation aside. But let's see who's going to be embarrassed now. Can you come up with a timeframe here? And are we talking, ah… about multiple opportunities for…?"

Kristie spoke first. "I was with Thomas when he checked in. It was sometime in the late afternoon. I stayed the night and left the next morning. And I'm sure we never left the room until I jumped into the taxi and headed for the airport."

The burning was much more apparent on Kristie's fair skin. "I wasn't counting, but I guess there would've been an adequate sampling to choose from."

Edie asked Thomas, "What did you do after Kristie left?"

"I was busy at the convention center. Didn't spend much time in the hotel suite."

"Would anybody have known your schedule?" Steve asked.

"Can't say for sure if—"

"You still syncing your calendar schedules on your computers and phones?" Edie asked.

"Yeah. So?"

"Somebody with the right computer knowledge might've determined when the room would be empty. Can you remember anything unusual that happened? Run into anybody who looked suspicious or out of place?" Edie asked.

"Jeez. I don't know. Who even pays attention to things like that?"

Kristie sat up a little straighter, eyes narrowing. "Thomas, when we got off the elevator, after you checked in and we headed up to the room?"

"What? I remember being a little preoccupied with getting settled in and spending time together before you had to leave in the morning."

"The room key card. Don't you remember? We were walking down the hall, turning the corner, and that man on the elevator called to you. You had apparently dropped it, and he must've picked it up. He asked if it belonged to you."

Thomas shrugged. "So? I guess I was even more distracted than usual."

"You were holding the card in your hand?" Edie asked.

"No. I stuffed it in my pocket when I bent down to grab the bags in the lobby."

Thomas stood up; head turned toward the ceiling as he paced. "Kristie. When we got to the room, you headed into the bathroom to turn on the water for your bath. So I killed the time emptying out my pockets and trying to organize stuff for the meeting."

Thomas stopped pacing and stared at Kristie. "I couldn't find my convention badge anywhere. I remember placing it in the same pocket with the room key. When I checked in, they asked to see the badge to confirm I was attending the convention. And they handed it back along with the room key. So I stuck everything in the same pocket."

"You never found it?" Kristie asked.

"No. While you were in the tub, I retraced our steps back to the elevator. I even rode it down to the lobby and checked with the guy at the desk. To make sure I hadn't left it there. But I never found it. It was gone. At the time, I didn't worry that much about it. More of a nuisance. I wound up showing my paperwork at the convention center, and they printed me a new badge. Guess anybody might've picked it up."

Steve looked at Kristie and then Thomas. "No. Not just anybody. What about this guy on the elevator? Anything about him seem out of place?"

Thomas shook his head and shrugged. "I never paid any attention to the guy. Kristie?"

"Seemed polite enough, I guess. Dressed in a business suit, but he did look a little uncomfortable. Scratched his neck a lot. I remember backing away when he began coughing."

"Could either of you describe him?" Steve asked.

Thomas shook his head.

Compressing her lips, Kristie hesitated and then said, "Well... on an elevator you do your best not to stare. If I had to guess, I got the impression he was young, in his mid-twenties. And I'd say he might've been overweight."

Steve flashed back to the incident in the Great Adventure parking lot last night, but it was dark, and he didn't get a good look at either of the two men. The impression he had of the guy doing most of the talking was entirely different than Kristie's description. The other guy hung in the shadows, and his image didn't register all that much. Besides, Kristie's description fit half the post teen male population in the state. They do enjoy their greasy fast-food restaurants here.

Thomas sat down again, his hands wringing. "I don't understand any of this. You make it all sound like a big conspiracy. To do what? Why would anybody want to hurt that poor little girl?"

"You're right, Thomas," Edie said, words slowly formed. "I don't think Leilah Harris was the target. Don't you see? Somebody might be out to destroy you."

Thomas's face scrunched up, but then his eyes bulged. "Oh my God! Could somebody be sick enough to kill Leilah—to what? Try to make me into a monster? For Christ's sake. I'm a high school science teacher. I've never been involved in any controversies. At least not anything to precipitate something as horrendous as this. But if that's true, then I'm just as responsible for this as if I had killed her myself."

Steve's and Edie's eyes locked on each other, and they both turned to Kristie, who had a haunted look on her face.

"I'm... so... sorry... Thomas," Kristie said, eyes downcast. She rubbed his neck. "None of this is your fault. This has nothing to do with you. The message was for me. I knew that fighting for what was right wouldn't be easy. But if all this is true, this fight has just gotten a whole lot uglier. What the hell are we up against here?" Faltering, she collapsed in Thomas's arms and sobbed.

Thomas said in a low, but solid voice. "Don't you dare count me out of this thing, Kristie. If there's going to be a fight, we do this together."

Unions, politics, and the mafia? Not a narrow list to work with, especially in Edie's home state. But Steve figured that trying to clear her brother's name would be a good place to start. What the hell kind of a monster is capable of casting aside a sweet, young, innocent girl… to gain what?

This investigation had just become more deadly than he'd imagined.

CHAPTER 33

TODAY, AL ROZANO AND PHILIP Lucchesi met in a more private location: thirty miles east of Washington, D.C., on an estate perched along a high bluff overlooking the Severn River. The third man in the room casually sipped his martini, glancing out at the distant US Route 50 bridge. The setting sun cast long undulating shadows off the outdated span while the snarled tail-end of the commuter traffic inched along.

Al Rozano, the head of the New Jersey chapter of the CBT, had been picked up at Reagan National Airport after the short commuter flight from Newark, New Jersey. The limo drove him and a second passenger, Philip Lucchesi, the national president of the same Consolidated Brotherhood of Tradesmen union, to their present location. They were meeting at the request of the man who'd been waiting for them in the spacious study.

This man was not the owner of the estate, but he had a vested interest in shaping the upcoming plans of the CBT. His clients represented a major segment of a growing list of unusual allies aligning themselves with the union's current goals. Their solidarity grew stronger after hearing the leaked news about Vice President Tyler Griffin's plans for relocating from the grounds of the US Naval Observatory to the White House.

This estate was one of many scattered around the globe and owned by Theodore R. Kravitz, a well-known entrepreneur who specialized in dealing with the petroleum industry and served on the board of directors for several large banking institutions and corporations. He offered this property to close associates who found it necessary to discuss politically virulent topics with individuals whom the established political parties usually dealt with at a discreet location.

Following Lucchesi's lead, Rozano took a seat in the other armchair across from the kidney-shaped antique mahogany desk. After sitting down, Arthur Constantine swiveled his chair around and placed both elbows on the inlaid leather surface of the desk, facing the two men.

Clearing his throat, Lucchesi's pharmacologically fixed smile masked any underlying emotions. "Arthur, when I got the message that someone with a significant interest in our mission wanted to meet, I never suspected it would be you. It was my understanding that the—how should I refer to your usual clients? Enemy may be too strong a word. So, let's call them adversarial opponents."

Arthur Constantine leaned back and nodded, his expression cutting off any further comments from Lucchesi. "There comes a time, Philip, when you need to lift your head out of the sand and look at the big picture."

Folding his hands and not waiting for an answer, Constantine pushed on. "But for our immediate purposes, it's in everyone's best interest not to dwell on the specifics of who I'm here to represent. Discretion on this subject is more appropriate to our discussion. At this point, you guys have no need to concern yourselves with those details."

Lucchesi turned to Rozano. "Whaddaya say, Al? Should we be insulted, or intrigued?"

Rozano shrugged and looked around. "Hey. In this kind of place, I find it hard to be insulted."

Constantine laughed. "And at least it gives you a chance to leave that hellhole of a state and experience how the rest of the country lives."

"Now, that might be taken as an insult," Lucchesi answered for Rozano. "It's been a long time since we last talked, Arthur. But it's good to see you haven't lost your stylish good manners."

"So," Constantine said with a terse nod, "I'll consider that the end to our small talk. Let's get down to business."

Both Rozano and Lucchesi parroted Constantine's gesture, signaling for him to proceed.

"What I can say, gentlemen, is that I represent a consortium of individuals who are well-placed in our government and have a strong desire to remain so for the foreseeable future. These delegates of our long-standing representative republic are of the firm belief that if Tyler Griffin succeeds in his bid to become the leader of our nation, the framework of the existing two-party system will be forever destroyed."

Constantine paused and raised his eyebrows. "At least in the format that's worked in such a lucrative fashion for those fine statesmen on both sides of the aisle. We can't have two diametrically opposed agendas in this town. We need to return to the old days when there was an understanding that for this system to work, both parties needed to share equally in stealing as much of the nation's revenues as possible."

Neither Rozano nor Lucchesi offered any response to that statement. Rising, Constantine moved his frame to the window, glancing at the lingering view of the setting sun and choosing his next words.

With his back still to Lucchesi and Rozano, he said, "I'm not one to criticize the failed efforts of those now disgraced former members of the executive branch—

most of them part of the inner sanctum of the White House—who tried to demonize the efforts of the Restraint in Government Alliance. While there first appeared to be a short-term success in stifling the RGA, a certain amount of bad publicity countered those efforts. Indeed, those failings led to the situation we are now facing. Instead of tearing down Tyler Griffin in the process, he rose above the initial damage done to the RGA and benefited from the whole debacle. And our current commander-in-chief had everything to do with keeping Tyler Griffin in the limelight. Not to mention the recent dilemma her health issues have handed us."

Interrupting, Lucchesi said, "Everyone here is mindful of our predicament, and I'm sure you're aware that we at CBT have been working hard to rectify it. Al has been spearheading our most recent efforts in New Jersey."

Rozano said, "We've been trying to strengthen our union's position in the state by putting pressure on the employees working in the vice president's family business. As soon as the Griffin family got a whiff of our efforts to unionize their people, the vice president's sister, Kristie Pauling, who heads the GMHC operations, began to take an active interest in politics as a platform to introduce legislation that would be devastating to the union's power in New Jersey."

"Once we got word that President Andersen was stepping aside," Lucchesi said, "and that Tyler Griffin would be throwing his hat in the ring, Al and I have been ramping up the heat to discredit the Griffin family once and for all."

Constantine returned to his seat. "Yes, we've been keeping an eye on what's been going on, and needless to say, you guys have stirred up a hornet's nest. Not to criticize, or second-guess your objectives, but do you really believe Tyler Griffin is going to sit back and let you destroy his family, his company, and their political ambitions?"

Constantine held up a hand, not giving Lucchesi a chance to answer. "We have evidence that Tyler Griffin is already involved in what's going on in his home state. On the surface, he appears to be hands-off, but behind the scenes he's been investigating everything you've been trying to do."

"We've got our people working from the inside," Rozano said, "covering most of the GMHC operations, and we haven't seen anything suspicious to worry about. The worst problem we've encountered appears to be a little irritating local blowback from one of our former partners. We've had a long-standing agreement in place, but this Casella family has resurfaced and is trying to interfere with our activities."

Rozano folded his arms and nodded before continuing. "My guys reported this back to me, and I've got no doubts they're capable of straightening out the Casella family. It's been years since we've heard anything from Vinnie Casella, the former boss of the family. He's been locked up so long we almost forgot about the rest of the family. But my boys can be very convincing, so once they sit down and have a talk with this new guy, I'm sure everything will be fixed."

"Is that so?" Constantine smirked. "You're not getting this. You should take a better look at your own damn operations. This name you mentioned? Casella? I don't know who the fuck this Vinnie is you're talking about. But I got solid information that Tyler Griffin has sent someone by the name of Steve Casella to look into certain aspects of what you guys have been up to."

Constantine's eye grew larger. "And by the way, when I said you stirred up a hornet's nest, perhaps what I should've said was you've stepped in a pile of shit deep enough to derail this whole deal."

"What are you talking about?" Lucchesi said. "And where in the hell are you getting all this information?"

"For now, not only do my clients wish to remain anonymous, but I'd rather keep my other sources to myself."

"That's bullshit, Arthur," Lucchesi said, leaning forward.

Constantine waved him off. "Besides, there's more for you to consider. You might be interested in the fact that Steve Casella didn't come out here by himself. Guess who happens to be with him?"

He stretched out his arm and raised hand toward the faces of Rozano and Lucchesi. "Don't bother to think too hard—I'll save you the trouble. It's the sister of the guy you framed for the murder of that little black girl. Her name is Edie Pauling. Ever hear of her? And again, don't bother. I'll tell you. If you recall the mess that led to our previous administration being removed from power and locked up, you might remember the two people who played a prominent role in uncovering the infamous conspiracy. What would you say if I reminded you that their names were Steve Casella and Edie Pauling?"

"Holy shit," Rozano said. "That would be one fucking coincidence."

Constantine barely restrained himself from reaching across the desk and choking Big Al Rozano. He opted to take several deep breaths, telling himself he needed these guys to be on the front lines, carrying out the plans of his current clients. Especially if things went wrong and they needed somebody to take the fall while he and the rest of them faded back into the woodwork.

He reached into the attaché case resting in the kneehole of the desk. Pulling out a folder, he slid it across the desktop, steering it in front of Rozano.

"You might find the contents of this helpful. There's detailed information about the vice president's upcoming plans and schedules. As more precise information is uncovered, I'll be passing that along."

Lucchesi grabbed the folder first, and after a quick glance, he handed it to Rozano.

"Let me reiterate this, Philip. I'm here to tell you that you've got the support of a lot of important players who represent a great deal of power in this town. And they'd prefer to keep it that way. I'll leave it up to you to work out the details of the end game. My clients are not concerned with the particulars; but they do expect results."

Long after Al Rozano and Philip Lucchesi had left, Arthur Constantine stood looking out the window. The night had fully taken over, and he regarded the never-ending stream of headlights and juxtaposed taillights crossing the bridge. He considered what options needed to be in place if the union's plan didn't work. With the stakes so high, he couldn't afford to gamble on the outcome. He feared the loss of important clients if they failed to accomplish the primary goal.

Chapter 34

The headlights on the Durango cut through the blackness as Steve navigated along the isolated country road.

"You doing okay?" Steve asked Edie as they drove back to Morristown following the emotionally charged conversation at the Griffin retreat in Stillwater.

Edie let out a deep breath. "Oh, I'm really getting pissed-off. You should feel sorry for the sonsofbitches who're responsible for setting this whole thing up. All this evidence has got to be contrived; I'll tell you that. What's got me concerned is how quick the feds stepped in and are pushing the case against my brother."

Steve remained silent and Edie kept talking. "Somebody had to pull the strings to return a grand jury indictment so fast. I'll go to that arraignment tomorrow to support Thomas, but you can bet your ass I'm going to do a hell of a lot more digging on my own. A lot of the information I've been working on for Tyler may hold clues as to what the hell is going on. No way this isn't related to why Tyler called you out here to begin with."

"So, you're assuming the union is behind this too?" Steve asked.

"My guess is they're somehow involved, but I can't be sure who's calling the shots. That reminds me—the call you got before we left the Griffin property?"

"Right. I didn't want to bother you about it until I knew your plans. It was Dominick. He heard the news about your brother—said to tell you how sorry he was. He also asked if I wanted to accompany him to the Federal Correctional Institution in Fairton. Thought it'd be worthwhile for me to meet Uncle Vinnie. I told him this might not be the best time, and—"

Edie turned to Steve and grasped his shoulder.

* * * * * *

The lime green Corvette throttled down for the toll plaza after taking the southbound Garden State Parkway exit off Interstate 78.

"Does she always win those arguments, Steve?" Dominick Casella grinned after asking Steve why he changed his mind about letting Edie go to Philadelphia without him.

"She considered this a good idea," Steve responded. "Important even." He threw a hard glance at Dominick. "You two plotting something behind my back?"

"What? Me and Edie? Nope, I never mentioned anything about this, but she sure is one tuned-in chick."

"Is that a Jersey term she'd want to hear you calling her?"

"Hell, no." A slight squeak underlined his response. "All I'm saying, is I got the impression very little escapes her scrutiny. That's all."

Steve stretched and settled back into the contoured white leather bucket seat. "Well, I guess I'm a little slower than the two of you. But we've got a good two-hour ride for you to bring me up to speed."

Dominick reached into the glove box, traded his Marshwoods for a pair of aviator sunglasses, and punched on the MP3 player. He selected a Frank Sinatra's greatest hits album and adjusted the volume to a comfortable background level. Steve folded his arms and ventured another glance at Dominick.

"Hey," Dominick said, "a little before our time, but this represents the height of, well the era when, well when the Casellas—thrived. When I was a kid, Uncle Vinnie would tell stories about his dad—or was it his grandfather?" He shrugged. "So, they'd go listen to this new 'crooner', Frank Sinatra, at one of the clubs down the street from where he lived. Hoboken. It's right across the river from Manhattan. From what I understand, Hoboken was a much different kind of place back then."

"Must've been before the Casellas moved in and took it over," Steve mumbled.

"Anyway," Dominick said, "that's where Sinatra got his big break. Back then he was a nobody. Hanging around with the regular guys. And Uncle Vinnie, he talked a lot about those golden days for the Casella family."

"Two hours won't be enough time, Dominick. Especially if you're gonna break into a song."

"Just kidding, Steve." Dominick switched back to his normal eyewear. But Steve noted Sinatra's greatest hits weren't canceled. Dominick finally nudged down the volume.

"I was in my senior year in high school when I went to work part-time at the Springfield Final Cut Beauty Supply store. One of the stores in the family's business. They viewed it as a rite of passage. Working there was supposed to be a real big deal as I recall."

"How many people did you have to kill on the job? Or was that only for the full-time Casella employees?"

Before Dominick responded, Steve continued, "Ah, never mind. But I'm curious. Since you mentioned these beauty supply stores and beauty parlors yesterday… well, it seemed kinda strange for, damn... I can't believe I'm even saying this—a front for the mob... mafia... or organized crime operations?"

"Hey, that's the beauty of it—*capisce*?" Dominick pounded the steering wheel and let out a shrilly laugh. "Sorry, couldn't resist. But I can understand how you'd see it that way. That's what made it so perfect for the family. Of course, I didn't have a clue at the time. I guess they were trying to ease me into the retail end of the operations. A lot of what went on in those establishments was way over my head. It wasn't until I got my accounting degree that I made any sense out of the financial aspects of things. And it's taken years to try and convert over the operations and make it all legitimate."

"Same go for the family's waste management company?" Steve asked, trying to bait Dominick. "By the way, what's the name of that particular enterprise?"

"The Guarding State Waste Management Company has undergone a similar conversion. But for fun, we kept the same old name." Dominick shrugged and winked. He jabbed Steve's arm.

Steve ignored the gesture. "So, all those people in your offices in Short Hills? That's what they're doing? Real accounting work? Not making book or anything?"

"Well, now and then... particular scenarios come up... and certain things need to be reworked and cleaned up. But we've made great progress." Dominick beamed. "In its heyday, those operations served a very large and serious clientele. Especially the beauty supply stores. By the time the Casellas got done funneling and massaging the transactions, their money was cleaner than the finest shampoo offered by one of the many Casella hairdressers. With all the ways to deal with wholesale, professional, and retail trade in the beauty supply industry, it was the perfect business model."

"If it was so perfect, why's Uncle Vinnie a guest of our federal government?"

"Hey. What can I say? Somebody's always got deeper pockets, or a government official opted to do his job. But I gotta tell you, that rarely occurred back in the golden days."

Steve reflected that things hadn't changed so much. There seemed to be enough corruption and incompetence around in the government for Edie to make a damn good living reporting on it.

"If you don't mind my asking, Dominick, why didn't you and the so-called enlightened generation of Casellas maintain the original family business model?"

"Can't speak for the others, but I can damn sure tell you what did it for me."

CHAPTER 35

(Dominick Casella's senior high school year)

DOMINICK CASELLA PARKED HIS DAD'S OLD Buick Skylark in the Grand Union's parking lot and walked across the busy boulevard to the store. Uncle Joey stood in the doorway looking at his watch.

"Hey, Dominick, I'm glad you're punctual and can follow instructions. As you can see, we got limited parking in front of the store. We're slow right now, which is good, 'cause it's just me and you. Your cousin hadda go to Newark for a last-minute delivery."

Dominick's jaw dropped. He assumed since this was his first day on the job, he'd be only observing and learning the ropes tonight.

"Couldn't be helped. Ya know how it is. Well, maybe ya don't. But I understand you're a quick learner. They say you're a little shy." Uncle Joey tapped an index finger against his temple. "But you got it up here."

Uncle Joey checked his watch again as he ushered Dominick inside. "Danny said he'd be back by now, but he's probably stuck in traffic. I still got time before I leave, so I'll give ya the quick run—"

"Before you leave?" Dominick said. His voice cracked while looking around the interior of the Final Cut Beauty Supply store. His first day on the job. A sense of panic fought to the surface.

"Yeah. It's dinnertime and Aunt Carla's waiting on me. She gets cranky if I'm not on time. But don't worry, the most I'll be gone is thirty, forty minutes... an hour tops. Unless Aunt Carla gets a little frisky. She sees me washing a dinner plate it sometimes gets her all—"

He gave Dominick's arm a quick jab. "Don't worry, I'll tell her she'll have to wait till tonight. I'll try not to turn her on."

This time, Dominick, ready for the arm punch, went with the hit.

"The house is right across town. Not far. And your cousin Danny should be here before I'm done explaining everything to you anyways."

"It's only me working in the store?"

Beads of sweat made Dominick's glasses slip down his nose. And not only because of the nightmarish images he grappled with about his aunt and uncle naked on the kitchen floor, slipping and sliding in pools of dish detergent and....

"Hey kid, why's your face all red?" Uncle Joey said, laughing. "Vinnie told me you were reliable and trustworthy. The whole family's counting on you, Dominick. Besides, there's nothing to it. Come on. We'll start with the register."

Five minutes later Dominick's head was still spinning, but he had to admit that operating the old-fashioned cash register looked simple. It surprised him the store still used one of those mechanical sliding imprint contraptions for credit card transactions. When he questioned his uncle about this, he was told the following:

"Ya see. This here process helps keep the transactions more secure. We don't want any electronic fingerprints. It gives us better control over what happens after the sale. *Capisce?*"

Dominick nodded, but with no real comprehension. He asked, "With this old-styled register, I don't see any bar code scanner for entering prices, so does that mean all the merchandise is clearly marked?"

Uncle Joey picked up a bottle of shampoo from one of the closer shelves. He put on his reading glasses and pointed to a large sticker on the shelf in front of the bottle he'd just grabbed.

"I'm sure your eyes are better than mine, so this shouldn't be too difficult. The big numbers are what we charge for retail. Now look closer. Underneath ya can see a series of letters, several numbers, another series of letters, and then more numbers."

By this time, Dominick had already asked Uncle Joey for a pen and notepad. He scribbled down the key information being fast-forwarded to him. The additional sets of numbers referred to professional and wholesale pricing information. There was one minor problem with this system, but Dominick wasn't anywhere close to the point of asking the key question.

"Any questions, Dominick?"

Dominick shrugged. Afraid his head would split open if he tried to say anything.

"I gotta go. Aunt Carla's expecting me in five minutes. Don't worry. I'll keep it in my pants."

This time he left out the arm punch.

"Danny should be here any minute. And if ya run into trouble, my number's on the wall next to the phone. If you have a problem, I got Vinnie's number in the register drawer. But I'd think twice before punching in his number."

Dominick stared into the display mirror behind the register. That last comment had him holding his breath until the redness on his cheeks took on a bluish tinge.

Uncle Joey whistled and chuckled to himself as he grabbed his car keys and headed out the door. Dominick had doubts about his uncle adhering to his promise of not fooling around with Aunt Carla. He looked too happy.

As his uncle's black Seville made a quick left turn out of the parking lot, Dominick could see him still smiling. The chorus to Frank Sinatra's *My Way* faded away as the Seville lurched through the intersection several seconds after the traffic light had turned red. Horns blared and Uncle Joey raised his arm out the window, flipping them the bird.

The store remained quiet for the next several minutes, so Dominick had the chance to walk around and acquaint himself with his new surroundings. The image of pumping gas at the Exxon station around the corner from where he lived looked better by the minute.

Two hot-looking young women wearing tight short skirts and low-cut blouses slinking through the door interrupted his thoughts. Pumping gas didn't look so good anymore.

The shorter woman with the deeper cleavage placed a can of hairspray on the counter, bending down in the process as she hunted through her flowered canvas bag for her wallet. Dominick remembered that he needed to check the item's price on the shelf and wrenched his eyes away from the biggest breasts he had ever come across. For a minute, he thought his eyeglasses had miraculously turned into magnifying lenses.

He returned with the price written on his pad and, in a trembling voice, told the woman what she owed for the hairspray. His eyes shifted to her face in time to catch her smirking expression transform into annoyance as she spoke.

"Hey, sonny. What the hell? That's not the price I pay for this. Besides, with the way you've been leering at the goodies here—you should be paying me."

She turned to her companion and winked. "Ain't that right, Sheila? These," she said, and paused with both hands cupped under her breasts while jiggling them, "are worth a hell of a lot more than a lousy can of hairspray."

"Aw, come on, Angie, give the kid a break. You're embarrassing him."

To Dominick, Sheila said, "Don't mind her. She's always sticking her boobs in people's faces. She just got 'em. Whaddaya think? They look real to you? A lot of guys say they're a little too firm."

Dominick's face got so hot it puffed up and blurred his vision. He didn't dare attempt an answer. His head bobbed up and down several times as he tried not to stare at Angie's breasts.

"Yeah, I'd say he appreciates 'em, Sheila. But he won't be getting the chance to squeeze 'em. Least not tonight…."

Angie turned to Dominick. "You're charging me the wrong price. That price is for the public. I'm a hairdresser." Dominick felt her eyes scanning his slender frame. "Who're you anyway? We've been coming in here for over five years, and I've never seen you before."

As Dominick slipped around the aisle to check the label for the professional pricing information, something came out of his mouth he immediately regretted.

"Can you show me something to prove you're a hairdresser?"

"Haven't I fuckin' showed you enough? I show you any more, you're gonna be walking around with that wet spot all night." She held a hand to her face and giggled.

Dominick's eyes shot down to his crotch. He stopped himself before cupping a hand over the bulge. That made Angie laugh even harder.

"Just leave the kid alone, Angie. You've stunted his growth enough for one night."

Angie remained silent; eyes riveted on Dominick's crotch.

Dominick fumbled through the transaction without further incident and listened to the door close behind the two women. He glanced out the window but saw no sign of either Danny or Uncle Joey.

He had settled down by the time the next customer shuffled through the door—relieved to see the latest patron was a man. In his early thirties, he wore a puffy pink shirt and white slacks. Perched atop white Docksides, no socks.

This time Dominick took the proactive approach when he rang up the sale. "Sir, I assume you're a hairdresser. Let me—"

"You smart-assed little turd. Why don't you say it to my face? Huh? Fag. That's what you really want to say. Isn't it? Where does Joseph come off bringing in snotty-nosed homophobic little shits like you?"

The man's lower lip puckered up. "I have a good mind to take my business elsewhere."

But he didn't. And Dominick worked his way through the second sale of the evening.

Alone again, Dominick tried to keep busy straightening out items on the shelves. A booming voice coming from behind startled him.

"Who the hell are you?"

Trying to grab the falling bottles of shampoo before they landed on the floor, Dominick jumped and looked at the source. "Ah, my name's Dominick. This is my first day on the job. My Uncle Joey hired me."

Dominick felt as if he'd been trapped in this store for half his life, though he'd only walked through the door thirty minutes ago.

"Where the hell is Joey? I'm kinda in a hurry here. He told me everything would be ready. There should be four cases with my name written on 'em. The name's Sal."

"I... I—" Dominick stuttered.

Sal pushed aside the curtain to the back room and pointed as he barged through. "Those are the cases right there. But where's the fucking invoice... and all the paperwork? He said it'd be right on top. I gotta have it all tonight."

Dominick found his voice and tried to find a way out. "Ah, sir. I don't know anything about any of this. Let me get Uncle Joey on the phone. I'm sure if you talk to him, he'll tell you where everything is."

He picked up the phone and dialed. He prayed he was only interrupting Uncle Joey's dinner.

"Okay, but while I'm talking to Joey, go load those boxes into the car. I'm parked right out front. In the no parking zone, so hurry it up. It's the black Town Car. Put everything in the trunk. The door's not locked, so reach into the glove box and pop open the trunk. Go on. Give me the damn phone. I don't got all night."

Without another word, Dominic did as he was told. His hands shook the entire time. As he gingerly closed the trunk, that same booming voice startled him again. A firm hand grasped his shoulder. Dominick's face had long since lost the red-hot embarrassment over his reaction to Angie.

Now his face was snowy white and as cold as ice.

"Hey, kid," Sal said, staring at Dominick's face. His words sounded soft but were edged like the blade of a knife. "Look at me. Forget whatever you saw. I just got back from a little hunting trip. You're young. You'll work things out. You want a little free advice?"

Dominick figured he'd already gotten enough advice for a lifetime, but his head nodded.

"The way to get older is to mind your own fuckin' business. *Capisce?*"

The word sounded more menacing than when Uncle Joey had used it earlier. Dominick nodded his head again.

He caught a glimpse of his dad's Skylark parked at the far end of the Grand Union's parking lot and felt the keys stuck in his pocket. All he wanted to do was to get the hell out of here. But Sal's steely grip on his shoulder kept him anchored in place.

"Just fuckin' with ya kid." Sal released his grip, a little slower than the moment warranted.

Dominick's knees buckled like rubber, but he kept himself upright. The Skylark might as well have been on the other side of the moon. When his eyes stole a glance at Sal, he saw a slightly more human image than he'd just imagined. Maybe he was overreacting. His legs felt like the skeletal structures might be returning, and most of the icy layers on his skin had turned back to good old sweat.

"Joey said to tell you that when he gets back, he's gonna write up all the paperwork. He didn't have time to finish it before he left. I need you to drop it off at my place after work. Can you do that for me? It's real important."

Finding his voice, Dominick said, "Yes sir, I'd be happy to."

Dominick would've preferred driving his dad's Skylark over the Palisades into the Hudson River.

Two hours later, after following his Uncle Joey's directions, Dominick turned onto the street where Sal's barbershop was located. His eyes blinked from the array of flashing lights on the ambulance and squad cars scattered about the street and sidewalk, blocking the front of the barbershop.

Stupidly, as if none of this registered, Dominick pulled over near the edge of the police barricades. He picked up the paperwork and got out of the Skylark, heading toward the center of the activity. He didn't get very far when a uniformed police officer stopped him in his tracks. Dominick peeked around the beefy officer in time to see a gurney being wheeled out of Sal's barbershop with a black body bag strapped on top.

A sobbing woman struggled alongside and grasped at the zippered bag, screaming, "Sal! Nooooo… Sal!"

Someone in coveralls, trailing behind her, carried a long clear plastic bag containing a familiar object.

Dominick slid the papers up and under his shirt and scurried back to his car. What he wanted to do was to scream and run as fast as his legs could carry him. And get the hell out of there. Call the number for the gas station job. And tell Uncle Joey—he quit.

CHAPTER 36

(present day)

STEVE WATCHED DOMINICK'S KNUCKLES TURN white as his grip tightened on the wheel of his Corvette. When Dominick stopped talking, he took two deep breaths and shook his head.

"Steve, I'm telling you, I was scared out of my mind. When I reached in the glove box to find the trunk latch—there was a damn pistol sitting in plain sight. Not only that. A bunch of extra magazines were tucked in there too. And... oh... a large black plastic bag lay on the floorboards in the back seat. Something dripping out onto the rubber mats. I didn't look any closer. I probably should've been wiping off my fingerprints as I closed the door."

Dominick, a haunted expression glued to his face, glanced into the rearview mirror. He flexed his fingers and tapped them on the wheel. "Then guess what? When I opened the trunk and tried to find space to put in the cases? He had a damn arsenal in there. Rifles, shotguns, canvas bags with boxes of ammo sticking out. And more plastic bags—but at least they appeared empty."

"So, you say Sal was a hunter?"

"What? Yeah, right. Only a moron would believe that story. And I swear the gun they carried out behind Sal's body? It sure looked like one of the shotguns sitting in his trunk."

"Ever find out why he killed himself?"

"Suicide my ass. That, of course, was the official designation. There wasn't much of an investigation. What a freakin' joke. And let me tell you, Steve. No way in hell that guy would've killed himself. There was a story talked about in the family. About what *really* happened. And then Uncle Vinnie called me to his house. He hammered me on what I did with the paperwork that night. He put his arm around me and explained how things worked. I won't bore you with the details, but needless to say, he motivated me to make a career change."

Steve shrugged. "Hair coloring and getting too many permanents can be unhealthy. I guess you made a wise choice."

Steve settled back in his seat and closed his eyes. His first reaction: Blow off Dominick's family history lesson as an exaggerated teenage tale of wannabe bad guys. Then his mind jumped to a different place. If Dominick could be taken at his word, the Casella family had been involved in a number of sordid activities. At least he hoped it was all in the past.

What was he dealing with now? The Casellas may have taken a different path, according to Dominick, but these guys Steve had run into the other night had stuck with the program. If they believed he was interfering with their turf, they had a lot to lose from his meddling. And that meant so did he.

And then there was Uncle Vinnie.

This should be one memorable family reunion. He turned to Dominick, about to say something, but changed his mind. He reached for the volume control and then leaned back again, listening to Sinatra's voice bleeding out of the audio system. The Corvette didn't have a rear seat, but it did have a trunk.

CHAPTER 37

A DOE AND TWO FAWNS SPRINTED across the groomed landscape, disappearing down a ravine leading to the pond on the northwest corner of Griffin's property in Stillwater. Edie stared at the back of Vice President Tyler Griffin's head. Kristie and Thomas Pauling stood by her side. Tyler Griffin took a deep breath, exhaled, and turned away from the window. For a moment, he didn't say a word; his eyes fixed on the three people in the great room.

"Kristie told me Sampson wouldn't be here, but where's Steve?" the vice president asked Edie.

"He's tied up with some, ah, family business." Edie's eyes darted away, avoiding his trademark dark stare.

"Humph, maybe I'm wrong, but isn't Steve the last surviving member of his family?"

Edie relented, realizing eventually the vice president would need to be informed. She told the story of her discovery regarding Steve's relatives.

With a slight tilt of his head, the vice president said, "AND…?"

Frowning, Edie said, "I've got a hunch this family reunion may be helpful in getting a better grip on what you've been up against, Tyler."

Edie stole a glance at her brother who had moved away from the others. He stared out one of the floor-to-ceiling windows, and his hand periodically reached for the GPS locator strapped to his ankle.

"And maybe some clues as to who's behind framing Thomas," Edie added.

Tyler nodded. "Yeah, Kristie filled me in on last night's discussion. Things are getting downright nasty since the political stakes have risen."

Earlier today, Thomas Pauling was arraigned at the James A. Byrne US Courthouse in the Eastern District of Pennsylvania and formally charged on the indictments returned by the grand jury. There had been little doubt as to the outcome of today's proceedings based on the unprecedented haste the US Attorney's office had acted on this particular case. Thomas had pleaded not guilty to the multiple charges of the sexual assault, kidnapping, and murder of Leilah Harris.

After the arraignment, Kristie, Sampson, and Edie met with Thomas and his attorney to make sure his lawyer was on board with what the family's role would be regarding any forthcoming investigations. Before heading to the Griffin retreat, Sampson opted out of the trip to Stillwater. Edie later learned from Kristie that he decided to take a different approach to the problem.

Tyler Griffin gave a terse nod to Kristie. She turned to Edie. "When Sampson brought you and Steve here from the airport, I understand Tyler talked about upcoming plans to announce his candidacy for the presidency. And, as we discussed in my office, I've already declared myself to run for the state legislature."

Kristie paused and smiled at her brother. She stepped closer to Thomas, who still faced the window. "With the president just revealing her decision to retire after this term, it would be prudent for Tyler to step up and indicate his intentions. Alice planned to endorse him as her choice last night, but Tyler talked her out of it. He didn't want to take away from the gravity of her own revelations."

Kristie took a sip of her drink. "After what's happened with Leilah Harris, it seemed logical for me to either drop out of the race or face an onslaught of media outcry and humiliation in the court of public opinion." She placed her glass on a nearby table and then stood behind Thomas, positioning both hands on his shoulders. "But Thomas pointed out that to do so would be playing right into the hands of the bastards who're behind all this."

Kristie's gaze turned out the window, parroting Thomas. "I considered dropping out of the race and distancing myself from politics to shift the spotlight so Tyler would stand a better chance to put this mess aside and gain support for his nomination."

Edie had been looking keenly at the three of them. With a rueful smile, she focused on Tyler and said, "My guess is Tyler wasn't buying this. Were you?"

"You can bet your ass on that," Tyler said. "I'm not going to abandon my family and let these sonsofbitches get away with using Thomas. When I stand up and make my announcement, Thomas and Kristie are going to be right by my side. And you can be sure I'll take the opportunity to give my sister one big endorsement."

Thomas turned back to the room and responded with a shaky voice. "Whoa… I don't remember agreeing to be out there in public with you guys. Standing up on the podium? Are you sure you want to be so in-your-face with my problems? This could backfire on you."

"Bullshit," Tyler retorted. "This whole thing is going to backfire on whoever the hell is behind it. They'll have to try a lot harder to put a stop to our plans."

Staring at Edie, Tyler's eyebrows rose. "Isn't that right, Edie? I'm counting on you and Steve to keep digging into whatever the hell you've already started. Since you two have come on the scene, things have gotten a lot more interesting. And now this possible connection to Steve's family. You guys are like the cheese drawing in the rats."

Edie returned the stare. "Yeah? And who set the trap?"

"Is that any way to speak to the vice president of the United States?"

"Just think what I'll say when you become the president."

Edie's mind shifted into overdrive as the words of the vice president echoed in her head. How much more did these bastards have up their sleeves?

CHAPTER 38

DOMINICK PARKED THE CORVETTE IN the visitors lot for the Federal Correctional Institution and turned to Steve. "It's not a problem as long as I sign a written voucher for you. At least that's how it's supposed to work. But there is a small chance of a slight delay in you getting in to see Uncle Vinnie."

"What do you mean by a slight delay?"

"A week or two, but—"

"And you waited until now to tell me this?"

"As I said, it's probably not going to be an issue, that's why I didn't say anything before. And I knew you wouldn't want to wait to follow the official procedure with all that's happening. Right? One way or the other, a guy with your reputation would find a way to finagle the system. Besides, if they don't let you in, you can drive away in my Corvette."

"What the hell are you talking about now?"

"Oh, didn't I say? You wouldn't be allowed to remain in the parking lot while I'm inside visiting with Uncle Vinnie."

Steve narrowed his eyes. "Once you give me the keys, what the hell makes you think I'd come back for you?"

After entering the front lobby and filling out the required Visitor Notification forms, Dominick and Steve approached the officer in charge of verifying the visitor information profiles, and Dominick handed him the paperwork. As the officer ran the names through his system, Dominick requested a waiver for Steve. Looking up from the computer screen, the officer stared at Dominick from above his reading glasses.

"Son, what are you trying to pull here? Let's see your identification. NOW." He pointed over at Steve. "You too, buddy. I'm gonna be looking at them real close."

The officer scrutinized the picture IDs, and for an inordinate amount of time he glared at the two men standing in front of the window. He did additional work on the keyboard before granting them both approvals to enter.

"As if you didn't know," he said to Dominick, with a threatening glower. "You're both already on the approved list of visitors for Vincent R. Casella. And by the way, son, we don't appreciate your little attempt at humor. Seeing you all appear to be related, you guys might share the same incarceration genes as the inmate you're visiting. So, while you're here, take a good look around and make yourselves at home. You never know."

The officer shook his head and pointed to the waiting area. He let out a noisy breath and called out for the next person in line.

After settling into the vinyl and metal chairs, Steve turned to Dominick, poised to ask the obvious question when a loud voice called out their names. They were efficiently processed, hands stamped, and escorted through a series of corridors and into the crowded visitors room.

He bared a noticeable resemblance to Steve's dad, but Uncle Vinnie's features were decidedly harsher. As he shuffled over to where Dominick and Steve were seated, Steve detected a definite favoring of his right leg. When he spoke, Uncle Vinnie's voice was eclipsed by a raspy garbled overtone from years of smoking unfiltered cigarettes or from a damn good imitation of Marlon

Brando's role in *The Godfather*. After brief embraces, they all took their seats.

"So, gentlemen, to what do I owe the pleasure of your company? Dominick? You got anything hidden in your hanky you'd care to pass along?"

Dominick's neck twisted so fast Steve swore he heard it crack as he checked to see if any of the guards had caught those remarks. "Uncle Vinnie, please... I—"

"Ah... Dominick, don't wet your pants. I'm messin' with you. You straighten out those books yet?"

Uncle Vinnie lowered his voice and leaned toward Dominick. "At least the ones you show the feds?"

This time Dominick thinned his lips and remained mute.

Uncle Vinnie turned his attention to Steve, a broad smile transforming his face. "Tom Casella's little boy. Anybody ever tell you, you don't look anything like him? Not that I'm accusing Penny of anything...."

Uncomfortable, Steve shifted in his seat. Uncle Vinnie shook his head, the smile remaining. "Penny, your mom, a wonderful girl." Uncle Vinnie placed a hand over his heart. "Saddened me when I heard how she died. And then what happened to your dad. Damn feds. Framed him like they did to me."

He uttered those last words loud enough for two of the guards to hear. The closer one chuckled and turned toward the second one and started talking. Both shaking their heads while walking further away.

Steve leaned forward; his eyes wide open. "You were framed?"

Uncle Vinnie waved his arm. "No. I'm messin' with you, too. I guess I was too stupid. Pockets weren't deep enough. But times have changed. Now the feds are fleecing everybody themselves. No room for family enterprises anymore. Can't tell the politicians from the union bosses. But enough reminiscing."

Uncle Vinnie settled back in his chair and wagged his finger. "Steve, it's about time you came to visit your dad's favorite cousin. I was beginning to think I'd be dead before you showed up. It's been almost three years since I first got here and added your name to my personal list."

Dominick's jaw dropped. "You knew all along we're related to this guy. And you never said anything to me?"

Uncle Vinnie shrugged. "I was a little preoccupied with my own legal problems back then. So, sue me. Oh wait, I'm the attorney—you're the accountant. Do I have enough funds remaining to hire someone of my caliber?"

Leaving Dominick with his mouth still open, he turned back to address Steve. "When your dad and I were kids, we were inseparable. He was always trying to keep me outta trouble, getting beat up defending me. As kids, your dad was tough. In high school, I was kinda small, like Dominick here, so I usually wound up with a good ass-kicking trying to muscle my way around. Didn't mature physically till I got older."

Uncle Vinnie laughed. "Hey, you still got a chance, Dominick. Anyway, Steve, your dad moved on after we graduated high school. He kinda drifted apart from the family. Best thing he ever did. He was different from the rest of us. Like his older brother, Bob: the cop. They both had principles. Where the hell did those genes come from? What about you, Steve? Hey, at least you're not a cop." Uncle Vinnie shook his head. "A shame what happened to your Uncle Bob too. Sounds like Idaho can be a dangerous place."

Uncle Vinnie continued with a smile. "So, you're a fireman. A fireman I can deal with. In fact, we did a lot of business with a number of fire departments. The family's interests were wide open in those days. Plenty of room to work with."

"Uncle Vinnie," Dominick interjected in a quiet tone. "Some things have happened. It's possible the union bosses are resorting to their usual nasty activities. You see, the vice president—Tyler Griffin—asked Steve to look into—"

"You think I don't know who the hell the vice president is? That all we get in here is the Food Network? Or NPR? By the way, this Tyler Griffin character, even before he got to be such a bigshot in Washington? He was impossible to deal with when he was still a local boy around here. His whole damn family's the same way. A bunch of missionaries trying to straighten out the entire state. Making us businessmen look bad."

"Right," Dominick said, "but that's not what I mean. Something—"

This time Steve placed a hand on Dominick's arm. "Let me explain, Dominick."

Steve described in detail what had been going on at the GMHC locations and the tactics being utilized to persuade their employees to join the CBT. He wasn't sure that outing this information in a federal prison to a convicted felon was a breach of the vice president's desire to keep a low profile, but he had a strong premonition something needed to be done to move things along. As he spoke, Steve was under the impression Uncle Vinnie had been grading the success of his former colleagues' performance. From time to time, he'd either nod or shake his head as he absorbed Steve's story.

"So the other night, I was at this union event over at Six Flags—"

"You mean Great Adventure," Dominick interrupted Steve.

Steve scrunched his forehead. "What?"

"We call it Great Adventure, not—"

Steve placed a hand on Dominick's shoulder. He lifted his head back and sighed. "Yeah, right. I sometimes forget. It's another one of those Jersey things. Sorry. So, I was at… Great… Adventure… and when I headed back to my SUV, two guys stopped me. They were convinced I worked for you, Uncle Vinnie. That I was meddling around in their territory or something. They said their boss—Big Al, I think they called him—wasn't happy with you interfering in their business. That there were agreements in place, and the Casellas were going to be held accountable for reneging on the deals. At least, that's my interpretation of what they told me."

"You left one thing out," Dominick said. "The most important part. Uncle Vinnie, listen to this. That's why I needed to bring Steve here. Tell him about the girl. And Edie's brother."

Steve felt a little confused at first, but then outlined the story of Leilah Harris's death and the events leading up to Thomas Pauling's arrest.

When he finished, Uncle Vinnie turned to Dominick. "Don't tell me you bought all those stories about the bodies being buried and never found in the Pine Barrens?"

"What? Well, yeah, sure. You're saying it never happened?"

"No, it happened."

Uncle Vinnie leaned closer to Dominick. "Maybe you're not the naïve do-good mama's boy we all thought you were. And, I hate to admit it, but from what I been hearing, what you've done with the family's business? Well, being legit hasn't exactly ruined things for the company. From what I understand, you've been working hard and turning good profits. And we haven't had to kill anybody in a while. Unless I've missed something?"

Dominick beamed and nodded. For an instant, Steve wasn't sure if he was admitting to more killings or better business practices. A further look at Dominick's demeanor had Steve reassured it was the latter.

"But," Uncle Vinnie said, "you didn't hear any of those compliments from me. Clear?"

Uncle Vinnie scanned the room and lowered his voice. "Steve. You said it was dark, but can you describe anything about those two guys? Anything at all?"

Uncle Vinnie gave Dominick a quick glance and listened to Steve as he sifted through whatever he recalled about the two men.

Chapter 39

THE FRONT DOOR SLAMMED SHUT. Marty Calebrese walked into the living room of the house he shared with his associate, Tony Funetti. He grabbed the remote, punching one of the buttons.

"Hey!" Tony responded. "That's the season four finale. Junior's just got off. But now Carmella's learned about Tony's mistress. She was about to whack him with a golf club and boot him out on the street—"

"Jesus, I only put the damn thing on pause. It's a rerun, a recording, you moron. Besides, you've seen the damn show a dozen times. By the way, *TONY*, you ain't no Tony Soprano. You been studying the series for years now and nothing ever rubs off."

"What the hell you mean? I've learned plenty from his mistakes. No bitch has ever thrown me out of my own house."

"Yeah? Well, maybe that's because the only ones who ever set foot in this...." Marty spread his arms around and made a point of showing his distaste for Tony's sloppiness in the house they both shared. "...lovely establishment—are the whores. At least you pay 'em good enough not to cause any scenes with the neighbors on their way out."

"Hey, what can I say? I'm a generous guy." Tony eyed the remote. "But enough about me. Now that you've interrupted my show, tell me, how's Big Al doing?"

Marty walked into the kitchen and came back with two beers. After handing one to Tony, he settled down on the faux leather Lazy Boy and twisted open his bottle. He took a long draw and wiped a wrist across his mouth.

"We may have been underestimating the tenacity of the Griffin family."

Still holding the unopened bottle, Tony said, "You think by using those big college type words, you're impressing me? Just 'cause I barely graduated from the eighth grade doesn't mean I'm stupid. So, if you're trying to say the Griffins are bigger stubborn sonsofsbitches than we figured, why don't you just fucking say it in English?"

"You're right, Tony. Barely graduating the eighth grade only scratches the surface for what the hell's wrong with you. And you may be exaggerating a bit. The way I remember is you got your ass thrown out before you got anywhere near a cap and gown. But we can save that for another time."

"Son of a bitch," Tony said, springing off the sofa. Not in protest to Marty's statement, but to the suds erupting from the bottle that sprayed him with a direct hit as he twisted off the cap.

"Listen up, Tony. We're gonna have our hands full for a while. Big Al just got back from a meeting outside of D.C. He's being real secretive of where it took place and who else was involved." He smiled. "I'm guessing our freeze-faced leader Philip Lucchesi was one of 'em though."

Shrugging, Marty continued, "He did say there are important people watching what we've been doing and are interested in making sure we're successful. I guess the New Jersey chapter of the CBT is on the national radar screen."

Tony wiped his face with the dirty handkerchief he'd pulled from his pocket, eyes narrowed on Marty. Marty had the habit of shaking the bottle before handing it over to him. Tony fell for it every time.

"Okay, I'll bite," Tony said. "Can you be a little more specific on the meaning of success? I mean, I can come up with a list that's fatter than my dick on Viagra. We've all but nailed this Pauling guy. That's gotta put a damper in the wife's political plans. The whole family's gotta be running for cover. And with a little more pressure in the right places on the GMHC operations, the union vote should be a shoe-in. And right now, we got fire marshals and safety inspectors sniffing up the asses of half the managers at GMHC, trying to slap 'em with as many violations as they can for ignoring a bunch of safety regulations."

Tony tried using his fingers to tally up their achievements, but Marty noticed that holding the dripping beer bottle in his wet hand made him lose count. "So where am I going wrong? The biggest trouble spot I can see is the crap with Vinnie Casella, and him sending this goombah sniffing around our territory. Christ, there should be no problem setting that asshole straight. We probably scared the little shit away the other night anyway."

"So, was he scared away before or after his dog almost bit your nuts off?"

Tony waved his arm dismissively at Marty. "Dogs love me. They can sense I wouldn't hurt 'em. You, on the other hand...."

Marty had thrown down the papers he'd brought home on the coffee table between them. Luckily, they were out of range of the frothy fountain from the beer bottle. He leaned forward and tapped the pile with his index finger.

210 • Ron Vergona

"You may be interested in hearing that this guy we bumped into last night is a different Casella; nothing to do with Vinnie's family." Marty frowned. "Well, he actually is related, but what I'm saying is, Vinnie didn't send him. Not sure if Vinnie even knew he existed. It says here he's from San Francisco."

"What the hell you talking about? He's part of the family, but they don't know him? Then he comes all the way from California to mess up the agreement we've had with Vinnie for all these years? But Vinnie didn't send him?"

Nodding, Marty said, "That about covers it. Except for one little hitch. From what Big Al found out at his meeting, the vice president brought him out here."

"That bastard. Since when is Tyler Griffin trying to meddle in our business? Doesn't his hands get greased enough by sticking 'em in the federal banks and the treasury and the IRS and the—"

"Jesus Christ. The vice president got him out here to investigate what the hell we've been doing to mess up his family's business. He doesn't trust the local officials to do any serious examinations into those so-called accidents. Suspects they're all in our pockets."

Tony gave him a 'ya think?' kind of look, but Marty ignored him and kept talking. "The vice president's been trying to keep his connections quiet. He wants everyone to think he's not involved and using his clout to interfere with the investigations."

"Are they suspicious of any tie-in with us and the bitch's black husband being arrested for murdering his underage student?"

Marty hesitated. "I don't think so." He pointed a finger at Tony. "But here's the kicker. When this Steve Casella character showed up, he brought his girlfriend with him. Apparently, her family's living in Jersey, and she happens to be the sister of our favorite science teacher, Thomas Pauling."

"Holy shit, that's a fucking boat load of coincidences, if you ask me."

"A word of advice." Marty's face scrunched. "Don't use that phrase around Big Al. I kinda said the same thing about coincidences, and he turned beet red. I was afraid he'd have a stroke right in front of me."

"Well, he could stand to use a little color. He's always reminded me of a chubby little vampire."

"You got the vampire part right. But I'd say he's a bit on the north side of chubby."

Marty took a deep breath and turned serious. "The bottom line, Tony? The word from D.C. is nobody believes the Griffin family is gonna back down. And now with the vice president about to announce his plans to run for president, the family is only gonna unite even stronger. A little bad publicity isn't gonna cut it."

"So, what the hell they want us to do?"

"Well, for one thing, we gotta break the back on this right to work propaganda the Griffins have been pushing. They want the heat turned up. Gotta make sure GMHC is under the union's thumbs. We've already got most things in place. But we need to step up the pressure to make something happen sooner rather than later. Let's discuss those plans first. Then we can work on these latest orders I got from Big Al. This is gonna be our big break. As long

212 • Ron Vergona

as you don't screw things up. Now, listen up. We gotta do this right."

CHAPTER 40

THE SUN HAD LONG AGO BURNED off the earlier fog, but the humidity still hovered near the danger zone. Steve entered Edie's air-conditioned condo and paused after closing the door to allow the frigid environment a chance to chill the dampened shirt against his skin.

"How long have you been at that damn computer?" Steve asked, bending over the chair and folding his arms around Edie.

Edie eased back into the clammy warmth of Steve's embrace. "Not long enough to find a way to clear Thomas's name."

"How'd the arraignment go?"

Edie shrugged. "About how you'd expect when the government is hell-bent on ramming it to someone. Just got back from Stillwater. Tyler was there today."

She rubbed her eyes. "Right now, I'm still working on what we learned from Thomas and Kristie yesterday. I keep going over the same things, trying to make sense of the events leading up to when the girl disappeared. We can put together a plausible theory of how this could've gone down, but there's no way to prove any of it, unless we find the damn people involved. Even then, we'd need something concrete to prove the whole thing was a set-up. The physical and circumstantial evidence against Thomas is overwhelming."

Steve exhaled and kissed the top of Edie's head. "Sometimes it just takes pulling one little thread for the whole thing to unwind. There's nobody better than you in grabbing on to even the thinnest leads." He massaged

Edie's shoulders and stood back, stretching his arms. "How's Thomas dealing with this?"

"On the surface, he's holding it together, but he's always been good at keeping his emotions inside. There was a faraway look in his eyes that had me worried. It was there even when he talked about being opposed to changing Kristie's or Tyler's political plans."

Steve pulled up a chair and swung it around. He leaned against its back, facing Edie. "That's what this all comes down to, isn't it? One big power play. And the stakes keep getting higher. The state politics sparked it, but now this thing has evolved to the national level. Tyler Griffin. President Tyler Griffin. That represents fighting words to a lot of angry people in Washington."

Edie nodded. "There're more than enough people who don't want Tyler Griffin in the White House."

"Has the vice president decided when he's going to make the announcement?"

"Yeah. That's what they discussed today. Since the president addressed the nation, all the talking heads have been busy speculating on what's going to happen. And Tyler wants both Kristie and Thomas standing on the stage right next to him when he makes his declaration. Kristie and Tyler endorsing each other and at the same time showing their support for Thomas. You know Tyler, if he's going to do something, he's going to do it big. Right in their face."

"And you have doubts about this?"

Edie pursed her lips. "Well... I'm not sure if Thomas can handle much more pressure. Inside he's torn apart. On the other hand, I think he wants to make sure this doesn't stop what Kristie and Tyler need to do. He talked

Kristie into fighting back the union bosses by going into politics in the first place. It was a long and difficult fight to convince her this was the right thing to do."

Edie paused and closed the lid of her laptop. "I need a break from these searches. Right now, I'm just spinning my wheels. How'd things go today with Uncle Vinnie?"

Steve stood up. "I'll grab a couple of beers. Let's sit outside on the patio and talk. I'm determined to get used to this damn humidity. Besides, my shirt's already soaked through, and it's freezing in here."

"Okay, but I'll get the beers. You grab two chairs and take them outside. Remember? I haven't gotten around to furnishing that part of the condo." She got up and headed into the kitchen.

"I hadn't noticed," Steve called out.

"Other than my king-sized bed, what have you noticed?"

"Well there always seems to be a pair of nicely shaped legs supporting a deeply tanned—"

"Can't hear you… I'm in the kitchen."

As Edie walked onto the patio, Steve's phone rang.

"Damn. Where? No. But I'm sure Edie can get us to Kearny. We're on our way. Yeah. That might not be a bad idea. We'll bring Amber along too."

CHAPTER 41

MUCH EARLIER THAT SAME DAY, as the first light peeked above the horizon, Andrew MacAteer's two synchronized alarm clocks resounded harsh tones across the quiet apartment in Kearny, N.J. Transitioning from a blissful sleep to instant alertness, the young man jumped out of bed and proceeded with his morning routine.

"I'm right on time. It's six o'clock. Time to get up," he said with confidence. "I'm right on time."

His feet padded into the bathroom. "Okay now. Here's my comb." After checking his image in the mirror, he got to work. "Nice and neat. I'm right on time."

Andrew MacAteer had been living on his own in this studio apartment over a detached garage in the back of a long, narrow lot on Elm Street for almost six months. Although he had just turned twenty-two, this experience, which would've been ordinary to most his age, presented him with one giant adventure.

Andrew's parents had helped him pick out this apartment. The owners of the property, good friends of the MacAteer family, lived in the Dutch colonial house in front of the garage. Most of the houses in the area stood on lots much narrower than this one, requiring their garages to be located under the main dwelling. This home, one of the older, original properties in the neighborhood, had been built on a wider lot, allowing for the detached garage with the small apartment above. It gave Andrew MacAteer an air of privacy in an otherwise crowded environment.

The police department had a station right down the street, making his parents more comfortable with Andrew living away from home for the first time. But the primary benefit of this location was that one of GMHC's newer retail stores was also located in Kearny, approximately four blocks to the east. Andrew's parents had been extremely proud when he became one of their new employees. Living in this apartment allowed him to walk to work, but he dreamed of getting a driver's license and buying a car of his own.

Andrew paused and again checked himself in the mirror. He was shorter and heavier than the average young man of his generation. A few body parts appeared slightly out of proportion, but that didn't concern him. He stared at his wristwatch and then looked back to the mirror.

"Okay, I'm almost ready. I'm right on time. Not going to be late." Andrew once more ran the comb through his thick and curly light brown hair.

It accomplished little, but if anything, he was persistent. He backed out of the bathroom to finish getting dressed. In a painstaking fashion he buttoned his bright green work shirt, counting each button as he went along. He rubbed his fingers across his embroidered name sewn over the breast pocket to make sure it was still there.

As taught, he tucked the shirt into his tan chinos and slipped the silver-plated belt buckle into position. Finally, he settled down on the tiny bench next to the door and labored over the laces of his black work shoes with the concentration and precision needed to restring a Stradivarius. After glancing at the checklist on the wall, Andrew gazed one more time at his wristwatch and headed out the door, leaving plenty of time for his daily walk to work.

"I'm right on time. Right on time. All the lights are off. I locked the door. I'm right on time."

While none of these daily tasks was considered remarkable, for Andrew MacAteer they represented major accomplishments. An expanding list of definitions branded Andrew's uniqueness. Many of the classifications and medical terms describing his disabilities had changed over the years and would continue to do so as the science and the politics evolved. His brain processed things differently, but no specific name existed for the myriad of learning difficulties he battled to overcome.

Although no tangible connection linked his IQ to particular learning disabilities, the fact remained, with an IQ hovering in the low sixties, Andrew was usually classified as being mentally handicapped, but educable. Andrew faced a constant strain to perform everyday tasks. His mastery level of skill objective remained anchored at the level of the average third to fourth grader. That said, Andrew, from an early age, supported and encouraged by a loving family, not only conquered those challenges, but also succeeded to the point of where he was today.

That translated into him working at a good job, living independently, and dreaming of the future.

"I'm right on time. I'm right on time."

CHAPTER 42

THE KEY TO AVOIDING SUSPICION is to avoid a singular point of attention. The problem needs to arise in a random pattern, or one dependent on unrelated circumstances. A key factor is the appearance of neglect. Rain could be both good and bad. A light rain or high humidity might accelerate the process, while heavy rains could wash away all chemical traces and slow the desired effect.

The actions of Chuck Kolinsky, while not rocket science—were based on the precise science of the oxidation reaction in metals. The imprecision of this particular objective stemmed from the unpredictability of weather, contact time, number of applications, and concentrations of the applied acidic gel compound.

Impatient for results, as the game plan had changed, Big Al Rozano now demanded immediate action. Chuck Kolinsky, a supervisor in the garden department at the GMHC retail center in Kearny, was also on the payroll of CBT. He'd just learned that the need for results had grown more serious. A point driven home earlier this morning when the two CBT representatives, Marty Calebrese and Tony Funetti, made a rare appearance at the GMHC Kearny retail center. They gave Kolinsky the nod, which he correctly took to mean the waiting period had ended, his choices limited. When Marty Calebrese bent over and placed a shoe on the lower shelf of the exact cantilevered unit in question, Kolinsky found himself wishing for an immediate result himself.

Instead, once Marty finished tying his shoelaces, he and Tony headed toward the store's exit. On their way out, Tony handed out a number of sports and theater tickets, and scores of restaurant vouchers and other goodies to any GMHC employee within reach. As Andrew MacAteer walked through the door, reporting for work, Marty slipped a logoed union cap over the young man's head. For another fifteen minutes, the pair hovered outside the store's main entrance passing out additional union propaganda before the manager coaxed them off the premises.

Chuck Kolinsky walked over to the work schedule board and smiled after double-checking the shift's work assignments. Right after Marty and Tony left him standing alone in the garden department's storage area, Kolinsky had swung over the wheeled ladder trolley and checked the inventory numbers on one of the outdoor cantilevered shelving units. While performing this routine task, he accomplished his primary mission to confirm that the applied chemicals had achieved their goal. When he moved the ladder back to the storage area, he noticed the floor had nearly dried after last evening's downpour. The morning sun playing its role in what would soon transpire. The floor drains had done their job, which in this case washed away something much more telling than rainwater.

CHAPTER 43

THE GRIFFIN FAMILY ADVOCATED FOR hiring the handicapped. Besides the required accommodation provisions for their special-needs employees, Kristie Pauling had contracted with outside training companies and put together several innovative programs custom-tailored to a specific employee's needs. The concept was similar to the individual education program, or IEP, used by elementary schools to maximize a student's potential in their special education classes. Although the programs challenged the handicapped person's abilities, they also provided a rigid level of safety criteria. Once an employee completed a training program and was certified in a specific job function, the company assigned a personal coach at the employee's work site to assure strict adherence to the guidelines learned in the program.

Andrew MacAteer was one of the first to complete the forklift training program offered by GMHC for a select group of handicapped employees. This turned out to be a daunting task for the training facility, as well as for Andrew. One of Andrew's major impediments, diagnosed as dyspraxia, meant he had a problem concerning messages from the brain being delivered to the periphery, resulting in poorly coordinated muscle activity. The fieldwork, a critical part of the training classes, needed to be supplemented by intense physical therapy sessions to achieve the muscle memory framework necessary to perform the required tasks.

Andrew beamed as he walked out of the classroom on the last day of the training session, clutching the certificate in his hand. Kristie Pauling had invited his parents to attend this session which evaluated his forklift operating skills. They were incredulous with the outcome of this program and now felt they too could share in Andrew's dream of getting a driver's license and owning a car. In fact, his dad had already talked to Andrew about looking at used cars. That was several weeks ago.

CHAPTER 44

IN A PANIC, ANDREW MACATEER yanked the cap off his head and threw it in his locker. Caught off guard, he hadn't noticed the two men walking by until after one of them pushed the union cap over his neatly combed hair—without breaking stride—and continued muscling their way through the store. He hoped no one saw the infraction to the company rule of not wearing anything with a logo when reporting to work, especially one with those three large letters centered above the brim: CBT.

Unobserved, Chuck Kolinsky had entered the locker room and watched Andrew's nervous mannerisms. He nodded to himself and edged closer. Andrew closed his locker, turned, and bumped into him.

"Oh! I'm sorry, Chuck. I just punched in. I'm not late, am I?" Andrew stared at Kolinsky and swallowed hard.

"No, Andrew. But after you put on your apron, go grab a forklift and head over to the garden department. We gotta move the older stock. There's a new shipment of fall supplies coming in later this week, and we need to make room."

Andrew's face lit up. Kolinsky knew he was always eager to utilize his brand-new skills. "Great. I'm on my way. I'll pick up the checklists from the office and meet you in the equipment storage area. Right on time."

"Ah, yeah. See you there, Andrew." Kolinsky had forgotten about those particular details. As Andrew's assigned coach, he was responsible for documenting that Andrew followed the safety requirements. After considering his options, Kolinsky came up with a way to make this fit into today's plan.

Fifteen minutes later, Kolinsky strolled up to Andrew who was clutching the clipboard and writing his signature on the first form, which included the checklist for all the major systems on the vehicle. It looked like Andrew had gone over the check-off procedure twice. Technically, Kolinsky was required to witness this inspection, but he banked on the fact that Andrew wouldn't question his coach's behavior in brushing off a few of the guidelines. Andrew wet his lips and lowered his head when Kolinsky grabbed the clipboard and scrawled his own signature.

Handing the clipboard back to Andrew, Kolinsky pointed and said, "Drive over to the end of aisle six, all the way to the rear fence on the right side of the gate."

Andrew's face brightened again when Kolinsky half-heartedly added, "I'll be walking behind you, checking up on how you're doing."

Andrew arrived at the specified area and secured the forklift. Pulling the clipboard from its holder, he jumped out of the vehicle and crouched beside the first of the three pallets. His eyes glanced up at the stacks of large ceramic planters.

"I already verified the gross weights on all the pallets and applied the shrink wrap to secure the loads," Kolinsky said as if reading his mind. He placed a hand on Andrew's shoulder. "Sign the papers and get to work."

Andrew's face clouded over. He hesitated but did what he was told. "Ah, I guess that's okay. Do you want me to look at the numbers on the shelving unit and make sure it can hold this heavy load okay?"

With an air of impatience that he knew made Andrew nervous, Kolinsky said, "Let's not waste any more time, Andrew. I've got it covered. I checked and double-checked all load ratings for these units earlier this morning. Make sure you've signed everything and give me the damn clipboard so I can finish the paperwork. While I'm doing that, swing those safety gates into position. We need to get this done. Jack expected those pallets out of here by now. Let's move it."

Andrew backed away. After a few jerky steps he rushed to move the bright yellow accordion safety gates to block the periphery of the forklift path and the area on both sides of the shelving unit. A required procedure, even though they were working in the overstock storage area of the garden department, technically off-limits to all customers and employees not engaged in specific activities. Andrew MacAteer and Chuck Kolinsky appeared to be the only ones working in the garden area this morning. Kolinsky knew that keeping Andrew busy eased his anxieties and always put an extra bounce in his step.

After fixing the gates into position, Andrew returned as Kolinsky placed the clipboard into its holder on the forklift.

"I've got you signed-off and you're good to go," Kolinsky said. A lie, because all he did was make sure the required check marks and numbers were filled in, and Andrew's signatures were completed in all the proper places. Kolinsky had only signed the initial checklist performed back in the equipment storage area.

"Okay, Andrew, those pallets go on the top shelf of the middle unit. Let's see how you handle this simple job. Jack's been saying he still didn't think you were up to running this equipment."

Kolinsky reached out and tapped Andrew's shoulder, working a smile onto his set jaw. "Go prove him wrong.

Can you do that, Andrew? Remember, we're a team—the two of us—now go and do your part. We need to get this done. I'll tell Jack you got it done right on time."

Andrew nodded his head again and scrambled onto the forklift.

"Right on time," Andrew repeated.

Andrew fastened his seat belt and started the motor. As he concentrated on the task, Kolinsky stepped away from the overstock storage area.

Since the Occupational Safety and Health Administration, or OSHA, mandated safety requirements for forklift operations in 1999, they monitored the number, the circumstances, and the locations of fatal accidents.

Of the eighty to ninety fatalities recorded each year, almost half resulted from vehicles tipping over due to operator error. Less than nine percent of all fatalities occurred in retail situations. Due to the requirements for overhead safety guards protecting the driver, being struck by falling objects was a greater risk to people standing near an operating forklift than for the operator.

Andrew took several deep breaths and focused his entire mental faculties on the job. Inching the vehicle forward, he lined up the forks and advanced the machine until the loaded pallet slid up against the mast. He lifted the load and tilted the forks back. He followed these important steps without knowledge about center of gravity or the stability triangle. Andrew's training didn't involve theoretical components, but his brain had mastered the practical sense of the requirements. Like buttoning his shirt or tying his shoelaces.

In his head, he counted off each tiny step before performing any of the incremental pieces of the operation. This shaping pattern was one of the key techniques used in the specialized training program. It broke down complicated tasks into a series of simple movements that after a painstaking amount of practice could be repeated in the proper sequence. To prepare the special trainees for any unexpected circumstances that changed the normal paradigm and potentially posed a danger, the program included a variety of proofing drills. These were necessary to assure a solid foundation for each individual exercise.

Andrew lifted the first pallet onto the upper shelf with ease. As he pulled back the forks, his mind hiccupped, imagining something terribly wrong. He swore he felt a shudder. Not likely with all the normal vibrations and noise of the forklift. With his shirtsleeve, he wiped away several beads of sweat from his forehead. The moment passed and he resumed his activities. Focused on his work, Andrew never realized Kolinsky had disappeared. He was alone.

Andrew finished placing the third and final pallet on the upper cantilevered shelf. Withdrawing the forks, his eyes registered a subtle movement—had the planters shifted? He felt a slight vibration as the tips of the forks cleared the edge of the pallet. Light reflecting from the shrink-wrap rippled slightly. Even if he had questioned how that could happen with the load properly secured, no amount of training would've helped.

The next event occurred with such intensity that no one behind the controls could have reacted in time. The sudden rumbling and screeching of the failing shelf swallowed up Andrew's entire universe. The overloaded and weakened upper shelf tilted forward. Shards of multicolored pottery fragments flew through the air in a deadly pattern of destruction. The shelf completely gave way, crashing to the ground with a thunderous explosion.

Andrew's mind froze and processed only one thing. The sound bite stuck in his brain from the horror movie he'd forced himself to watch last night. He relived the scene where the evil, brain-consuming zombies pushed open the rusted gate to the crypt. They were coming to eat him.

Right on time.

He never heard the sickening crunch of the shelf smashing into the ground.

Andrew MacAteer was already dead.

A flying razor-sharp fragment severed his carotid artery as the sliding planters crushed him.

Chuck Kolinsky walked back to the storage area while shouting into his handheld for someone to call 911. When he approached the scene and saw the blood covering Andrew's body, he dropped to his knees and vomited.

CHAPTER 45

CHUCK KOLINSKY HAD CONVINCED HIMSELF that a few planters would bounce off the steel-meshed roof safety cage on the forklift. Andrew would have been shaken up, but not severely injured. In Andrew's confused state he'd never remember whether Kolinsky had signed off on the operation. Kolinsky was confident his own version would've prevailed. Now none of that was going to be an issue.

Wiping his face with his sleeve, Kolinsky swallowed back the remaining bile and stared at the devastation. Chemistry and physics had unerringly performed their roles. The acid-weakened cantilevered shelf gave way with the heavy load, but as it unhinged, the pallets slid and tumbled on a precise vector based on that momentary, but fateful angle, causing the bulk of the fracturing planters to fly through the open front of the forklift, not blocked by the top steel-meshed safety cage. Andrew sat at dead-center of the trajectory.

Kolinsky recovered from his momentary lapse of guilt and reported Andrew MacAteer's negligence to management, citing Andrew's failure to follow all safety precautions and wait for him to supervise the operation. The recovered clipboard substantiated his allegations.

When the OSHA inspectors arrived, Kolinsky recited chilling reports of unsafe policies endorsed by the company. He emphasized their programs for allowing handicapped people to operate dangerous machinery and perform other tasks beyond their limited capabilities. He further explained that fearful of repercussions, he had refrained from reporting this litany of infractions—not believing whistle-blower laws served as a sufficient safety net.

When Chuck Kolinsky left work for the day, a full contingent of the local press, as well as cable network crews, hustled to set up their satellite uplinks. Big Al Rozano undoubtedly played a role in making sure the gang was all there. Chuck Kolinsky had just gotten off the phone with Marty Calebrese, who didn't seem surprised by the fatal outcome of this accident. Marty had ordered him to suck it up and stick to the follow-up instructions as planned.

As the reporters swarmed around him, shoving microphones and cameras in his face, Kolinsky, after a suitable pose of reluctance, spouted out a tale of company neglect and complacency. He hinted at the likelihood of other safety violations being found. This was his final day on the job. He no longer worried about being saved by any whistle-blower laws.

According to Marty Calebrese, his promotion at CBT: a done deal. The union representative appreciated his performance and congratulated him on a job well done.

CHAPTER 46

INSTEAD OF DRINKING THEIR BEERS on Edie's tiny patio, discussing Steve's conversation with Uncle Vinnie, and deciding what to have for dinner, Steve and Edie drove to the GMHC Kearny retail store. Amber cozied up in the back seat of the Durango.

On Kristie Pauling's suggestion, they parked in the employee lot behind the store and entered the GMHC facility via the rear loading dock. This allowed them to bypass the media rampage just winding down at the front entrance. Kristie greeted them right inside the door and led them to a quiet corner of the huge warehouse storage area.

Kristie looked exactly how Steve expected the shaken CEO to look at the end of a long and trying day: Her color paler than her normally light complexion; her voice dull and distant as she talked them through the tragic death of Andrew MacAteer.

They had picked up the major details of the accident on the radio during the drive to Kearny. In addition, local news channels and the twenty-four-hour news stations replayed the dramatic interview with a disgruntled employee of GMHC. Steve and Edie listened to Chuck Kolinsky's damaging claims about the company's negligence and lack of safety guidelines for its employees. Kolinsky demonized GMHC's attitudes and policies for taking advantage of their handicapped personnel.

As they huddled together in the GMHC warehouse, Steve struggled to hold Amber on a short, tight lead, something he rarely had to deal with at this point in her training. Her agitated motions made it difficult for him to focus on Kristie's dialog.

"Can I speak to this guy who's been doing all the talking to the news media?" Steve said. Amber's agitated behavior continued to escalate.

Kristie sighed. "Too late. Kolinsky just quit. Told the authorities it wasn't safe for him to return to work. He claimed management would reprimand him for exposing the truth."

Kristie stopped, as if losing her train of thought. She looked around the vast warehouse complex and rubbed her eyes. Appearing dazed, she backed against a stack of crates for support and continued, "Kolinsky claims Andrew MacAteer, on his own, decided to move those pallets before he could stop him. Said he did it without anybody's permission. And that Andrew and others with similar disabilities working in the company don't have the capacity to make such decisions, let alone operate dangerous machinery by themselves."

Kristie remained quiet for several moments, and then her whole posture tensed. Hand going to her mouth, eyes wide open, Kristie said, "My God. What if this wasn't an accident? Like the fires you're investigating." Her eyes darted between Steve and Edie. "You've both seen those reports Tyler prepared. Not only the fires, but all those incidents at the other stores."

Kristie stared at Steve. "Ever since the union began pressuring our employees, we've had a rash of accidents. Tyler asked you to concentrate on the fires, but do you think somebody deliberately caused this to happen? Someone who works here...?" Her voice trailed off.

Steve glanced at Edie. "Edie, you've dug through the timelines, trying to link together a pattern. What've you come up with?"

"Difficult to say. The events appear unrelated, except for the speed of the union's responses. They always seem to be first on scene to throw accusations at GMHC's management." She shrugged. "And even before today, the seriousness of the incidents has been escalating; especially after Kristie announced her political intentions. I'm suspicious, but there's no evidence for the authorities to pin anything specific on the union."

Edie looked at Kristie. "But the union has got to be somehow involved. We know Tyler suspects them. That's why he asked Steve to investigate those fires." She paused as Amber ramped up her barking and pulled harder on her lead. Frowning, Edie said, "What's wrong with her, Steve?"

Shrugging, Steve kneeled and grabbed Amber's harness, trying to calm her down. "Kristie, what do you know about Kolinsky? His rantings sounded too orchestrated for someone supposedly shocked by the death of a co-worker."

Instead of responding to Steve's question, Kristie choked up. "I just got back from visiting Andrew's parents. They're obviously taking this hard. And I'm being seen as the bad guy in this. I understand that. I wish I could do something to help them."

Kristie's assistant rushed in, handed her a piece of paper, and vanished without a word. She glanced at the paper. "I expected this. OSHA has compiled a list of activities we must stop at once until they investigate the situation. On top of the list, they're calling for a shutdown of our handicapped training programs."

Kristie stopped talking and gazed at the entrance door to the garden area. Her dialog suddenly switched gears. "The local authorities have removed Andrew's body and the entire accident scene has been cordoned off until OSHA completes their investigation. A full complement of investigators will return tomorrow morning. I'm not sure why I asked you guys to rush over here, since no one's allowed anywhere near the accident scene."

Steve pulled over a chair from a nearby worktable and Kristie sunk down into it. Staring at the floor, she said, "Before OSHA arrived, I ordered the store manager to check out the rest of the overstock shelving units in the garden department. He found problems on several of the other units."

She glanced up at Steve as if she'd just noticed him. "There are definite signs of corrosion. At first the patterns appeared random, but his gut told him it looked suspicious. OSHA's going to do a complete inspection and check into our maintenance records. They already confiscated the safety checklists and the required forms Andrew filled out."

"Did you learn anything from those?" Steve asked. "It should at least demonstrate whether he followed the correct procedures."

Kristie sighed. "On the surface, they substantiate Kolinsky's claims. At first, I thought his blustering was done to cover his own liability. As Andrew's coach, it was his responsibility to check and sign off on all the paperwork before Andrew operated the forklift. Kolinsky claimed he witnessed and signed the vehicle safety checklist, but Andrew drove to the garden department and moved the pallets without his knowledge. And the paperwork shows the only form signed by Kolinsky was just as he stated. Andrew had signed all the other forms." Her voice sounded flat.

Edie placed a hand on Kristie's shoulder. "Kristie, I understand you can't give me this guy's personnel records, but it's important to check him out."

"I guess I'll need to talk to our lawyers," Kristie said, her words again not tracking the conversation.

Edie tried again. "Kristie, mind if I snoop around and talk to a few of the employees who knew Andrew and Kolinsky? It might help in understanding what happened."

Kristie nodded and appeared to regain her focus. She wrote on a pad and ripped off the top sheet.

Handing it to Edie, she said, "Take this. It gives my people permission to cooperate with you. The police have already taken official statements from everyone. Nobody witnessed the accident."

Kristie stood, inhaling a deep breath. "I need to pull myself together. Andrew's death has hit me hard. I initiated those specialized training classes for our handicapped employees. I saw Andrew graduate from our first class." She swallowed. "I can't believe he's dead."

Edie gave Kristie a hug and grabbed her notebook. She walked out of the warehouse storage area and headed onto the retail floor. Steve turned back to Kristie, poised to ask her a question. He momentarily loosened his grip on Amber's lead.

Amber broke free and bolted toward the overstock area of the garden department. She crashed through the flimsy plastic mesh barriers set up by OSHA.

Steve caught up to Amber near the damaged shelving unit. She bypassed the fallen upper shelf and focused on the lowest intact shelf, digging through the rubble. A low growl emanated from Amber, and she sniffed aggressively at the lower shelf. Her nose pressed against a particular spot. She circled out in wider and wider arcs and headed away from the site of the carnage. Steve grabbed the lead and encouraged this new scenting activity. Amber pulled him through the retail section of the store and out the front entrance. Amber screeched to a stop and focused on an area to the right of the door, next to a steel bench. Her determined overtures intensified, and once again Steve lost the struggle to maintain control. By this time the media crews had packed up and left. And except for the sudden outbursts of Amber's barking, the front of the store had turned quiet.

Amber's intense behavior made Steve think of the time she reacted this way several years ago. He hadn't understood it at the time, but Amber had picked up the scent left by someone placing a tracking device underneath Steve's SUV. She had attempted to pursue the intruder by pulling Steve down his driveway, but Steve had misread Amber's intentions and dragged her back into the house.

Steve recalled a more pleasant part of the story: The first night he had made love to Edie. The desire to return to Edie's arms caused him to ignore Amber's instincts to go after any would-be trespassers.

Steve read Amber's actions today as an indication of aggression against the source of the scent and not her trained responses for identifying particular chemical traces. Understanding this, Steve followed the training guidelines and rewarded Amber for her performance.

He wanted to sneak Amber back to the accident scene and give it a more thorough going over, but Kristie had already secured the area using portable chain link fencing modules instead of the plastic barriers placed by OSHA.

After talking to the employees, Edie caught up with Steve.

"Hey, mister. Don't you wanna talk to anyone?" Edie said while wiggling her phone in his face.

Puzzled, Steve dug a hand into his pocket. "Oh damn. I guess I left my phone in the Durango. What's up?"

"Well, it's not actually me who wants to talk to you. Dominick left you a message on my phone too. He sounded excited. More squeaks per second than usual. Here, use my phone," she said, hitting the redial key.

CHAPTER 47

FOLLOWING DOMINICK CASELLA'S DIRECTIONS, STEVE drove down Bergen Street, passing the New Jersey Medical School and making a left into a quiet residential neighborhood in the Fairmont section of Newark. A short trip from Kearny, but a complicated series of turns made the drive seem longer. Steve couldn't find a parking space close to the café where he was to meet with Dominick, so he double-parked the Durango next to a cream-colored Ford Econoline cargo van and got out of the vehicle. Edie scooted around into the driver's seat, and Steve closed the door.

As he leaned in the window to kiss her goodbye, Edie said, "Good parking job. I didn't even talk you through it. You're positioned to block in at least two cars."

She patted him on the cheek. "One thing… if you don't mind a little criticism?"

Edie paused, taking a breath. Steve held off on the kiss and waited.

"The stop signs? You have a habit of coming to a complete stop. Can't remember what the California law is, but you need to work on rolling stops. If you don't get the hang of it, you're gonna get rear-ended. Anyway, once we finish these lessons, I'll take you through the Lincoln Tunnel and you can learn the New York taxicab game."

"Why don't you take your Jersey attitude and—" Steve pressed his lips against Edie's, canceling the remaining words.

She uttered a stifled cry when he stood back from the SUV. Recovering, she said, "Play nice and don't let

Dominick get into any trouble. Remember he looks up to you. You need to concentrate on being a good role model."

Edie drove away; face flushed from the remaining traces of Steve's kiss. Unimpressed by the whole incident, Amber paced in the rear of the Durango checking out the neighborhood for any potential threats.

Steve stretched his arms and watched Edie disappear around the corner. He walked past the Econoline van and glanced at the painted-over name and logo on its side. Poised to take a closer look, he heard Dominick's shrilly voice calling him to hurry into the café. Once inside, Dominick ushered Steve along to a corner booth by a window.

"So, sonny, you ready to order something more substantial than that Pepsi you been nursing for the last hour?" The voice came from an ancient and imposing bulky form looming over the booth, tapping a hefty foot on the grimy and faded linoleum floor while her pencil rested over a yellowing order pad. "This ain't no social club where you and your boyfriend here can make time and gaze at the scenery while hogging our best booth. We need to make room for the paying customers."

Steve cast his eyes around the empty dive while Dominick's face sprouted vivid red streaks that spun around his neck. Dominick swallowed and coughed out the words. "This is Steve; he's like my cousin. He's not my—"

"What do I care if he's your sister? Now, what's it gonna be?"

"We'll take two orders of the Jersey dog specials, two chocolate malts, and two more Pepsis," Dominick uttered in one breath.

Before Steve could revise the order, Bertie, the name embossed on the pin sitting on top of her sagging left breast, let out a loud huff and spun away with remarkable dexterity.

Steve's eyes dug into Dominick.

"Don't worry, Steve. You're in for a real treat. Jersey's famous for their deep-fried hot dogs, and Newark is ground zero for the best tasting dogs in the whole state. And if you've never tried the cheesy fries that come with the dogs—you're gonna die and go to heaven. By the way, you keep tabs on your cholesterol levels?"

"So you've eaten here before?"

"Ah, not in this particular restaurant."

Steve nodded and leaned back in the duct-taped vinyl booth. In spite of the surroundings, his stomach growled as he absorbed the greasy, but enticing smells bombarding his senses. From behind the counter, he heard a cacophony of crackling and sizzling sounds in rhythmic accompaniment to the aged, oily aromas. The grease-laden atmosphere already elevated his cholesterol levels by at least ten points.

Aside from the brief, embarrassing diversion Dominick encountered with Bertie, Steve noticed Dominick's eyes remained focused through the grimy side window. He observed Dominick's nervous demeanor, which appeared underlined with a peculiar air of excitement.

Bertie dropped off the Pepsis and two humongous thick glass mugs topped with mounds of whipped cream and a cherry. The short-order cook, the male version of Bertie, smacked down two huge platters in front of them. Their unctuous fragrances beating them to the table.

Dominick smiled at Steve and whispered, "Now that's the real meaning of fast food, right? The secret is—"

"Keeping the hot dogs in the oil since last Tuesday?"

"That's one of the secrets... you wanna hear the others?"

They both dug in and made substantial headway into their meals. Steve was surprised at how good everything tasted. As he washed down the dogs and fries with alternating gulps of his malt and Pepsi, he mused about paying the price before too long.

Between bites, Steve confronted Dominick. "I gotta admit... this turned out to be an interesting spread, but maybe it's time to come clean on what you wanted to see me about. That's if you can stop spying out the window long enough to face me."

Dominick picked up his shredded and soppy paper napkin and wiped a splotch of mustard from his chin. In an uncharacteristic show of strength, with a deep, loud voice, he called out to Bertie for the check and a doggie bag. His machismo shriveled when Bertie marched over and slapped the check down in front of him, bouncing the plates, mugs, and glasses in response. A Styrofoam container slid off the table and landed on the seat next to Steve.

Dominick counted out the cash, stuffing it under the check before Steve could protest and grab his own wallet. Steve shrugged and dumped the remains of his fries into the container.

Getting up and out of the booth first, Dominick grabbed Steve's arm. "Come on, Steve. Let's go. I'll fill you in on the way."

Once outside the café, Dominick pulled Steve down the street, stopping in front of the cream-colored Econoline van. With a shaky movement, Dominick slipped the key into the passenger's side door and urged Steve inside. Before Steve had closed the door, Dominick dashed around the vehicle and sat in the driver's seat, turning the key to start up the engine. He pulled away, making a left at the corner, and then a right at the next block. Two blocks later Dominick made another right and pulled over behind a rusty old pick-up truck, scraping the front tire against the curb.

Through the windshield Steve eyed the café they had just eaten at about a block and a half away. At a loss for words, Steve said the first thing that popped into his head.

"You never came to a complete stop at any of those stop signs."

"Wh…what?" Dominick sputtered as he twisted his body around and swung open a narrow door behind the two front seats. He wiggled through. "Come on back here, Steve. Hurry it up."

With more difficulty than Dominick, Steve squeezed through the door. Dominick slammed it shut. There was a split second of darkness before the windowless cargo area became bathed in a surreal glow of light.

CHAPTER 48

WHEN EDIE LEFT STEVE AT the café, she had all intentions of heading straight home and sinking into a warm, soothing bath. Before reaching the interstate, her eye caught the familiar sign of one of her favorite department stores. So instead, she detoured into a nearby parking structure and caught up on a little shopping.

Feeling guilty for neglecting Amber, before returning to the Durango, she picked up a bag of high value dog treats at a boutique pet store. After driving out of the parking garage, Edie cruised back toward the highway. Stopped at a red light, she killed time by playing with the Durango's radio.

"Nah, I don't like that one either," Edie said to Amber while she scanned through a bunch of channels. "Let's try this one. Oh-oh." Edie's voice changed tone.

Amber sprang up, a low rumbling growl building. The last channel she'd hit made Edie's face harden as she listened to Reverend Jefferson Carter's closing remarks from his daily syndicated radio show. His voice rang in full campaign mode, spouting out his hateful rhetoric and using the murder of Leilah Harris and Thomas Pauling's arrest as his platform of the day. Edie reached for her cell phone to call into his talk show to verbally spar with this lunatic before realizing she had been listening to a replay of an earlier live performance. Good thing. Lending any more credence to Carter's ranting should've been beneath any real journalist.

While the reverend's final wrap-up blared through the Durango's speaker system, Edie steered the vehicle toward the studio where Carter's show originated from in the heart of downtown Newark. Maybe she'd catch

Carter still hanging out, sharpening his fangs for the next rally. With everything going on, Edie felt feisty, looking for a fight. Returning to her condo and relaxing in the bath—long forgotten.

She pulled into the studio's parking lot, almost empty at this time of day. The setting sun had disappeared behind the taller buildings in the business district. Several overhead lights were burned out; dim shadows lost in the far corners of the lot. She parked under one of the remaining bright lights.

"I'll be gone for a minute, sweetie," she said to Amber, "and it's better for you not to hear what Mommy has to say. Don't worry, Carter's probably already gone."

Edie kissed Amber's snout and locked the door. Dodging puddles left over from an earlier series of showers, she walked toward the side entrance of the building, digging into her purse for her press credentials in case she had trouble gaining entry. Off to her left she sensed movement, and then her eyes were drawn to the echoes of strained voices. Her hand closed on the Ruger's grip, but she kept the handgun inside the concealed holster pocket of the purse.

She walked toward the sounds.

Edie picked out two distinct voices. One sounded familiar. Annoyingly familiar. Except his normal condescending tone was absent. Only a pleading, whining, and sobbing display of words remained. Both men, immersed in a heated confrontation, failed to see Edie closing in on their isolated encounter. The two men stood eye-to-eye next to Reverend Carter's personal automobile: not his usual chauffeured Town Car.

As Edie tried to grasp the situation, the man pointing the knife toward Reverend Jefferson Carter's neck spotted her. She heard Carter utter the man's name and she figured out what was going down.

Still brandishing the knife at Carter, Leilah Harris's father turned to Edie and said, "Young lady, why don't you keep on walking and let me finish my business with this low-life leech."

In a thin voice, Carter squealed out, "Help. He's gonna kill me. Call the police. Hurry."

"You're a hypocrite," Mr. Harris said. "Asking the cops to help you after your indictment of all white authority."

"He's crazy. Lady, you gotta help me," Carter begged.

Edie glanced down at the fresh puddle forming between Carter's feet, tracing the origin back to his crotch.

She took several shallow breaths and tuned out Carter. She focused on the stricken father of the innocent young girl caught up in this vile, disgusting mess.

"Mr. Harris," Edie said, voice strong and confident. "I know what happened to your daughter. It's horrible, and I can't begin to understand what you're going through."

Mr. Harris's eyes fluttered, but the knife remained steady.

"This piece of shit isn't worth it," Edie added.

"You hear how he's taking advantage of what happened to Leilah... for his own political gain? What he's been saying at those rallies? Instead of focusing on my daughter, he made everything all about him and his sick ideas. And now this filth spewing from his radio show—that was the last straw."

"Mr. Harris," Edie said, stepping closer. "Please don't do this. Think of your family. You want Leilah's memory to be tied with you going to jail? You have another daughter, don't you?"

Mr. Harris nodded, the knife eased back from Carter's neck, but still close to his intended target.

"Listen to me, please." She nodded toward Carter. "He isn't worth destroying the rest of your family."

"I-I… I don't know. The things he said." Mr. Harris's voice cracked.

Edie stared into Mr. Harris's eyes. "Let me take care of this. You need to drop the knife and go home. Mr. Harris, nobody can fix what's happened, but don't make it worse. Please, turn away and go home. Go home to your family. They need you." Her eyes pleading to the distraught father.

The air remained quiet for a good ten seconds.

The knife clattered to the ground, echoing in the deserted parking lot.

Mr. Harris was long gone before Carter took a breath.

Edie picked up the knife and wiped it clean with tissues from her purse.

Finding his voice, Carter said, "I mean… what the hell are you doing? We gotta get the cops here and arrest that lunatic. That's evidence you're destroying. You got no right."

Finally getting a look at the person he was talking to, Carter gasped. "It's *you*. Pauling. Edie Pauling. The sister. What the hell are you doing? I'm not gonna let that guy get away with this. You're damn lucky Harris didn't recognize you. Or he would've tried to kill you too. I have a mind to call him back here. Then we'll see who's in trouble."

Edie stepped forward, looking up at Carter's face and making a sniffing sound with her nose, eyes turning to his crotch. She stepped back, inhaling again.

"You're a pitiful example of a human being, Carter. And an even worse role model for the black communities you plunder through to beef up your hateful agenda."

"Pauling, you got no business speaking to me like that. I'll have you arrested as well. Aiding and abetting." He spoke with no real commitment.

Carter continued on several different venues, but Edie waited him out, holding her ground.

After hearing enough blubbering from Carter, Edie raised a hand to silence him. "If I ever hear a word about any of this from you, your new political ambitions will be as useless as your bladder. So, why don't we call it a night and go home?"

* * * * * *

Edie's phone rang as she dropped back into the driver's seat of the Durango.

"Sampson. What have you been up to?"

"Saving your ass again, sis."

After Sampson explained he was on his way back from Washington, D.C., Edie offered him a quick dinner of Vietnamese takeout from a restaurant around the corner from her condo. She called in the order and headed back to Morristown. They pulled up in front of her condo at the same time, Sampson losing the battle for the closer parking space.

Sampson grabbed the bag of takeout from Edie, and they headed inside her condo. He strode directly into the living room and dug into the aromatic cartons.

"What the hell are you talking about, Sampson?" Edie prodded after waiting for Sampson to stop inhaling his food.

Sampson stood up from the sofa and cleared the empty takeout cartons from the coffee table. Leftovers didn't exist with Sampson at the table.

"Kristie said you were up to something, but she didn't mention anything about D.C." It had been like pulling teeth getting Sampson to put two sentences together while he devoured the food. So far, she had made little progress in reaching the heart of his story.

Sampson walked into the kitchen and dumped the cartons in the trashcan. "I'm grabbing another beer, Edie. You want one?" No answer. "Okay. Suit yourself."

When Sampson returned to the living room, he found Edie sitting on the sofa with her arms crossed and foot tapping.

"I can see how you been putting those gray hairs on Steve."

Before Edie responded, Sampson held his free hand up in surrender as he gulped down the first third of the bottle.

"So, like I been trying to tell you all evening," Sampson said, smiling and wiping his mouth with his sleeve. "When we found out about the president's health problems and Tyler Griffin running for the presidency, I got to thinking... things could get a lot more serious for the Griffins. And then this bullshit with Thomas scared the hell out of me."

Sampson finished what remained in the bottle. "You've been working on how this stuff ties together and concentrating on the CBT being the center of the firestorm. Well, from what I understand about this Rozano character, he might be a big deal here in New Jersey—he's one mean motherfucking bastard, if I might add. But Rozano, or Big Al, as his friends call him, doesn't pass gas without approval from Washington."

Edie interrupted. "I agree. I discovered that on numerous occasions he's unofficially met with Philip Lucchesi, the national head of the CBT. In fact, I've been digging into the background of Rozano and his crew. You remember Agent Mike Finley? He's been helping me improve my computer skills in accessing restricted databases."

Sampson arched his eyebrows. "That sounds dangerous. Or at least illegal. That's why I prefer to let the professionals do the hacking for me."

"Isn't that a little costly?"

"Not when I walk into the lady's office with this big smile and my sought after charm." Sampson's formidable chest puffed out. "You remember Beth Dawson? We developed a close friendship when she worked in that law firm in Woodbridge. We met through my bail bond firm. Three years ago, she moved to Washington. Beth now works in the Office of the Clerk in the US House of Representatives. From time to time, we still keep in touch. That's where I've been since yesterday."

This time Edie raised her eyebrows. "I'm glad your love life is strong enough to encompass the beltway, but...?"

A smile spread across Sampson's face. "Yeah. When you work hard, you gotta play hard. If you'd stop interrupting, I'd have gotten to it by now."

Edie put a hand over her mouth as she tucked her legs under, settling back on the sofa.

"Beth pulled up files from one of their primary databases."

"Are you referring to the registration database lobbyists are required to file on behalf of their clients?"

"Jesus, Edie. You ever gonna stop doing that? It's like you're reading my mind. Gives me the shivers. But if Steve can handle it, he's a better man than me."

"Sorry. I mean, sorry I didn't think about looking into this myself." Edie picked up a pad from the coffee table and jotted down some notes. She kept the pad and pen on her lap.

"Beth compared the union's lobbyist client list to a different database. This one's not as official as the lobbyist registration database. Beth told me certain government agencies have compiled lists of known activists. You might want to ask Mike Finley about these files if you haven't already."

Edie shook her head. "Haven't come across them yet, but I've only started on this track. This all sounds promising."

"I'll give you the facts. And you can determine what they mean. I'm just the pretty boy part of this operation."

Sampson paused and glanced briefly at the empty beer bottle. "These agencies also have access to the phone and email records of individuals on the lists. Unfortunately, Beth's access to those records is limited. But like you, I believe she too is working on improving her computer skills."

He smiled at Edie, tapping the bottle. "At any rate, I doubt you'd be surprised at most of the names of the individuals and organizations associated with Philip Lucchesi's activities. All the usual suspects involved with the CBT union. The special interest groups, activists, and several esteemed members of congress. Not to mention key officials in the executive branch. I'm sure the vice president is aware of most of this and makes sure things don't get out of hand."

Edie nodded. "I'm guessing that's another reason why Tyler wanted Steve here to look at things under the radar. And I'm sure he's concerned with who's been leaking information about the president's health and his own plans to run for the top office."

"Right. But here's where things get a little more interesting. And timely, especially regarding the political fallout from him considering the run for president." Sampson paused and leaned forward. "You ever hear of a character named Arthur Constantine?"

Edie shook her head and wrote the name down on her pad.

"Well, it seems he's a nefarious figure in our capital. One of the more heavy-handed powerbrokers. But nothing to link him to Lucchesi or any other leaders from the CBT at this point. In fact, Constantine's, let's call them associates, for lack of a better term, would probably show up on an enemies list for many of the unions. Their left leaning adversaries describe them as a bunch of rich, old, racist white men who hate women and gays."

"Do they have blue eyes too?"

Sampson raised his arms. "Hey, not my definition. Some of my best friends have blue eyes. Does that make me an Uncle Tom?"

"No, that assignment will go to your brother Thomas."

"You trying to tell me something little sister?" A wolfish grin overtook Sampson's face, and he rocked his arms like cradling a baby.

"Back to this Arthur Constantine, please." Edie unconsciously placed a hand over her stomach.

Sampson stared at the gesture. "Yeah. Beth didn't find any direct connections to the CBT. But another name popped up. Theodore R. Kravitz. He's a dubious businessman with ties to a lot of politicians in Washington. Beth says he's been pulling the nuts on many of the house and senate leaders for as long as anyone remembered. And one of his top ball-busters is Arthur Constantine."

Edie didn't take the bait at Sampson's sexist choice of words and let him continue speaking. "According to Beth, if there are any threads existing between Kravitz and Lucchesi, Constantine's got his hands on the rope. As you might suspect, we didn't find any smoking gun, only several recent communications between Lucchesi and Constantine."

Edie stepped into the kitchen and brought back two more beers. She handed one to her brother and said, "Everything's getting more complicated, but it's finally falling into place. Best case scenario is there's more money behind the local efforts here in New Jersey. Worst case, they're planning to accomplish a lot more than we first thought."

CHAPTER 49

STEVE BLINKED, ADJUSTING HIS EYES to the dim overhead lighting in the cramped interior of the Econoline van. Dominick flipped switches with one hand and cranked open the roof ventilator with the other. Shelves holding specialized electronic gear lined one side. Several bins filled with a variety of not so normal looking sundry equipment hung on the opposite wall.

Steve tried not to bump into Dominick who busily worked at curious looking tasks. "I'm guessing you didn't buy this equipment at your neighborhood Radio Shack like a normal red-blooded American geek. So instead of asking you where you found this stuff, why don't we cut to the chase, and you tell me what it's for and why we're here?"

Steve looked around the cramped interior and pointed his finger toward the ceiling. "And about to sweat our asses off—by the looks of this useless vent in the roof."

"Well, I wouldn't worry about it getting too hot; I understand some thunderstorms are about to—"

"Dominick. If I wanted a weather report, I'd turn on the damn radio. What the hell are we doing in the back of this van, which if I'm not mistaken used to be part of the Final Cut Beauty Supply fleet, judging from the shoddy paint job covering the company logo? But I'm guessing a better choice than commandeering an old garbage truck from the family's waste management company."

"You're right. You should be a detective. I've had the van and the idea for a while, but it wasn't until we visited Uncle Vinnie that—"

"You got thirty seconds to come clean, or I'm turning you over to the waitress down the block."

The first of three flat screen monitors came to life as Dominick talked, his fingers never slowing as they twirled across the equipment.

"Steve. What we're looking at on monitor number one is a house you might find interesting. And stop staring at me that way."

Steve glanced down at his watch and then refocused his gaze on Dominick.

"Okay, okay," Dominick said. "Remember when you described those guys who confronted you at Great Adventure to Uncle Vinnie? Your descriptions were kind of vague, but it got Uncle Vinnie thinking. He did some checking and put a few things together. Back before Uncle Vinnie got hammered by the IRS, FBI, and several other federal acronyms, he, and by that, I mean a good portion of the Casella family, did a lot of work with the unions. They helped each other to keep things lubricated and running smoothly. If you get what I mean. Remember what I told you about how the beauty supply business fit into the greater scheme?"

"Can we go for the shorter version? The one that convinces me why the hell we're here, and I'm not jamming your head through the roof vent?"

"I was about to get to that."

Dominick bobbed his head. "As I explained, Uncle Vinnie is, or I guess you would say was, an attorney. There were these two young guys he worked with from time to time. Uncle Vinnie referred to them as two-bit hoods. That was back then."

Steve shook his head. "Under the circumstances, I'll take that under advisement. Given the source."

"Uncle Vinnie got them out of a couple of tough jams. Bailed one of them out of jail more than once. And this guy, Tony Funetti; he'd done time before working with Uncle Vinnie. Still in his teens when he got nabbed. I guess the other guy, Marty Calebrese; he was a little smarter. In fact, Uncle Vinnie sounded impressed by his intellect. And he had a clean record."

"Sounds like two nice upstanding Irish gentlemen," Steve said.

"What? Ah... where was I? So, later they sort of parted ways with Uncle Vinnie. And the terms weren't so good. Uncle Vinnie recalled they got arrogant, pretending to be real important. They bragged how they were going to make names for themselves with all the big shots in the organization." Dominick paused. "So, here's the thing. Uncle Vinnie was almost positive the one guy you described was Marty Calebrese, the brains of the operation. And listen to this. They called him Marty The Mouth."

Steve smiled and said, "I guess the other guy must be Tony Two-Step?"

"Holy shit. You've heard of him?"

"Just keep talking," Steve shook his head, covering his face.

"Oh, right. Hey. That's why you're the detective."

Dominick tapped his finger on screen number one. "Did I mention this is the house where these two goons live?"

"I'll bet you've been waiting to say 'two goons' ever since we got in this damn van."

Rolling thunder bracketed Steve's words, and the first large and heavy raindrops echoed off the metal roof.

"Steve, if I didn't know better, I'd think you were making fun of me. Remember the Pine Barrens episodes I talked about with Uncle Vinnie? Well, these two goo—I mean these two gentlemen. Well, I did a little checking on my own. That was their trademark. Delivering stiffs to the Pine Barrens. This is a little too much to be a coincidence."

Steve was now alert and staring at the screen, his eyes widening. He ignored the beads of sweat forming on his forehead.

"Nice work, Dominick." No hint of sarcasm in his voice. "Let's take a look at these two goons." He waved his arm around in the close quarters. "So, what's the rest of this gear used for?"

Dominick beamed and resumed working as the storm moved in with a sudden blast of wind, cooling things off.

"The second and third screens give us thermal imaging inside the house. And it appears we got only one heat signature. Can't tell who it is though," Dominick said. "And over here... I need to... there we go."

He cranked up the dials on a piece of equipment underneath a black speaker enclosure, and a belching of static spewed forth.

"What's with the audio? Don't tell me you snuck inside the house and planted microphones?"

"Nope," Dominick replied, "but I did get my hands on these directional mikes. As long as there's a window nearby, we're good to go. Except this rain presents a problem."

The storm masked most of the sounds from inside the house until the torrential rains passed through. When the scattered rain squalls eased up, they finally discerned more distinct audio.

"Guess the TV is on," Steve said. "I'm surprised we're not hearing any Sinatra tunes. Maybe they're not real goons. Or perhaps the younger generation of goons never heard of Frank Sinatra."

Dominick didn't have time to take the bait as the first screen came alive with action. A car pulled up in front of the house. Two girls in clear ponchos hurried through a sudden downpour to the shelter of the covered porch.

Squinting, Steve saw little additional clothing underneath the dripping ponchos. Dominick did his part to zoom in and fine-tune the focus.

The girls disappeared inside the house just as the rain subsided. The TV sound vanished, replaced by giggling voices. Those sounds faded too. Dominick checked the infrared sensors and pointed out movement on the second story. At first, Steve imagined watching a video game with ghostish blobs cavorting on the screen. Dominick readjusted the directional microphones as the blobs converged into one fuzzy, palpitating image. The giggling picked up again, along with tortured breathing and gasping. Steve wasn't sure if he didn't prefer the heavy downpours drowning out these sounds.

"The guy is going to have a heart attack," Steve commented. He could see Dominick lost in an erotic daydream. Steve smacked him on the head.

The last of the storms moved through and the skies cleared, but the air remained cool and crisp as darkness swept over the van. A bright moon rose and provided a backdrop of dim shadows rippling from the quivering tree branches catching the residual post-storm breezes. Steve and Dominick tried shifting positions in the cramped van and, in spite of the cooler air, an increasingly suffocating environment.

Dominick fidgeted with the directional mike controls, trying to adjust the positions as the action shifted. "Jesus Christ, Steve, this guy's got great stamina—they've been at this almost an hour."

Steve tilted his head to one side and said, "Listen a little closer to the background sounds. I hear snoring. I guess they didn't kill him after all. And I believe the ladies are having a little fun on their own. Maybe warming up for their next customer." He patted Dominick on the shoulder. "Why don't you give 'em a call? I'd be happy to wait in the café so you can utilize this van for what you doubtless intended it for in the first place."

By the look on Dominick's face, he'd probably been thinking along those same lines, but he never got the chance to reply. From outside the van, the sounds of a decelerating engine resonated with crying tires as glaring beams of light reflected off the house's windows. On screen number one, a black Cadillac lurched to a stop in the driveway, and the driver's door swung open.

The figure emerged from the car and paused, staring up at one of the second story windows. The man's face, caught in the glow of the porch light, revealed a shaking head and growing scowl. Steve leaned toward the screen as he stared at the image of one of the guys who he'd encountered in Great Adventure's parking lot.

Dominick said, "If I'm not mistaken that's Marty Calebrese. Tony Funetti was always a little heavy. This guy looks fit and trim. And at the moment he also looks pissed off."

Steve regarded the man, watching him pat a hand under his jacket and walk across the lawn, taking the porch steps two at a time. Several moments later the sounds from the black speaker enclosure changed. The giggling turned into startled screeches. The snoring stopped; replaced by loud grunts and curses. Thirty seconds later the two girls erupted from the front door, ponchos fluttering behind them.

"Either they're late for their next appointment, or Marty Calebrese isn't into girls," Steve said in an unnecessarily low voice.

Clear words jumped from the black speaker enclosure. "Tony, if you don't put something over your fat belly and pathetic shriveled up dick, I'll shoot the fucking thing off. Even with my skills it'd be a difficult shot to hit something so small. You got five minutes to get the hell ready and meet me in the car. We've got work to do."

An interior door slammed and within seconds Marty Calebrese stood in the driveway. He lit a cigarette, blew smoke into the moonlit night, and climbed into the driver's seat. Several minutes later, Tony Funetti emerged from the house. Right before the porch light clicked off, Steve picked up a glint of metal while Tony struggled to unsnag his jacket from his shoulder holster. The passenger door hadn't even closed when the Cadillac's tires gripped the tarmac as it reversed down the driveway and sped away. Steve exited the van and watched the taillights fading and disappearing after an abrupt left turn.

Dominick said, "I'd say Tony Two-Step stepped in it this time."

Steve didn't respond as his head spun from trying to process the situation. Dominick yanked at his sleeve, pulling him back in the van.

"Let's see what we need," Dominick said, eyes twinkling behind his glasses.

"Here's a pair of night vision goggles. I'll grab the flashlights and this tool kit." He threw a pair of gloves at Steve. They bounced off his chest.

"Come on. We might not have much time."

Steve stared at the goggles sitting on top of Dominick's head and the toolbox in his hand. "What the hell are you doing?"

"We're checking things out while they're gone."

"Are you out of your mind?"

"What could it hurt? A quick look. Maybe we'll figure out what they're up to."

"Dominick. This is no game. All these toys here are one thing, but breaking and entering is something far more serious. Besides, if we wanted to find out what they were up to, we should've followed the damn Cadillac instead of sitting here arguing about snooping around their house."

Steve chastised himself for not moving on that plan when they still had a chance to catch up with them. Dominick scrambled out the door.

Steve grabbed a flashlight, picked up the gloves from the floor, and tried to keep up. If he couldn't stop Dominick from doing something stupid, he could at least help him out. The idea crossed his mind that it was time to put his attorney friend, Joe Wilton, on speed dial. But he didn't need a lawyer to tell him this was not the best way to handle things. On the other hand, he was concerned they needed answers, and they needed them sooner rather than later. This line kept getting easier and easier to cross, and he was surprised to realize it didn't bother him as much as it should.

They crossed the street and ducked into the shadows without being observed. Scattered clouds floating across the night sky sporadically blocked the moonlight, giving them a false sense of cover. Dominick peered into several windows as they worked their way around to the back of the house. Steve thought that with the night vision goggles, Dominick looked like a character out of a bad science fiction movie. Dominick was digging into his tool kit when Steve tapped him on the shoulder.

"I hope you're not going to try and pick that lock. The house is equipped with a sophisticated alarm system." Steve pointed to the metal alarm box tucked under the eaves above them.

Dominick grimaced as he stuffed his instruments back in the bag. Steve proceeded to walk around the house. He heard Dominick call out in a low voice. Following it to the source, he saw Dominick peeking out the side door of the detached garage.

"Steve, come on. The door wasn't even locked. Hurry it up."

Steve slipped inside the garage and closed the door. Since the garage had no windows, Dominick turned off his night vision goggles, and they both clicked on flashlights. Swinging the lights around the interior of the oversized one-car garage, they exposed various garden tools hanging on one wall and an uncluttered workbench across the back. Layers of dust covered everything, and invisible spider webs tickled their faces as they explored the recesses of the garage. Ancient remnants of grease and motor oil drifted up from the stained and cracking concrete floor.

The garage looked relatively unused and empty—except for the metallic silver Lexus.

The car had been washed and waxed since Steve had seen it fleeing Great Adventure's parking lot. And the entire license plate was now visible. The two numbers he'd memorized from the other night were stamped in the middle of the plate.

"The car's not locked either. Why would they be so careless?" Dominick asked.

Steve shrugged. "Marty Calebrese looked to be in a real hurry, and Tony Funetti barely got his pants on."

He recalled they also had their guns and again regretted not moving fast enough to follow them.

After they gave the car's interior a once over, Dominick opened up the glove box. Finding nothing of interest, he activated the security switch and popped the trunk open by leaning over to the driver's side and hitting the valet button. Steve looked at him inquisitively but said nothing as he headed to the back of the vehicle.

The trunk looked clean and almost empty. In the netted side pocket over the wheel well, Steve spotted a small leather case tucked inside. With gloved hands he lifted it into the center of the trunk and placed it on top of the imprinted Lexus logo on the carpeted floor covering. Dominick came up behind him and focused his flashlight on the interior of the case as Steve opened the top; being careful not to disturb its contents.

The blood drained from Steve's face. He snapped it closed and returned it to the netted compartment. He turned so rapidly he almost knocked Dominick on his ass.

"We need to get the hell out of here. Now!" Steve said. "Close this thing up. Don't disturb anything else."

As Steve said this, he tried to work out a way to deal with what he found and avoid any further compromising of the evidence. If that was even possible.

Chapter 50

On the quiet, deserted street, Steve stared at the Econoline van disappearing around the corner. He looked toward Edie's condo, noticing the glowing light from her laptop, shadowed by movements behind the lacy curtains. He expected the sun to peek up over the nearby rooftops long before he and Edie sorted through the latest activities. This was getting to be an unsettling habit.

While in the van with Dominick, Steve had sent Edie several text messages to let her know he'd be late. He gave no details as to what they were up to, nor had he texted her after finding the leather case in the trunk of the Lexus.

Edie's eyebrows arched as Steve closed the condo door and walked over to her desk.

"You sneak home in the middle of the night after dining in one of Newark's finest hot dog establishments and you don't bring me flowers?"

Steve gave her a brief kiss and said, "I suppose if Dominick hadn't cleaned out his van so thoroughly, I could've grabbed you a bottle of hair dye or bleach or whatever product would work. Did I ever mention being partial to blondes? How about a nice shade of Champagne blonde? A perfect fit for your popular segments on FOX News. Help you blend in."

Before Edie answered, Steve added, "Or even better, what if I told you who framed your brother?"

Edie turned to face Steve. "Are you talking about…." She glanced down at her notes. "Marty Calebrese and Tony Funetti?"

Steve bit his lower lip and nodded, wondering why Edie's words didn't surprise him. "Would you prefer the long-stemmed roses?"

"I changed my mind. I'm craving one of those famous boiled-in-oil hot dogs instead. Is that what you're carrying in that greasy looking box?"

"Not unless you want to eat the remains of my cheesy fries, which have been sitting in Dominick's hot van all evening. I saved these for Amber."

"Don't you dare give that crap to her."

Steve sighed, walking into the kitchen. The lid of the garbage can slapped down. Steve returned and sat on the sofa. Edie cozied up at his side. Although he wanted to concentrate on the girl seated next to him, his eyes locked onto the papers spread across the coffee table. Instead of reaching around Edie for a needed embrace, his arm swung over to the coffee table and picked up the top sheet. The official-looking emblem on the upper left side of the paper made his hand tremble. He was about to ask her she got her hands on documents from this clandestine federal agency when he focused on another sheet of paper. A collection of Tony Funetti's mug shots stared back at him.

"Edie. Please tell me you printed these out from the latest version of Facebook?"

After propping herself up with one of the fluffy pillows, Edie snuggled closer and placed an arm around Steve.

"Well, I have been getting pointers from one of the computer geeks who works for Mike Finley. And somehow, he also forgot to cover several password links on his desk when he left the room to bring me coffee and a chocolate donut covered with scrumptious little nutty things."

"If he'd brought you a hot dog, I'd be jealous. But let me see if I got this straight," he said, while thinking he probably didn't want to understand several parts of this story.

"You're saying the vice president's security chief, Mike Finley, one of the top agents in the secret service, DHS, or whoever he claims to be working for these days, is a part of… of…." Steve couldn't finish the sentence.

"Just because Tyler's keeping a low profile, doesn't mean he's not providing the necessary support tools," Edie said, pausing. "I'll start up the large coffee pot and thaw out the bagels. I doubt we'll be going to sleep anytime soon."

Steve looked at the open bedroom door. He saw Amber spread across the middle of the fluffy blue comforter. He'd had other things on his mind for Edie's king-sized bed. After a quick greeting when Steve got home, Amber headed right for the bedroom. Probably knew exactly what Steve had in mind. She had even turned her nose at the greasy box in his hands. Before he returned his attention to what Edie was doing in the kitchen, Steve took notice of several distinct chuffing sounds coming from the bedroom.

As Steve and Edie compared notes, they learned more about the backgrounds of Marty Calebrese and Tony Funetti; the two thugs who appeared at the center of all the problems they faced. The things Dominick had related to Steve complemented what Edie had pieced together through a variety of restricted government databases. Steve came down with a bad case of heartburn to show for all his efforts.

Tony Funetti's early background painted a picture of a hapless bully. A school dropout, he was always in trouble and had served jail time on two occasions for minor offenses. He'd been arrested a number of times after his earlier convictions, but none of the subsequent charges ever stuck.

Tony, with the help of his new friends in the CBT, procured a competent attorney. Vinnie Casella. Things transformed when Tony teamed up with Marty Calebrese and eventually led to an obvious rift with the Casella family.

While reviewing Marty Calebrese's background, they found a more cunning and potentially violent opponent. His IQ scored higher than his ethical sensibilities. He possessed a keen understanding of computers and other electronic devices. His marksmanship abilities meant that if he had you in his sights, your survival chances were non-existent. Edie's highlighter pen marked the more troubling aspects of his brief stint as an Army Ranger and subsequent early career choices.

Steve pointed at another yellow highlighted section and looked up at Edie. "This helps explain a few things."

Smiling, Edie said, "I thought you'd find that interesting. I considered highlighting it in red so you wouldn't miss it, but I guess that wasn't necessary."

"So, Marty washed out of three different fire academies," Steve said, "and all for the same reason. I'd attest to the fact that a lack of theoretical and technical understanding wasn't high on the list. Took him a while, but he finally got to use his knowledge and put together that little firebox timing device. It was his troublesome attitude and aggressive tendencies that got him kicked out. Exactly the right qualities for his current work with the CBT."

All this fit with the concept of Marty Calebrese and Tony Funetti being the heavies for the more questionable tactics of the union. They had obvious strong ties with the local union leader, Al Rozano. And although the links were more tenuous and difficult to substantiate, Edie disliked what she saw regarding Rozano's connections in D.C. The recent revelations from Sampson had added several more layers to the conspiratorial nature of their problems.

Edie told Steve about the two union guys hanging around the Kearny GMHC right before the so-called accident resulting in Andrew MacAteer's death. She had talked to several employees, and the descriptions she'd gotten matched Tony Funetti and Marty Calebrese. If Edie had asked Amber, she too could have confirmed their presence. She planned to dig into Chuck Kolinsky's background and find out if he had any union ties.

A little past dawn, Edie's phone rang.

CHAPTER 51

STEVE WATCHED EDIE'S FACE PALE, seeing the death grip she held on the phone.

"Slow down. Take it easy," Edie said.

Edie paced about the room, one hand clasped and buried in her hair. "Wait, wait. Let me put you on speaker phone so Steve can hear this."

Kristie Pauling's voice crackled from the tiny speaker. "Thomas drove to a little all-night gas station store on the county road. About an hour ago. He's not answering his cell phone." She paused and swallowed hard. "The bodies of two US marshals have been found about ten miles further down the road from the gas station. The GPS locator they'd attached to Thomas's ankle was on the ground next to the bodies. It'd been cut off."

"Did Thomas notify the authorities when he left the house?" Edie asked.

"No. He didn't need to. The store is less than five miles from here. He's only required to notify them on anything beyond the five-mile limit. He must've gone outside the zone, and that triggered their response. But Edie. There's no way Thomas would've shot those officers."

There was silence and then Kristie's hollow voice resumed. "Why would he? He's not a cold-blooded killer. None of this makes any sense. He's been miserable about Leilah's death but believed his name would be cleared."

They listened to muffled sobs pouring from the phone. "Edie... after we met at the retreat... it was all coming together... related to the conflicts at our stores."

Steve asked, "Did he say anything else before he left?"

"We'd been talking about this afternoon's rally after the dedication ceremonies. I guess he was still uncomfortable about standing next to me and Tyler, but he wanted to do whatever he could to help. Said he needed to get out and breathe some fresh air to clear his head. Oh my God! I shouldn't have pressured him so much. He's always holding things inside. Thomas was so broken up about Leilah. Maybe he still believes he's responsible because he was the target. And not Leilah. Oh my God, Edie. It wasn't even his fault. My family— no, I was the real target. They used that poor girl and Thomas to get to me."

Edie closed her eyes and tilted her head back. "Kristie, listen. Let Steve and I work on something. We need to follow up on a couple of ideas." She let out a deep breath. "Have you talked to Tyler?"

"Tyler wants everything to go on as planned. He's sending a car. We were supposed to meet up with Marine Two at Newark Airport and all fly to the site of the rally. Tyler's insisting that I still go. He said we can talk things out on the way. He's hoping to have more information by then so he can make a public statement. Try and stay ahead of the media. Oh God, Edie. What the hell's going to happen? Where could Thomas be?"

CHAPTER 52

EDIE ENDED THE PHONE CALL from Kristie Pauling. She and Steve had barely started to discuss their options when Edie's phone rang again. This call left her looking more frantic than Kristie's. Steve had seen the gamut of emotions course over Edie's face before, but her current expression had him scared out of his mind. Her voice sounded vacant as she relayed the conversation to him.

Steve shook his head, slamming his fist on the table. "Edie, you can't be serious. Why the hell would Thomas want *him* involved? Do you honestly believe this moron? And by the way, I don't give a damn if that's racially insensitive."

Edie ran shaky fingers through her hair. "Steve. I don't know what to believe. I've never trusted Carter—and I refuse to call him reverend—to do anything not in his own best interests. It pissed me off when he used Leilah Harris's disappearance and death as a political platform. At least he got what he deserved when that imam sideswiped his press conference."

Edie stopped for a moment and slowly composed her next words.

"There is one other thing I need to tell you about Carter." She looked straight into Steve's eyes. "And with his twisted egotistical mind, I can't be sure how this plays into what's happening."

By the time she finished her story about running into Reverend Jefferson B. Carter and Leilah Harris's father outside the broadcast studio, her body shook and she continued rubbing her hands roughly through her hair.

Steve closed his arms around Edie, absorbing the tension surging through her. He had no idea what Carter could be up to, let alone why Edie's brother would have involved him in the first place. He sure as hell didn't trust what he'd just heard.

"Edie, I don't understand. Why didn't Thomas talk to you directly? Why Carter?"

"Carter said Thomas was on the brink of a complete breakdown. He had a gun and vowed to kill both of them if Carter didn't make the call. And if I didn't do as he said and come to him in the next two hours, he'd pull the trigger on himself anyway. He specifically told me not to tell Kristie or Tyler about any of this. The rally has to go on as planned, or he would kill himself before I got there."

"Again. How is Carter involved? You think he contacted your brother after the confrontation you had with him last night?"

Edie's lips trembled. "Look. None of this makes sense, but if it's for real, I'm sure I can talk Thomas out of it. If there's even the slightest chance to save him, I gotta try. And if Carter's doing this to get back at me— that makes it even worse. There's no way I'm sitting this out."

Steve held her tighter, thinking that's what the bastard probably counted on. "Then we better grab Amber and get going. What about calling in back-up?"

She exhaled and pulled away. Her shoulders slumped. "I didn't mention this, but Carter suggested you might want to join me. Actually, it was more than a request. But he also insisted if there's any evidence that we're bringing in reinforcements, Thomas wouldn't hesitate to pull the trigger. Carter said once we show up, Thomas told him he'd be free to leave. Thomas wants to talk to the two of us alone."

Her face contorted and she grabbed Steve's hand. "Besides, Steve—there are two dead US marshals. And every law enforcement authority in the state is on a manhunt for my brother. They're convinced he killed those cops. You think they'll hesitate to shoot first?"

Her body slackened and shrunk as Steve looked on. She took a step back but stared into his eyes. He imagined a helpless child standing lost and afraid.

Edie's next words were quiet and pleading. "We've come a long way since Rosa Parks, but I'm not sure what the hell would happen if a bunch of pumped-up cops came face-to-face with an African American male who's a suspected cop killer—with a gun in his hand. They'd probably do the right thing—that's what my head tells me—but I'm not about to gamble with Thomas's life."

Steve had no answer. He looked at Edie and his heart broke knowing he'd seen a part of her he'd never fully grasp. Something he couldn't fix. He nodded in agreement, but nothing changed his mind that listening to Reverend Jefferson B. Carter was one bad idea.

"Okay, we do it alone."

CHAPTER 53

TERROR ATTACKS IN THE UNITED STATES are nothing new. They didn't start with Al Qaeda or any other radical Islamic terrorist groups. Our nation faced terrorist attacks well before World War I, but certain activities during that particular struggle are important to current events.

Before the United States entered World War I, it represented itself as a neutral nation in the conflict. However, the Germans understood we were supplying the allies with the necessary tools of war. Fuel and munitions held in warehouses and ships in key ports along the New York Harbor awaited export. From 1914, until the time the United States entered the war, almost four years later, numerous acts of sabotage were perpetrated on our nation under the covert direction of German intelligence operations. More than half of the targeted sites hit by the German agents during that period were located in the New York area.

One of the most devastating attacks executed by the Germans occurred during the early morning hours in late July of 1916: the Black Tom explosion, set in a warehouse location and a ship docked at a pier across the narrow expanse of water from the Statue of Liberty. A series of violent explosions thundered across the harbor, shattering windows in both New York and New Jersey, thrusting shrapnel over a widespread area.

The Statue of Liberty was closed after sustaining minor damage as a result of the blasts. Most of the damage was confined to the torch-bearing arm of the statue. Since that day, public access to the arm and the torch's platform has been prohibited.

* * * * * *

Thomas Pauling shot back, "You can kill me right now because I'll never do what you want."

He looked around the cramped quarters where he'd been dumped. Hands and feet wrapped with duct tape. Thomas felt his fingers and toes going numb. Everything had happened so damn fast. All a blur since he'd walked out of the minimart and gotten into his car.

Someone concealed in the back seat stuck a gun to his head. Gave him directions where to drive. Then those two federal officers, US Marshals, came out of nowhere—lights flashing, sirens screaming. The guy with the gun to his head ordered Thomas to pull over. What the hell was going on? How did the feds turn up so fast?

Thomas realized they must've picked up the warning from the GPS signal—that he'd violated the conditions of his bail arrangements. The guy in the back seat told him what to say. If he didn't, the gun concealed under the coat on his lap was pointed right at Thomas's spine.

Two US marshals walked over to the car. No reason to be concerned. He'd tell them he made a wrong turn. Didn't know he'd gone beyond the five-mile limit. Like the gunman said to do. A simple mistake.

And there was no way to warn them.

Then as one officer leaned over to look into the car....

Another vehicle came out of nowhere, careening around the corner. Thomas heard the crying tires. A semi-automatic pistol held in the driver's hand spit rounds at the officer standing back from Thomas's car. He went down quick and hard. The gunman behind Thomas pulled his weapon up when the officer leaning in the car spun around to the sound of the shots. Two slugs hit him in the back of the head. Thomas was surprised when instead of falling forward, the officer kicked backward and slammed against his door. Trails of blood traced the dead officer's descent to the ground. They never had a chance to draw their weapons.

It was an execution.

Before knocked unconscious, Thomas remembered the two thugs yelling at each other. The guy who'd driven up shooting yanked him from the car, pushing the dead officer's body out of the way. They shoved Thomas around, tearing at his clothes and going through his pockets. He watched his phone crash to the ground and shatter. They found his ankle bracelet and cut it off; tossing it aside.

How long ago did all that happen? And where the hell was he now? Earlier, as he floated in and out of consciousness, he had sensed loud engine noises and vibrations, but no jarring bumps or anything like riding in a car. Everything kept shifting around and swaying underneath him.

Marty Calebrese looked at Thomas with a menacing smile. "Why don't you shut the hell up. We don't need you to call your damn sister anymore. If my asshole partner didn't break your phone, we could've texted the bitch. She's a suspicious little jerk, so she probably wouldn't read any messages from an unknown number."

Marty walked over, pulling a knife from an ankle sheath with the hand not holding the pistol against Thomas's head. He sliced off the duct tape securing Thomas's hands and feet.

"But not to worry, Tony's persuaded a more willing pawn to get things rolling. Somebody who convinced your meddling little sister you were in trouble and needed her help. You never can tell when assholes like that will become useful. I keep telling Tony. Networking is important."

Marty's smile turned into a sharp laugh. "No matter which way you look at the situation, I guess you do need help. Wouldn't you say, Pauling?"

He didn't wait for an answer. "We're a little behind schedule because of your lack of cooperation, but Tony just called and everything's set. After he's taken care of a few little details, he'll be back to help finish up."

Marty stepped back and pointed his pistol toward the doorway. Thomas hesitated at the sight of two bodies stacked in the far corner of the room.

"A little collateral damage," Marty said. He shoved Thomas Pauling and directed him to climb.

Thomas looked up at the narrow spiral staircase and the scaffolding covering large sections of the cavity. What in the hell were they doing here? His gut clenched as his mind processed and projected the consequences.

CHAPTER 54

AFTER FOLLOWING THE DICTATED ROUTE, Steve parked the Durango at Liberty State Park. They could see the next ferry getting ready to depart. Edie ran over to buy the tickets while Steve attached Amber's harness and service jacket. Steve had the appropriate credentials to back it up, and he didn't want any delays about bringing a dog on board make them miss the ferry. Steve knew Edie had her own way of dealing with a different federal restriction. Asking for forgiveness was always better than trying to gain permission.

Due to the timing of the vice president's arrival and appearance, the scheduled ferry stops at Ellis Island were canceled until Marine Two left the island. Thus, the ferry they boarded headed directly to the Statue of Liberty, on Liberty Island.

Critical renovations to the Statue of Liberty had been completed several years ago but recent safety concerns were raised when authorities discovered a considerable portion of the work involved substandard materials and the contractors had bypassed a number of code provisions. Inspectors and union officials were indicted after several whistleblowers came forward. This had come in spite of the grave danger to any individual trying to expose the corruption. Several suspicious deaths occurred during and after the work on the statue had been completed. Those deaths were now being investigated, and the people who had come forward with the accusations against the union leaders had been taken into protective custody.

For the last three months, and for at least the next six months to follow, access to the interior of the Statue of

Liberty would be prohibited as the corrective work proceeded.

Obeying Reverend Carter's instructions, Steve and Edie walked around to the south side of the pedestal and used the park service maintenance entrance on the extreme left at the bottom of the ramp. Carter had given Edie the access codes to gain entry. Steve's head ached trying to quiet the alarm bells racking through his brain. As the green light flashed and they pushed open the door, Steve registered the low distant thumping sound of approaching helicopters. Checking the time, he knew it was Marine Two and its squadron carrying Vice President Tyler Griffin and Kristie Pauling to the ceremony and rally on Ellis Island. He wondered how they would handle the maelstrom of questions from the media. On their drive to Liberty Park, they listened to the first breaking stories regarding the ambushed US marshals and the search for the fugitive, Thomas Pauling. They had all but run out of time.

The heavy door clicked shut and their eyes adjusted to the dim lighting.

Steve strained to hold on to the lead as Amber reacted with a growling lunge. His eyes riveted on two bodies heaped in the far corner of the room, but Amber's escalating reaction appeared directed at something else.

A figure emerged from the dark shadows inside a caged storage area. An ominous voice followed. "Won't do you a damn bit of good to let go of the dog, Casella. As you can see, it's not gonna be any threat to me. And I'd have to shoot it. Marty's exact orders. He's still a little pissed off with your dog's antics from the other night. Me, I'd rather not kill a dog."

After staring at the two bodies, Edie responded. "You didn't have any problem killing these park service security guards. Plus, I'm guessing those two US marshals. Or even better, causing the death of a helpless, handicapped boy. And what about killing Leilah Harris and discarding her body in the Pine Barrens? Yeah, you're a real saint... aren't you, Mr. Two-Step? And where the hell is my brother?"

Steve could see the realization sprout on Edie's face as she grasped the situation.

Tony Funetti smiled. "Too many questions. Marty said you were a little bitch. You do make a few good points but, in our defense, you shouldn't be mourning those two gentlemen in the corner. They were paid well for their cooperation. Too bad they were expendable. So listen up. First, Pauling. Toss your purse across the room.

"NOW!"

Edie complied, giving Steve a helpless look.

"Casella. Keeping your hands where I can see them; I want you to take your dog and put it into the electrical closet over there and close the door. Use your best command to settle the dog down. That's for its own good. If Marty hears the dog barking, he'll shoot both me and the dog."

Steve followed Tony's commands, closing Amber in the closet after quieting her down.

"Okay, Casella," Tony said as he opened the fence gate and stepped forward out of the caged enclosure. His handgun trained on the couple. "Move closer to your girlfriend. Now, nice and slow, empty your pockets. Both of you. Good. Pull up your pants legs. Good. Lift up your shirts and turn around."

Tony shook his head. "Not very well prepared. Are we now?" He winked at Edie. "Nice tits. I understand some girls even try to hide weapons up there."

Steve gave Edie a quick glance.

"What's the matter?" Tony said. "Am I boring you? Too bad. It's time to go." He smiled. "By the way, I wasn't sure our favorite reverend could convince you to follow his instructions. Me? I never considered him trustworthy. More of a blowhard who did anything to accomplish what he wanted. Does that make me a racist? Oh well." He looked straight at Edie with that last remark. "Now you, Pauling, you're an annoying self-righteous bitch. As are all the talking heads on TV with their fake blond hair. At least you're not a blonde. Haven't stooped that low yet?"

Steve stole another quick glance at Edie.

Pointing with his gun, Tony said, "Casella, you take the lead. Through the door and up the stairs. Remember I'll be right behind your girlfriend. You wouldn't want me to put a bullet through her ass before she gets to say goodbye to her brother."

Edie spun to face Tony. He smirked. "That's right. We're all going on a private tour right up Miss Liberty's arm. The rest of the group is waiting on the torch platform. Oh. And by the way, in case you're wondering? The good reverend won't be there to greet you. He won't be speaking to anyone else ever again. Too bad he didn't live long enough to become our first African American reverend to be president of these United States. Couldn't resist feeding his tongue to what's left of the fish population in the Hudson River. Would've thrown in the rest of the body, but the river's polluted enough."

As they climbed up the stairs and then onto the narrow, steep ladder to the torch platform, Tony never spoke another word. Steve listened to his labored breathing and prayed he'd suffer a heart attack. At the top, Marty Calebrese greeted them with a gun to their faces. Thomas Pauling's cuffed hands were secured to the railing.

CHAPTER 55

FROM THE PLATFORM, STEVE GLANCED skyward at the sound of the oncoming helicopters as they turned, starting their approach and descent to nearby Ellis Island. He recognized the modified Sikorsky S-92, the latest iteration of Marine Two. Originally designed for search and rescue operations and for use by the oil and gas industries, it now carried the vice president and his sister. Two Blackhawk tracker helicopters flanked Marine Two. The starboard Blackhawk slowed, and the gap in the formation expanded.

"Good job, Tony," Marty Calebrese said, taking several steps back from the open doorway leading down the arm on the Statue of Liberty. "It's getting cozy up here, but it's almost showtime. Don't bother cuffing these two. Just keep an eye on them while I set the stage for what will look like Thomas Pauling's last desperate act."

"You're a goddamned lunatic," Thomas spit out, struggling against the shackles restraining him to the outer railing.

Tony Funetti signaled for Steve and Edie to sit down beside Thomas. He leaned back against the wall of the central shaft below the torch, his head momentarily craning toward Ellis Island.

Steve noted the tripod and the twenty-inch barreled SR25 fitted with a maximum-range tactical scope set up by the railing. He recalled the Navy SEALs had employed this same firearm for more than a decade. Edie still had her dad's old rifle, a similarly set up version, and on several occasions, he had joined her at an outdoor range to shoot practice rounds with it.

Marty settled in behind the tripod and gripped the sniper rifle.

"A real tragic situation," he said, glancing over his shoulder, hands still clasping the rifle. "Thomas Pauling, the distraught and troubled accused rapist and killer, who has already gunned down two US marshals, a couple of park service guys, and a civil rights activist—in a desperate rage, shoots the vice president and his own wife."

Marty continued to talk, but he no longer looked at the people on the platform.

"It's fortunate Thomas Pauling comes from a family priding itself on firearms proficiency." He chuckled. "And then the troubled man grabs a handgun and fires at his sister and her boyfriend, killing them both before turning the gun on himself, and with a final bullet—ends the madness."

The rest of the world no longer existed for Marty Calebrese.

He took several deep breaths and lined himself up behind the scope on the SR25, waiting for his targets. There was only the narrow trajectory from the steel-railed torch platform on the Statue of Liberty to the designated landing spot on the open field at the southern tip of Ellis Island. In the peripheral vision of his left eye, he noted Marine Two flare out as it glided onto the precise laser-guided landing spot. Swirls of dust shrouded the immediate landscape.

The pneumatic shock absorbers shifted slightly as the landing struts kissed the ground. The blades spun down, allowing the buffeted air to clear. Marty waited, and at last the side door slid open and the stairs dropped down. If the angle and positions were ideal, he might be lucky enough to hit both targets with a single shot. But he was prepared to take them out individually. The primary target was the vice president. Pauling's wife would be his bonus shot.

As they came into view, Marty moved his finger from its indexed position to the trigger. The open doorway of the helicopter momentarily framed both targets. Once their feet hit the ground, he would pull the trigger. The distance was close to the limits of his ability, but the weather conditions had been cooperative. Marty was confident he would not miss.

Steve racked his brain to come up with a plan.

He earlier heard one of the tracker Blackhawks break formation but could no longer locate its position. Although Tony kept his handgun trained on Steve and Edie, he appeared mesmerized by the vice president's helicopter landing on Ellis Island.

Steve watched Tony's eyes flick back and forth, his attention torn between Marty's targets and his responsibility to keep the prisoners in check. The exit door to the statue's arm was behind Tony. Tony edged a little further around the central shaft, probably trying for a better view of Ellis Island.

Waxing and waning engine noises reverberated around the torch platform. Steve picked up another sound; behind Tony's position. It was almost, but not completely obliterated by the fluctuating din of the helicopters. Steve focused his attention on the familiar rasping and snarling coming from the open doorway.

The slight hand signal went unseen by everyone on the platform, but not to the white German Shepherd who responded instantly by springing through the opening. Amber drove Tony onto the metal floor, his gun tumbling through the steel railing and dropping three hundred feet to the ground.

Fixated on Marty's trigger finger, Steve watched it slowly squeeze back.

Steve and Edie both leapt at Marty.

Steve hurtled his body against the tripod at the moment Marty fired, catching the brunt of the discharging projectile's concussive forces in his right ear. His head crashed into the steel railing, stunning his senses.

Edie latched onto Marty's back and shoulders. Her strength and weight combined presented no major hindrance. He lifted himself up and tore at the determined female clutching at his neck. With an agonizing grunt, he extricated himself from her wriggling arms, catapulting her on top of the railing.

The leverage and momentum flipped Edie over the side.

Shaking off the downward spiral into unconsciousness, Steve struggled to his feet and rammed his battered head into Marty's side. The jolt stopped Marty from prying Edie's fingers off the bottom of the latticework on the outside of the railing. The inertia thrust Marty tumbling back.

Amber used her powerful jaws to keep Tony pinned to the ground. He stretched a bloody arm to his calf and pulled a hidden knife from its sheath.

Tony no longer looked concerned about killing the dog.

Amber pivoted her body away from the gleaming object. She clamped her jaws onto the man's wrist, neutralizing the threat. Tony's body slackened. Amber pressed her front paws on his chest and anchored widened jaws against his neck. She held the position, filling Tony's ears with low growls until he lost consciousness.

Steve stretched over the railing and locked a hand around Edie's arm as she slipped free of the latticework. Her legs flailed as Steve clutched the slippery arm, trying to coax her to reach up and grab his other hand.

Steve sensed a movement behind him, but his entire focus remained on Edie. Marty had recovered and inched forward. Reaching under his jacket, he chambered a round in his Glock and raised it into position, sighting in on his target.

Two shots rang out.

Blood and brain matter splashed across the back of Steve's head. Edie's other hand clasped onto his wrist as his body arched backward and his lungs contracted with an agonizing groan. Edie's legs slapped over the top of the railing, her body crashing into Steve.

His body twisted and he landed face down on the unforgiving metal floor.

Edie's eyes widened and a scream stuck in her throat. She stared at Steve's still figure.

She gaped at the blood and flesh oozing down the back of his head and neck. A shriek surfaced as Edie struggled to turn him over.

Amber released her grip on Tony's flaccid body and scooched over to Steve, licking his face.

That was when Edie saw Marty Calebrese leaning crookedly against the railing. She guessed it was Marty. He no longer had a face, and he was missing a good portion of his skull. Startled, she looked around, feeling the air pounding, the tiny platform vibrating. She saw nothing but heard the sound of chopper blades spinning down.

Edie looked over at her brother shackled to the railing. He had watched the entire drama unfold. Edie saw the fear in his eyes as he stared at the distant turmoil on Ellis Island.

Tony Funetti's body lay motionless on the platform.

In response to Amber's licking, Steve's eyes fluttered open. "Closed doors… never a problem for you, Amber… are they?"

He looked at Edie. "Not so easy holding on to you. Must be all that greasy food you've been—"

Deciding on whether she should punch him or kiss him, Edie settled on a tight embrace against his chest as Amber continued cleaning Marty Calebrese's brains and blood off Steve's head.

From behind them came an out-of-breath sounding voice. "Jesus… Christ. Didn't anybody tell you… the interior of the Statue of Liberty… is closed for repairs? And you guys are… trespassing on federal property. Do you have any idea… what the penalty is for that?"

Edie turned and recognition spread across her sweat and tear drenched face.

Agent Mike Finley gave them the thumbs up as he edged onto the narrow platform.

"Everybody on Marine Two is fine. The shot went wide. When we were making our descent, I caught a glint.

Didn't seem right. So we dropped back to take a look. We just got into position near the statue when I saw the muzzle blast. Guess we were a tad bit too late. But I succeeded in wiping the smile off that asshole's face before he put a slug in your head, Steve."

Steve hefted himself up on his elbows. He glanced at the remains of Marty Calebrese and then back at Mike Finley. "Next time don't stop for coffee first. But you're forgiven, Mike. Especially after those shots you took. So maybe we shouldn't quibble about a few seconds. Let's consider you right on time."

Steve paused, wincing. "Hey? Can you believe it? That guy you shot? He didn't like the Casella family."

Finley shrugged. "Imagine how he'd feel if he got to know you. But guys—we need to go. That is if you want a lift out of here."

As he said this, another agent burst through the doorway and got to work in the cramped space. Back on the ground, Liberty Island was already being cleared of tourists who'd soon be replaced by the investigative teams swarming to the scene.

Edie helped Steve to his feet and gave him a nudge. "Hey. You saying I'm fat? At least I can climb down the ladder. But Amber, although she learned to climb up? I doubt she can get back down on her own."

Edie bent over and patted Amber's stomach. "So good luck, Mr. Firefighter. Let's see you in action."

CHAPTER 56

LESS THAN A MILE TO the north on Ellis Island, a team of determined secret service agents thrust Vice President Tyler Griffin and his sister back inside Marine Two. This was against his insistence on continuing the final leg of the journey to address the attendees of the reopening ceremonies for the immigration museum.

Due to the damages to the island's infrastructure caused by Hurricane Sandy, Ellis Island had been closed to the public until today. The secret service agents now confronted a storm of similar proportions in the name of Tyler Griffin. After pointing his sister back up the stairs to Marine Two, the vice president attempted to disregard his secret service agents' mandate to sequester him on board and cancel his engagement. He never got the chance to reconsider his decision. Two motivated agents physically dragged Tyler Griffin up the stairs and through the door.

None of the secret service detail sustained any injuries; the vice president suffered a prominent bruise on the left side of his forehead while being deposited back inside Marine Two.

In the aftermath, those standard evacuation procedures would undergo careful scrutiny by the Monday morning quarterbacking fed by the media's twenty-four-hour news cycle.

* * * * * *

Back on Liberty Island, the Blackhawk's pilot shouted, "Finley, I want you and your two new passengers buckled up. They're moving Marine Two out. Show's over for today. We're getting our boy out of here. Tracker two's taking the east flank. You guys better hurry,

I gotta move into position. We're widening the outer perimeters for Marine Two until the fighter jet escorts show up."

The co-pilot swung his head around to address Steve. "And mister, you need to strap that dog into one of those seats. You can clip the snaps right onto the harness. Can't have the dog flying through the cabin if we need to make any abrupt maneuvers."

They were still buckling up when the craft shuddered and rocketed into the air—jarring its occupants down into their seats. The heavy Blackhawk made a half circle around the Statue of Liberty before it vectored a path to the west of Ellis Island as Marine Two pulled back the stairs and throttled up its engines.

Mike Finley indicated for Steve and Edie to don the wireless headset communicators hanging above them, doing so himself. Before saying anything, Finley topped off the magazine in his rifle and placed it back in the rack next to the sniper platform. Coincidentally, it was the military version of the same SR25 sniper rifle Marty Calebrese used in his attempt to assassinate the vice president.

Edie watched Steve give Finley a look. "Hey," Finley said, smiling. "Italians aren't the only ones who make good snipers. The Irish have been known to produce some credible marksmen."

Adjusting the mike on his headset, Steve asked, "Didn't it take you two shots?"

"The second one was meant as a goodbye kiss."

Edie had been silent since she'd climbed down to the base of the pyramid and retrieved her purse. She had stoically stood by as the authorities prepared to whisk away the injured and dead assailants, along with her brother—technically still a bail jumper and now wanted for questioning in the deaths of two US marshals. The authorities denied her request to accompany them. Before catching up with Steve and Finley and boarding the agent's helicopter, they gave her a moment to hug Thomas.

On board the Blackhawk, she at last found her voice, but it came out so low, the noisy environment masked her words. Mike Finley gave her a sign to repeat it.

Clearing her throat, in a stronger voice, Edie said, "Do you really think this was their best shot?"

Steve shrugged. "After all, it was just a bunch of union grunts and wise guys doing their thing. Right?"

Edie didn't buy Steve's attempt to lighten the moment.

With a serious expression, Edie stared at him. Back on the platform she'd felt an overwhelming wave of relief at the sight of Marty Calebrese's dead body and Tony Funetti incapacitated by Amber. It was over. Her brother and everyone else at risk were safe. She knew enough evidence existed to steer the authorities in the right direction and eventually exonerate Thomas.

But as the euphoria subsided, a flood of unwanted shadows filled the voids. Like flipping the pages of a book, Edie recalled the conversation she had last night with her other brother, Sampson, and the threads of information she'd been wading through while examining her own sources. A terrible nagging suspicion pushed her deeper into her seat than the gravity-defying liftoff.

Using her headset and mike to communicate in this noisy environment gave Edie a surreal sensation. "Guys, listen-up here. From what Sampson and I've dug up, there's way more power and money behind this operation. This goes deeper than what we've seen. Mike. You gotta make sure the feds focus on D.C. See who's sleeping with whom on this thing. What we've unraveled so far barely scratches the surface. There's no way these guys would only rely on a couple of two-bit wannabe mafia hoods. No offense, Steve."

Steve appeared lost in his own world, but Edie imagined the wheels turning as his brain tried to catch up with her logic. He was staring out the port window when his eyes bulged. He clutched the back of Finley's seat and gestured for him to take a look at something erupting from the rear deck of a large yacht cruising below in the Hudson River.

Finley grabbed his binoculars. It took only a moment for him to react.

"Holy shit!"

Finley unbuckled the harness and in one fluid motion strapped himself onto the sniper platform while grabbing the SR25 out of the rack.

"Those motherfuckers launched a Switchblade," Finley shouted into his mike. "That's a tube-launched suicide drone meant to explode on impact. They're flying it right above the water where it's all but invisible."

Finley issued instructions to the pilot. Once on course he lined up the shot. "Keep it steady, I've just about... got it...."

Finley, focused on his target, didn't see it coming. Edie did, but a second too late.

The co-pilot, silent throughout most of the exchanges of the last several minutes, released his harness and swung around with his 9mm pistol. He fired at Finley. Edie drew the concealed handgun from her purse and placed two rounds into the co-pilot, but not before he turned the gun on her and returned fire.

A round hit Edie as the co-pilot slumped forward in his seat; dead from a slug through the heart.

Amber, barking and straining against the harness secured to her seat, couldn't break free. Steve scrambled to check on Finley's condition.

"There's a pulse, but it's rapid and weak." He dragged the inert body back into the cabin and looked over at Edie. He now grasped that she had also been hit. The handgun, while still trained on the pilot started to shake. Her other hand gripped her shoulder.

Blood oozed between her fingers.

"How bad?" Steve's voice cracked as he knelt beside Edie.

"It's only a nick, but my arm's getting numb. What do we do about this other guy?"

The pilot answered for her. "Hey, everybody relax. We don't have a lot of choices here. We gotta do this fast. I am *NOT* with the guy you just shot. You can believe that or not. So you decide for yourself if you wanna pull the trigger. If you do, we all die. You guys are smart enough to figure that one out for yourselves. But here's the thing. Nobody else is in position to stop that drone before it hits Marine Two and kills the vice president. And we don't have much time. So either one of you shoots it down, or I'm gonna drop this baby right on top of it."

Steve and Edie looked at each other.

"Not the choices I would've picked," Steve said.

Edie glanced at her shoulder and said, "I can pretend to keep him covered with my Ruger, but there's no way I can pick up that rifle, let alone shoot straight."

Steve glanced at Finley's unconscious body and stared at the sniper platform.

"Ah… no pressure here guys, but you got less than thirty seconds before I catch up to that pesky little bird and squash it into the river."

The pilot brought the Blackhawk about, trailing above and almost directly behind the drone as it skimmed above the waters of the Hudson by less than several feet. The rate of the Blackhawk's descent was alarmingly swift. The pilot matched his speed to that of the drone. In a few more seconds he'd punch the throttle and dive straight into it.

Marine Two was in the distance, taking evasive maneuvers. Communication channels were packed with well-controlled, but urgent chatter.

Edie had no doubt the pilot would do exactly what he had said. She nodded at Steve; confident he'd get the job done. She watched him pick up the sniper rifle and climb onto the platform.

He sighted in on the target.

The pilot's voice sounded louder and more urgent.

Steve exhaled and pulled the trigger. Again… and again… and again.

The fifth or sixth shot was the charm and the explosive charge on the drone detonated.

Dangerously close to the drone, the Blackhawk took a massive beating from the concussive force of the exploding warhead. The craft shuddered and listed, challenging the pilot's skills to stabilize the heavy chopper to avoid plunging into the river.

Through the static and chatters from her headset, Edie couldn't determine if the pilot was congratulating himself or had just turned religious. Her eyes opened wide. There was Marine Two, larger than life, and way too close. She swore the vice president waved at her. More likely he was issuing orders to someone.

Marine Two gained altitude after a dicey maneuver to avoid a near miss with the wobbling Blackhawk.

The scrambled fleet of F-15 fighter jets arrived on scene with an earth-shattering roar. They set up to escort the vice president out of the immediate area.

The pilot circled the Blackhawk back toward the yacht where the drone was launched in time to see one of the F-15s fire two Maverick missiles, disintegrating the vessel an instant before a second drone could be launched. The pilot turned and asked Edie to put the gun away, but it had already fallen to the floor.

Edie kept pressure on her wounded shoulder while Steve checked Finley's condition. She listened to the pilot radioing requests to find the closest medical facility to land this bird.

CHAPTER 57

EDIE'S EYES DROOPED CLOSED AS Steve tightened a makeshift bandage on her arm. There was nothing else he could do for Finley. Aware from his time served in the US Forest Service repelling into raging wildfires that all helicopter pilots were more or less insane, Steve spoke into his headset, in as calm a voice as possible, "I don't see any goddamned landing spot down there."

"Roger that," the pilot of the Blackhawk answered. "We passed the hospital's helipad about three-quarters of a mile to the east. The pier we just flew over. Figured we didn't have the luxury to arrange for admittance or provide any insurance verification. But I can see the front door coming up quick... and the boys are right there waiting below. Those trees need a little trimming anyway."

Steve felt his gut rise halfway to his eyeballs as the Blackhawk gave the distinct impression of dropping out of the sky like a rock. At the last instant Steve's gut wound up somewhere nearer to his ankles as the heavy bird hovered for a split second, inches above the rotor-swept turf, before the skids touched the ground.

Emergency room personnel removed Agent Mike Finley's unconscious body from the aircraft and transported him into the hospital, a few short yards away from the helicopter. Edie insisted on entering under her own power but succumbed to Steve's assistance in guiding her into the Port Authority Heroes of September Eleven Trauma Center, one of the newest additions to the Jersey City Medical Center.

Steve looked over his shoulder and gave a quick nod to the pilot who was absently bopping his head in time to unheard music. Even though Steve didn't read lips, he was almost certain the pilot mouthed the words to Frank Sinatra's *My Way*. Maybe the guy was older than he looked. Or was into the oldies but goodies.

While the potentially insane, but skilled pilot of the Blackhawk deftly deposited his passengers at the trauma center, Marine Two, following the successful evasive maneuver with the Blackhawk, and narrowly avoiding being hit by the suicide drone, made a beeline course to McGuire Air Force Base in central New Jersey. Before Marine Two landed, the vice president had shouted orders and established a command post to oversee an immediate plan of action. Air Force medics worked on patching up the nasty wound on his forehead, but Tyler Griffin never stopped issuing command after command to reestablish control of the situation and to jumpstart the investigation while things were still hot.

Kristie Pauling frantically tried to find out what had happened to Thomas. Details were sketchy after they informed her that he would remain in federal custody until the recent events could be sorted out.

Back on Liberty Island, authorities flooded the area and secured the site. In an ongoing stream of communications with the vice president's command post, Kristie learned Thomas had been taken to the New Jersey office of DHS in Hamilton Township. Until all this got straightened out, she was concerned that in the aftermath of his connection with the deaths of the two US marshals, some trigger-happy agents might take matters into their own hands. Tyler assured her he was handling that end, but got her transportation to the DHS office so she could be closer to Thomas.

Tony Funetti had been arrested, taken to a nearby hospital, and then released into the hands of the FBI after treatment for minor injuries. Amber, while being persistent in her endeavors to immobilize her target, had at least followed the guidelines of her training and exhibited a decent degree of bite inhibition. This was turning out to be an important issue since, as of now, Tony Funetti represented their best lead in chasing down others who might be connected with the assassination plot.

Marty Calebrese had been zipped up in a body bag.

The fiery remains of the renegade yacht from which the drone had been launched had settled to the bottom of the Hudson River. It would be next to impossible to track down any information on its ownership.

Edie's quick actions on the Blackhawk made sure the co-pilot wouldn't be testifying.

CHAPTER 58

THE NON-DESCRIPT CHARCOAL GRAY VAN with the company's name and logo imprinted on the driver's side door in small gothic-styled letters slowed as it reached the last northbound exit on the Garden State Parkway. It turned west onto Grand Avenue at the end of the ramp which roughly defined the eastern border of Upper Saddle River, New Jersey. The road the van now traveled on stretched to the western borders of this upward moving affluent community and metamorphosed into a cavalcade of differing names, imaginably as a tease to the old guard, even more affluent community to the south: Saddle River. The van slowed as it approached the summit and negotiated a hairpin turn in the road.

The driver double-checked the address before turning right onto an obscure driveway with a single estate sitting at the end. The owner, expecting the charcoal gray van, had already opened the heavy ornate gate. A hidden camera alerted the owner to the arriving van and the gate swung closed behind it. After about fifty yards of tall elms intertwining over and darkening the winding drive, the van emerged onto an open expanse. The portico of the French revival estate came into view. The sky mimicked the coloring of the approaching van as the sun set behind the ninth green on the posh country club located a short distance to the west. The two women who exited the van wore different, but professionally complementary outfits.

Before opening the door, the owner of the residence cinched his robe a little tighter, highlighting the expanding girth of his waist. He ran his fingers one more time through his wavy but thinning brown hair. As he got a look at the women standing in the open doorway, he pulled the cigar out of his mouth.

"Who the fuck are you?" The man glanced around them at the parked van to confirm the familiar name and logo on the vehicle's door. The subtle lettering read *Maid for You*. Although standing on the wide threshold, and a half-step higher than his visitors, his short stature made it impossible for him to see over their heads.

"Where the hell are Mandy and Del? I specifically asked for them."

The woman dressed in light blue hospital scrubs shrugged and spoke up. "Mr. Garrison didn't say, but apparently there was an emergency. I'm supposed to tell you he's sorry. You being such an important client, he asked us to give you an extra special treatment. I hope you're not disappointed in what you're seeing. I can assure you we're as qualified, or you may find out, better qualified than Mandy and Del to handle whatever ails you."

Scrubs took a step forward and stroked the front of his robe, below his bulging belly.

The man's eyes did a quick survey of his visitors. The second woman wore a skin-tight white nurse's uniform looking as if any minute it would lose the battle to hold her curvaceous body in check. He took a last puff on his cigar and deposited it in an ashtray on the small table in the foyer. He stepped aside, allowing Scrubs and Tights to enter. Scrubs carried a large leather medical bag at her side. As she brushed by, her loose-fitting clothing did little to disguise the promise of what hid underneath.

From reading the file and being briefed by Mr. Garrison, the women learned that except for this man, the large, secluded estate was empty. The man's wife wouldn't be returning home until tomorrow morning. She was participating in a two-day private tennis retreat in the Hamptons. Her tennis instructor, a young stud in his late twenties, handled only special clients. From the photos in the file that the women had reviewed, they doubted she would excel on the courts. Not to mention she probably wasn't much of an inspiration in bed. With what they had planned for the husband, it wouldn't have been fair to criticize the young tennis pro for how he earned a living.

Tights spoke for the first time. "I see you're giving us a good onceover. I'm guessing you're satisfied with what you see. So perhaps our new healthcare system ain't so bad. You didn't get to keep your doctor but wait till you see what you get from us."

A grin spread across his roundish face, making it look even more like a badly carved jack-o'-lantern. He ushered Scrubs and Tights to the doorway leading to the basement recreation room. The women had read up on the layout of this room. A hospital bed sat in one corner, surrounded not by the standard pull-around curtains you find in a real hospital setting, but a series of mirrored dividers on either side of the bed. There was a tall rack with several pieces of electronic equipment tucked into the corner. From an earlier briefing they learned that nothing on those shelves had any medical purpose, but apparently his wife liked to watch what her husband engaged in when she wasn't present. He accommodated her with the latest recording technology available. Today, there would be no lights or cameras—only action. The two women dressed in medical garb would make certain of that.

"Don't you worry now," Scrubs said in a low, husky voice. "We read the script. And we've added one or two new twists to the plot. Consider it part of the special treatment I promised you."

Tights rubbed herself up in front of the man as she undid the sash, opening up his robe. From behind, Scrubs lifted the top up and over his shoulders, letting the robe fall to the floor. Scrubs reached her arms around his short but bloated frame and fondled him, whispering the first orders to her new patient. He let out an urgent gasp and obliged her by lifting his naked body onto the bed. She adjusted the head section to about a forty-five-degree angle and raised the bottom so his knees were in a comfortable position with his legs spread apart.

He looked over at Scrubs as she unclasped the hinged top of the medical bag.

"What do you have for me in the bag, Doc?"

She smiled, at the same time nodding to Tights. "We're going to give you something you'll still be smiling about in the grave."

Tights had worked her way to the foot of the bed and grasped the zipper on the front of her uniform. The sharp buzzing sound as she pulled it down accentuated her body exploding out of the garment. The uniform disappeared, settling to the floor in a satiny rush. For the moment, the sweet fragrance of her perfume overcame the more animalistic scent emanating from the man's sweaty body. Tights climbed onto the bed and kneeled between his legs. She had his undivided attention as her hands danced up his calves, caressing his inner thighs.

Scrubs reached into the bag and pulled out a .357 magnum revolver. In a single motion she placed it against his right temple and squeezed the trigger. The transient perfume bouquet obliterated by the pungent nitro.

Tights jumped at the thunderous sound even though she was expecting it. Massaging her ringing ears, she turned to Scrubs, grinning, and said, "They must call him Big Al for another reason, wouldn't you say? I don't see much difference, even when he's dead. I guess as the top union boss he didn't concern himself with performance."

Tights worked her way back into her uniform, a more difficult task than popping out of it. The women then got to work and transformed the scene to one that better suited their purpose. Tights headed up to Al Rozano's office to locate his computer and printer.

Donning latex gloves, Scrubs wiped her fingerprints off the revolver and placed it into Rozano's right hand. The file had indicated he was right-handed. Twisting his arm and aiming the pistol around the side of his head above his right shoulder, Scrubs used his finger to pull the trigger, sending the round into the cedar-clad wall behind the bed. It would look like he was working up his nerve or was shaking so hard the first shot missed its mark. It also provided investigators with the expected gunshot residue on Al Rozano's hand. She then let his arm fall down to the mattress, and the gun clattered onto the ceramic tiled floor.

Tights returned with the ink-jetted note saying goodbye to his wife and regretting he could no longer live with the guilt. The Word file auto-saved onto his hard drive. With a smile, she placed the note over his groin. They wiped down any surfaces they had touched and drove the van out the gate using the codes from the file. The van picked up the Parkway at the nearest southbound ramp and sped away.

CHAPTER 59

THEY OFTEN MET IN THIS restaurant to discuss strategies. When Senator Henry Whitcome called and suggested they meet at the Angry Bird's Nest for a late dinner, the man didn't give it any serious thought. The timing of the call might have given him pause, but he was so far removed from the events that had transpired, he never considered the coincidence.

He had plenty of time to get to the meeting. Mixing himself a martini would be first on his agenda. He had approximately three hours before he needed to leave.

His third wife had left him three years ago. He pondered the meaning as he mixed the first martini, adding his customary three olives. His lucky number. Instead of settling onto his black leather recliner, the man walked over to the center of the large expansive floor to ceiling windows. He was on the thirty-third floor of the newest high-rise condominium building to spring up in Tysons Corner, an affluent section in Tysons, Virginia. Getting in on the ground floor with the developers of this project, he purchased the best of the three penthouse condos available with panoramic views of D.C.

As the crow flies, 1600 Pennsylvania Avenue was approximately twelve miles away. On clear nights he imagined looking into the bedroom window of the president. Not that he was into spying on the nation's first black spinster to hold the highest office in the land.

The expanded floor plan of the unit was too large for the single inhabitant who spent little of his time in residence. It was all about the prestige of owning the best, the biggest, and the most expensive in the area. Critics had argued that those buildings closer to, and within walking distance to the Silver Line station of the Metropolitan Area Transit Authority would be a better choice. The man laughed at that argument. He had no intentions of ever utilizing a subway train to commute to his office in D.C. His concession to the plight of the working man was to give his limo driver a decent bonus at Christmas. These admissions did not serve well for a man in his position, let alone the people he represented.

By the time he'd worked his way through the third martini, he'd maneuvered his aging body onto the recliner, trying to recall how many olives had made their way into the glass. He roughly calculated there was enough time for a quick shower to revitalize his senses before driving the twenty odd miles to the restaurant. Tonight, he'd drive himself, as this was his driver's scheduled day off.

Senator Henry Whitcome sat in a corner booth of the Angry Bird's Nest restaurant nursing his second gin and tonic. His sour mood escalated every time he eyed his Rolex. A man of his self-importance didn't tolerate waiting on anyone. After an hour of fuming, which included two additional gin and tonics, the senator cursed to himself and ordered a rare filet mignon, a loaded baked potato, and a Caesar salad with a crumbled bacon topping. He downed a carafe of Sonoma Valley pinot noir before paying the bill and storming out of the restaurant. The fine meal had sated his appetite but did nothing to diminish how pissed off he was at being stood up by someone he considered his inferior. He had followed explicit orders to schedule this meeting but had no idea as to its purpose.

Two days later, a local man heading down to a favorite fishing spot north of Potomac Falls, about four miles from the Angry Bird's Nest restaurant, came across an abandoned car at the bottom of a steep embankment next to the old railroad trestle. The authorities arrived and verified the exact coordinates via military grade GPS software. To the best of their calculations, the front wheels of the car were submerged up to the axles in the muddy shoreline of the Potomac River on the Maryland side of the border, while the rear wheels were fixed in the great state of Virginia. It was clear to the investigative teams from both states that the car was empty, and there were no signs of a struggle.

Philip Lucchesi, the national president of the Consolidated Brotherhood of Tradesmen, had vanished from the face of the earth.

CHAPTER 60

SEVERAL LONG AND AGONIZING DAYS after the failed assassination plot, the FBI dropped all charges against Thomas Pauling. Tony Funetti, who'd lawyered up, was now in protective custody as part of a plea-bargaining deal being worked out with the federal prosecutors. Trying to maintain an upper hand, he at first gave up only one significant name: Al Rozano, the head of the New Jersey chapter of the CBT. That had gotten the investigators nowhere since Rozano's wife had reported finding her husband dead of a self-inflicted gunshot wound upon arriving home following an overnight stay in the Hamptons.

Several other union employees planted at GMHC, including Chuck Kolinsky, had also been named by Tony Funetti as part of the conspiracies to undermine and sabotage the company, and were called in for questioning. But they knew nothing beyond their interactions with Marty Calebrese and Tony Funetti, the supposed representatives for the union.

Things had gotten more complicated regarding the potential jurisdictional handling of the numerous crimes attributed to Calebrese and Funetti. This was based on Funetti's own dispositions, and the evidence uncovered in his Lexus. Funetti's admission of their plan to use Leilah Harris to discredit Thomas Pauling and his presence at the scene in Thomas's hotel suite when Calebrese inadvertently killed the young girl with an overdose of sedatives was sufficient to exonerate Thomas. Forensics also helped clear Thomas Pauling in the death of the two US marshals.

On the advice of his attorney, Tony Funetti stopped short of admitting any culpability in the deaths of the US marshals, the park rangers, or Reverend Carter. The mutilated body of the reverend had been discovered in the aft cabin of a parks department motorboat moored at the service dock on Liberty Island.

Eventually, under increasing pressure from the authorities, Tony Funetti confirmed the name Philip Lucchesi as a possible co-conspirator. But any further evidence linking the leaders of the CBT union and their conspiratorial actions to power brokers in D.C. had stalled after Lucchesi disappeared. A law enforcement net immediately spread across the nation to determine his fate, but there were still no leads. Teams of investigators poured over phone and email records of Lucchesi and all known associates to look for any useful links.

When they brought Arthur Constantine in for questioning, a number of key politicians in Washington became nervous. While vowing to keep digging into his records and pursuing different lines of questioning with Constantine, their lack of success in learning anything of consequence frustrated federal investigators. In a show of arrogance, Constantine never retained an attorney during any of the interrogation sessions and, on the surface, appeared to offer his complete cooperation to the government. Still operating in the shadows with relative impunity, Constantine's associates were far from done in their efforts to stifle Tyler Griffin's political career.

Edie put together a series of reports criticizing the activities of key lobbying organizations and the covert operations of activist groups with supposed links to high-ranking congressional leaders in an effort to promote a public outcry for congressional subcommittees to open up an investigation. That pointed to how frustrated Edie was with the situation. She had little hope the congressional hearings would do anything more than give the members a chance to grandstand their positions. It was a miracle any of the elected leaders could find their own committee rooms without a Capitol tour guide, let alone question even the most simple-minded witnesses called to testify. The threat of such hearings eased the tensions of the remaining conspirators, since they were certain congress would bungle the whole mess.

Although the Department of Justice, under the urging of the White House, planned to open extended investigations into allegations of criminal activities orchestrated by the leaders of the CBT and the unknown coalitions in Washington, Edie was far from done in pursuing her own investigations into the matter. She had been impressed with the insights Sampson had gotten with the help of his friend in the Office of the Clerk in the US House of Representatives.

In a recent conversation with her brother, Edie suggested she could work directly with Beth Dawson, but Sampson preferred the current arrangement. Not that he was into all this spy stuff; but he did look forward to spending more time with Beth.

On another front, Edie became intrigued by reading the multitude of reports regarding Philip Lucchesi's disappearance. She wasn't entirely convinced of his death. And until someone discovered the body, she'd keep that chapter open. For the time being she wondered if looking into the Jimmy Hoffa case could provide her with any useful insights.

The Paulings and Griffins were relieved to see Thomas exonerated in the death of Leilah Harris, but

Thomas still harbored a deep and burning guilt for his student's death. One of the first things he did after being released was to visit Leilah's family, but he could do nothing to stop himself from feeling responsible for their daughter's death. Mr. Harris's stoic acceptance of his words of apology and sorrow wrenched Thomas's heart. He would've preferred the man had picked up a knife and stabbed him in the chest. That act at least would've been more appropriate after what had been taken from the innocent family.

Other than to Steve, Edie never mentioned the close encounter between Reverend Carter and Leilah Harris's father ever again.

CHAPTER 61

THE PERSISTENT SCRATCHING ON THE raised metal railing failed to awaken Agent Mike Finley, but the repeated high-pitched whining choruses did the trick. He opened his eyes and tilted his head to the side, which at this point represented his only capable movements. Except for the weak hand wave he tried next.

Mike Finley had taken two direct hits from the weapon discharged by the Blackhawk's co-pilot, Lt. Morgan, now identified as a back-up member of the assassination team. One round had passed clean through his left calf. The second and more damaging one lodged about a half inch from his spine, having collapsed one lobe of his lungs, scraping a path against the pericardium. Miraculously, it only bruised the left ventricle and avoided any major arteries.

Last night they removed Mike Finley from the respirator and released him from the cardiac intensive care unit. Steve and Edie had spent agonizing hours watching his vital signs shift like the Green Lantern roller coaster at Great Adventure.

"Thank Jesus the first thing I see is a pretty face," Mike Finley's raspy voice said, looking through the railing at Amber, before spotting Steve awkwardly holding an arrangement of flowers. "And not the ugly face of a glorified Guido disguising himself as a secret agent man."

When his eyes focused on the flowers in Steve's hands, Finley coughed, trying to summon up a weak smile. "Maybe I missed the signs, but are you proposing to me?"

Edie peeked out from behind Steve. "You can't have him, Mike, not unless you wanna fight me for him." A tear slid down her cheek as she reached over and patted Finley's hand.

She leaned over and kissed Finley's forehead. "Thank you, Mike, you saved our lives."

Not one to take a compliment, Finley scoffed, "Humph. At least you're outnumbered by two gorgeous females, Steve. By the way, I prefer my usual view from the hospital room. The one with me staring down at your sorry ass in bed—too slow to dodge any bullets."

Turning serious, Finley stared at Edie's arm wrapped in a thick bandage, covering the graze from the slug. She was lucky. The wound prevented her from picking up the sniper rifle and attacking the drone, but Steve had accomplished that task. Finley's sluggish mind began to process the sketchy images during the last moments before he lost consciousness on the Blackhawk's sniper platform.

"You doing okay, Edie? They told me you took a bullet from the son of a bitch. You saved my life too. Thanks, sweetie. How about the next time we get together; we try for a barbecue or something. I'll bring the steaks."

Steve said, "You think you could show up on time?"

"Why would I want to do that? Look what happens when I do."

Finley shook his head, remembering more of the earlier details. "Damn, I almost hesitated taking the shot at that guy on the Statue of Liberty. That wouldn't have looked good on my resume. Edie, you were so close to the line of fire. One little movement of the chopper—"

"Hey, my head was higher than hers," Steve said. "And closer to the trajectory."

"A tempting target, Steve, but there were other things to consider. Although from what one of my guys told me this morning, if I'm understanding it correctly, I probably killed the wrong goon. I learned the guy I shot was the one calling most of the plays. The guy who lived was just the muscles of the operation. We could've used Marty Calebrese to lead us further up the ladder, but at least this Funetti character has started singing."

Steve and Edie left Mike Finley when his eyes started drooping, tiring from their visit. They themselves still tried to come to grips with what had happened between the phone call from Reverend Carter and the hair-raising events that followed.

CHAPTER 62

THE VICE PRESIDENT'S VOICE BOOMED out from the podium.

"I am proud and humbled to be a citizen of this great nation and given the opportunity to serve as your vice president. And before that, to have had the honor of being elected to the senate and represent the great state of New Jersey.

"Due to an unfortunate incident, circumstances prevented me from speaking at the reopening ceremony that took place on this same spot. In the wake of the thwarted attack, the ongoing investigations, and the news stories that have already leaked out regarding my intentions, I am here to state the obvious. I had planned to step forward on the day after President Alice Andersen made her announcement. At any rate, as of today I am officially putting my hat into the ring…."

Vice President Tyler Griffin, against everybody's advice, had returned to Ellis Island to finish what he had started. Many media pundits questioned why the former senator from New Jersey, as well as a longtime resident and businessman from the same state, would select a site in New York to launch his campaign for the Oval Office. Let alone use this location as the means to endorse his sister, Kristie Pauling, for the state legislature in New Jersey.

The dispute of the boundaries and borders of Ellis Island had gone on since the original privately owned three-acre island in the New York harbor had expanded approximately ten-fold in size by the judicious use of landfill. In 1998, the landmark Supreme Court decision put the long-disputed claims to rest. It stipulated that while New York was correct in claiming the original island as within its jurisdiction, the almost ninety percent of the island as it existed today as a result of the landfill, belonged to New Jersey. Residents of both states tended to ignore the courts.

The exact site where the vice president delivered his speech, outside the front portico of the immigration building, which now functioned as a museum, was one hundred percent New Jersey property, built on landfill. However, right behind the podium, inside the doors, was the property of New York. A small portion of the interior section of the immigration building belonged to New Jersey, but the vice president chose not to make his remarks from either the kitchen or the laundry room.

Property rights issues aside, the vice president chose this location for a more sentimental reason. He was proud of the fact that his ancestors from Ireland, after years of struggling, had fulfilled their dreams to come to America. His family had entered the United States of America through Ellis Island.

The original point of entry on the island had long since burned down, but on January 1, 1892, a young Irish girl, followed by her two brothers, was the first of over twelve million immigrants to be processed in the over sixty years of operations at this center.

When people asked Tyler Griffin the next obvious question, he shrugged, allowing a small smile to spread across his face. Now that the museum had reopened again after repairs to the damage from Hurricane Sandy were completed, anyone could research the answer for themselves.

While Edie sat in the audience, she wrote down a memo to herself to check when the last landfill dump had been made on the island. Maybe she'd found her starting point in a possible search for Jimmy Hoffa.

Epilogue

Mike Finley, leaning against his crutch, turned back to Steve. "They make quite a pair. Looks like they just came back from the roller derby finals."

Steve tugged on his collar, stretching his neck in a vain attempt to find a comfortable compromise. "Yeah? And from where I'm standing, you must've been knocked out in the first round."

Capt. Jordan joined in. "Hey. Good choice not to cover it up. That bandage makes her look hot and sexy."

"Can't argue with that," Steve said. He noticed his captain had recovered from meeting Edie's escort in person for the first time earlier today.

"Hey guys… remember her big brothers are listening to what you're saying about their sweet and innocent little sister," Sampson said with a crooked smile.

Their attention returned to Edie as Vice President Tyler Griffin released her arm and gave her a light kiss on the cheek before taking a spot in the front row next to his wife.

The wound on his forehead no longer required a bandage, but the swelling and discolorations were still prominent. A white bandage covered Edie's gunshot wound. It blended in well with her gown, except for the bright hearts and flowers artwork drawn by Steve.

Edie joined the rest of the party, and they all turned to look as the final member started the procession. Edie wasn't the only one in white. Amber pranced proudly down the aisle. This time she was officially endorsed to be carrying the ring. But she decided not to stick with the usual program and plopped the ring in front of Edie, apparently wanting to bypass the entire ceremony.

Hundreds of acres of fertile fields, rambling meadows, and dense woodlands surrounded the lush and beautiful clearing that served as a cozy theater for the bridal party, along with their family and a select number of close friends. It would take a significant amount of time to clear the adjacent areas of all the pesky little varmints. Amber needed to get to work as soon as possible.

Steve and Edie had refrained from waiting for Uncle Vinnie to be released from the federal penitentiary in Fairton. In a hasty, but mutually agreed upon decision, the couple moved up the date for their wedding. Finding a suitable locale on such a short notice was proving to be a set-back until Nana stepped in and asked a close friend to help solve the problem.

Steve was grateful to Edie for introducing him to a family he didn't know existed. In the back of his mind, he tried to predict what she would help him with next. In a last-minute change with tradition, Steve suggested the bride's family should be seated on the right side of the aisle. All politics aside, Steve didn't care who sat where.

Looking out at the gathered loved ones, he snuck a quick glance at Edie and whispered, "I do prefer the right side of the bed. But as you may recall, I have no opinion about being on top."

Before Edie responded, a strong voice boomed out from the front right side of the aisle.

"You do remember I'm not deaf, Steve?" Nana said, failing to keep a straight face.

Nana, with a satisfied grin, turned to President Alice Andersen, seated to her right, and said, "I must say, Alice, your farm here in Virginia is a lot larger and much nicer than your old apartment next door to us in Hackensack. It's a long way from where you first started out."

The president said, "Not so far with all my loved ones surrounding me."

Always one to get the last word, Nana patted the president's hand and whispered, "I'm still looking to find you that special man. And I do see several gentlemen seated in the back that might be of interest."

Amber, bored with the ceremony, padded over and rested her head on Nana's lap.

THE END

AUTHOR'S NOTES

The Guarding State is the third book in
The Amber Restrained Series.

The series chronicles the escapades of two disparate individuals, Steve Casella and Edie Pauling, who surmount their differences and form an interminable bond that takes them on a journey to fight the injustices assailing the American dream. Together they challenge the seemingly unending barrage of incompetence and corruption that is ignored, facilitated, or orchestrated by the almost invincible power structure of an encroaching government. Along for the ride is Amber, a dog Steve has rescued from a fatal house fire. The sometimes disobedient canine companion is a constant source of frustration and amusement, but as part of their team, no one is more capable to assist when times get rough. As the nation and the world gather at the brink of extinction, Steve and Edie desperately try to gain traction against the slippery slope toward ultimate destruction.

<<ronvergona.net>>

Acknowledgments

I wish to thank AJ Wallace for the extensive feedback, corrections, and professional advice received for the first three books in *The Amber Restrained Series*. I am indebted to AJ's encouragement throughout the editing process, but most of all, the critical eye AJ used to transform these novels. As always, I am responsible for all remaining errors of judgment and oversights in the final versions.